IMMORTAL GENERATION

An Immortal Story of True Love, Truth, and Vulnerability

Book 7

The Immortals Stories Series

by

Linda Ashton Trott

Tagger Press

Copyright

ISBN 978-1-7782949-9-0

Cover design by: 100COVERS

First Edition, June 16, 2023

Adult Content, 18+

Dedication

I am dedicating this book to my husband, without whom it would have been impossible to complete this work.

A huge thank you to Lee Burton with OceansEdgeEditing for being my editor on my seventh book. I am still learning and he is a very good teacher and editor.

Thanks to you, the reader, as well for purchasing this book. I hope you enjoy it! If you do, don't forget to leave a review.

Contents

What did you miss?

In the last Immortal Stories Series book, here's what happened:

- A coven of witches were rescued
- Gwen tells Andrews she's pregnant
- We met Margaret and Abeo
- We learn Abeo is immortal and used to be Wendell
- Duffy does more investigating on the Order
- Margaret and Abeo move in near Mark and Falon
- Gwen and Margaret give birth the same day
- Lora and Rick have magical wedding
- Margaret has a second multiple birth
- The New Year's Eve party ends with a boom!

1—Tell the Kids

Lora

The last seventy-two hours were frightening. First a bomb blew up the new restaurant. It landed me in the hospital, where I risked being exposed as not human. This compelled us to decide to tell Anita and the kids the truth about who we really are.

But first the bomb. At the apex of our New Year's Eve party, we received a bomb threat that was delivered in a very strange way. It was on a slip of paper inserted inside the wrapping of the gift box given to one of our guests. How that slip got in there, we don't know. How the bomb got in the restaurant was also a mystery.

Putting the mystery aside, we called the police, who sent us a bomb tech and the fire department. We were assured they could defuse it, so we started evacuating the restaurant into the cold January night. Just as the staff started leaving, the bomb exploded, sending shrapnel and furniture flying in every direction. A table flew towards Rick and I. It hit Rick on the head, while my neck got stabbed by a huge shard of glass. Apparently, Rick managed to use that table as a shield, protecting us from more damage.

The resulting slaughter of most of the staff and a few firefighters was nothing short of a tragedy. To make things worse, Justin was missing. We didn't know where he was in the restaurant when the bomb went off.

The police took over the scene. The fire department used dogs to find bodies, which was sorrowful and gruesome. Most of our dear chefs died. That was a terrible loss of life and talent. Chef Marcel was spared only because he didn't leave through the kitchen before the bomb went off. He left through the back instead. Most of the wait staff was gone too. Some of the staff who had been standing up against the back wall managed to escape the worst damage because everyone fell on top of them.

Sadly, one of the firefighters who was helping people get out was cut in half by a pane of window glass. The newscast had footage of the damage to the neighboring heritage buildings. It was just a crime to see, and would cost even more to repair.

Memorial services were being announced for various victims. Rick and I planned on attending as many as we could. But we still had no word about Justin.

The wreckage was nowhere near the point of being removed. We were told it could be months before Rick could think about rebuilding. He had already been in touch with his insurance. They said they were going to cover it. But we didn't know to what extent.

The bombing dominated the news cycle for three days, but there was so much for them to dig into. I expected it would be another week before they got tired of it. We'd know when they got down to doing a bio on Rick … that would be close to the end of public scrutiny.

At least one good thing came out of the investigation: the police cleared the owners of the restaurant, aka Justin and Rick, of any wrongdoing. They were victims of a terrible crime, and the police promised to get to the bottom of the bombing as soon as they could.

I had a huge question though: just how did the media find out about a bomb in the first place? Mark said they heard the story on the radio and jumped in the car and drove into the city. They found us at the hospital not that long after we got there ourselves. So, how did the news know about it in advance? Who tipped them off? Was the cook who quit involved? Or did the other cook who called in sick have anything to do with it? Why?

At least we would be clear of lawsuits from building owners. Rick sighed deeply in relief after that announcement.

Next was the talk we had to have with Anita and the children after I ended up in hospital. When we got home, they were shocked that we were basically unscathed. They had heard that we had been inside the restaurant, close to the explosion. Of course, they were terrified we had been injured seriously, or worse.

Mark and Falon stayed with us to help with the explanation and serve as support.

“Come on, kids, let’s get inside out of the cold,” I said to them as they clung to us on the step when we got home.

All eight of us went inside. Mark lit a fire in the fireplace and we all sat down together.

“Anita, kids, we need to have a conversation,” started Rick. “I need to explain to you something about myself, your mom, and our friends. It’s not a bad thing, not at all. But it is a secret thing.”

“Ricardo, how are you okay?” asked Anita. “How? They said you were right inside the restaurant when the—”

“Everybody, take a deep breath,” Rick interrupted. “We’re all okay, not a scratch on us. We’re not dying, and not going anywhere. Okay? Now, I’m going to tell you a true story.

“A very, very long time ago, an alien race came to Earth because their home was dying. When they got here, they found humans. Eventually, the aliens and the humans had babies together and some of them became magical, like your mom.

Today they are called witches, but back then they were considered very special people. Others lived very long lives, so long in fact that humans came to think of them as immortal because they lived longer than the memory of most people.

"The aliens looked like humans, which helped them have babies together, but they had some hidden differences. They had fangs, which they used to use for hunting. But on Earth they didn't hunt like that. Still, because the aliens were predators like our big cats, they had a better sense of smell, could see much better, and could hear much better than humans. This, of course, helped them hunt as well—even without using their fangs.

"I am the descendant of one of those immortals," Rick concluded. He then fell silent, looking back and forth at Anita and my kids. Their faces showed they were each processing what he had said in different ways. Some had widely dilated pupils, Anita was squinting. My youngest looked a combination of intrigued and scared.

We waited for the onslaught of questions that would inevitably come. Minni was first.

"We know Mom is magical. Is that how, Mom? Is that how you guys survived?" asked Minni.

"Good question, Minni. As it turns out, yes. I have been tracing my lineage backward, and I discovered that the magical ability that I inherited through my family line originally came from these immortals."

"Are you immortal now?" asked Minni, drawing the right conclusion.

"Yes, but that is because Rick has changed me. I was born human, just like you."

I could see the wheels turning in their heads as they processed what we were saying. In many ways, our kids would accept this as fact much more easily than Anita.

"Does that mean I can be changed too?" asked Minni, again a leap in understanding.

Good girl. I knew you were smart!

"Yes, it does."

Anita had remained silent through all this, as she listened to the kids asking questions, and our answers.

"Rick, can we see your fangs?" asked Pascal.

"Of course. I'll show you," said Rick. He slowly elongated his fangs. My sons were saying things like awesome and cool! Anita was gasping in shock. When his fangs reached their maximum length, he purposely spoke to sound silly and break the tension.

"Noo, you thee thath I cannoth thpeath very dell dith my theeth like thith," he lisped.

"Rick, you sound like Sylvester on Tweety Bird!" They all laughed out loud.

He let his fangs retract. "Now, there is more to this. When I say we're immortal, I mean long-lived. It does not mean we don't or can't die. It really just means we live a very, very, very long time."

"How long?" asked Trent.

It was Mark's turn to answer. "Well, for example, my sister Gwen is over three hundred years old, and I am one hundred and fifty years old."

"Wow! Really? What's it like to live so long?" asked Pascal.

"I'll bet it can be lonely," said my daughter. *Again, showing how insightful she can be.*

"Yes, it can be lonely," answered Mark. "We watch all our human friends and acquaintances die. We don't usually allow ourselves the luxury of becoming involved with humans, because we have to leave before they discover our secret."

"What secret?" asked Trent.

"That we are not human," said Rick. "We can never tell anyone that we are not human. We cannot tell even our bestest friends. Because it would be very dangerous to us if humans knew we existed."

"What would they do?" asked Trent.

"I fear they would keep us in cages and experiment on us," said Mark.

"You mean like in the movies?"

"Yes, just like that."

"Now, there is one more thing about being immortal that is relevant right now," I said. "We heal very quickly. Only the most serious injuries, like losing our heads, will kill us. Other injuries we heal."

"Is that why you and Rick appear unharmed?" asked Anita, speaking for the first time.

"Yes, that's exactly why. We can show you," I said, "if you want to see."

My kids were all excited about that, Anita not so much, but she wanted to witness it for herself.

So I took a sharp pocketknife from Rick, and in front of them cut a deep gash into my arm. They all screamed together, and watched as I started to bleed, but it stopped almost immediately. A single drop of blood fell to the floor. Then the cut started to knit back together, until it had disappeared completely without a scar.

"Wow!"

"Amazing!"

"Oh my gosh!"

"Ah mon Dios!"

They all sat silent for a minute. Then an explosion of words came from their mouths.

"When can I be changed?" asked my daughter.

I looked at Rick and Mark. We hadn't talked about this yet. But according to Abeo, it would not require sex, so that was good.

"How about this: let us speak to another immortal who knows more than we do, and when we get the answer, we will tell you."

They all spoke at once, of course.

"Wait! Anita, you have a question?"

"Is this condition inheritable?" she asked. "When your baby is born, will he be immortal?"

I looked at Rick and he nodded. "Yes, Anita, he will be born immortal. But he will not have all his adult characteristics."

"Then I request to be changed, so that I can continue to care for the next generation," she said.

Tears formed in my eyes. This woman was amazing. She lived her life—more than fifty years—caring for another family. And she wanted to keep caring for their future too.

"Of course you can, Anita. It would be our privilege to bring you into our family."

"You need to understand, Mama, that when you change, your appearance will also change. You will become young again."

"Alabado sea Dios," she murmured. Rick chuckled.

"What did she say?" I asked.

"Praise be to God!"

"So let's recap," said Minni. "My mom is immortal like you, Mark, and Falon? You all heal very fast. You all have incredible senses. And we can become like you?"

"You can add Gwen and Andrews, as well as Abeo and Margaret and all their children," I added.

"So basically everyone who comes over here is immortal?" asked Trent. "Cool!"

"Is there anything else we need to tell them now?" I asked Mark.

"No, that's about it for now. Kids, Anita, if you have any questions, ask us. Anytime. Okay?" said Mark.

The kids got up and animatedly talked with each other as they went up to their rooms. Anita stayed sitting there for a few moments quietly.

"Ricardo, I would like to do this as soon as possible. What do I have to do?"

"Mama, we need to give you a few injections. I'll ask Abeo what he thinks the dose should be and how many. We can get started on it as soon as you're ready."

"*Gracias*, Ricardo."

2—Mama Anita

Lora

A week later, after consulting with Abeo, we had three syringes prepared for Anita.

"Anita," said Rick, "Abeo says it may take a while for the first phase of the transition to happen, and we weren't sure if there would be complications. Abeo told us to make sure you were in bed and relaxed before the first injection."

"Why?" asked Anita.

"Because the first one is a huge dose, 10cc of venom."

"Venom? Ricardo, are you sure this will be okay?" asked Mama Anita.

"Si, Mama, it's venom that we deliver to make the transition possible."

"Oh, not snake venom?"

"No, Mama, not snake venom," said Rick. "Si Mama, all will be just fine. Abeo tells me this is the easiest way to do this. The venom will burn slightly as we give it to you, but that will disappear quickly. Next you will feel slightly high, a sense of euphoria, and then you will fall asleep."

"What happens then?" she asked.

"Technically, your human body will start to die as the venom changes your DNA and rebuilds your body. You will need a second injection thirty-six hours later, and possibly a third injection within seventy-two hours. Apparently, we need to keep the amount of venom in your body at a maximum for this to happen quickly and smoothly. This means that physical changes will happen, and the first one is the ability to heal. As your body changes, there will be growing pains, like when you were a girl, except this is from the bones in your body becoming stronger. You may gain some height as well. After the initial process finishes, you will undergo subtle changes for the next six months."

"Will I become young again?"

"Abeo isn't sure. There is a high probability that you will. We've only transformed young people so far, so we don't know for sure."

"Will I die?"

"No, Mama, I won't let you die. I promise. Are you ready?" asked Rick.

"Yes, I guess so."

We took her up to her room and she lay down on her bed quietly. We opted to do just injections, because Abeo said they were more potent than a bite. It would happen faster and cleaner than the multiple bites would. Besides, we didn't have anyone who would do it the "traditional" way for Anita. So this would be very interesting.

Once Anita was comfortable, we called Abeo for him to come give her the shot. He had been waiting outside on the pool deck. The kids came upstairs too, to be with Anita while she transitioned.

"Will Anita change into something scary?" ask my youngest.

"No, hun, she will look like herself throughout the transformation," I answered.

Abeo came in with a syringe kit and a bottle of a slightly iridescent liquid. He measured out an entire 10cc syringe of the liquid and swabbed a spot on her shoulder with some rubbing alcohol.

"Ready? This may pinch because I have to get the serum into a vein."

"Yes," said Anita bravely.

Abeo carefully inserted the syringe at a thirty-degree angle into the visible vein in her arm. Slowly depressing the syringe pushed the sparkly blue liquid into her. Anita gasped as the concentrated venom hit her blood. Her eyes dilated wide as the high took her. Within a minute or so, she was knocked out. Minni, my eldest, sat there with Anita's hand in hers. The difference between the weathered brown hand and the teen's young hand was startling.

"Okay. Now we wait," said Abeo.

"Whose venom was that?" asked Rick.

"It was mine," said Abeo. "I figured mine was the most potent, and therefore the likeliest to change her quickly and smoothly."

"Makes sense."

"How long will she be out?" I asked.

"She will probably stay unconscious for at least three days. I'll be back in thirty-six hours to administer the second dose. That will be the equivalent of six bites, which should be enough. But, if we need it, I have a third dose prepared. Watch her, check her blood pressure and heart rate periodically, and take her temperature too. Just to make sure nothing untoward happens."

Rick and I left to go make some dinner for everyone, leaving Minni with Anita. The other kids went to play in the pool.

An hour later, Minni was running down the stairs yelling for me.

"Mom! Something's happening!"

"Are you good, Rick?" I asked.

"Yup."

"Coming, Minni."

When I entered Anita's room, the change was clear. Her hair was straighter and less gray. Her skin appeared younger too, as there were no spots on her arms and hands. When Minni put her hand next to Anita's, the startling difference wasn't there anymore. Anita's fingers were now slender and long, free of the arthritic bumps that used to bend her hands. Her skin was smoothing out on her arms like the wrinkles were filling in.

"Mom, look at this!" she exclaimed, pointing to Anita's skin.

"It's happening so fast," I said. "It must be because the injection is concentrated. Let's leave her to sleep."

I had taken her temperature before the injection, and now it showed her body temp was elevated a little. That was another clear indication the venom was working.

We checked on her after dinner and she was still sleeping—or unconscious. It's hard to tell the difference unless you try to wake someone. She was running a mild fever, but still not alarming, so we left her door open and went about our evening. The kids watched TV in their den while Rick and I cleaned up the kitchen. We decided to watch a movie afterwards, so we made some popcorn and settled in.

I think I fell asleep during the movie. In fact, I know I did, because I woke up the next morning in bed. So Rick must have carried me upstairs. Throwing on a robe, I padded down the hall to Anita's room to look in on her. The kids and Rick were already there.

"Lora, look!" said Rick.

Walking up to her bedside, I saw that Anita's face was that of a young woman in her mid-thirties. Her graying hair had lengthened and turned a lustrous chestnut brown.

"Her body is working hard. Let's leave her."

Anita hadn't regained consciousness by the time Abeo returned. I was a little worried. But when I brought it up, he wasn't concerned.

"The body has a lot to do, and she was an older woman, so it will take longer and be harder on her," he said as he gave her the second dose. "It will be easier on her if she keeps sleeping."

"Is there anything I should be watching for? A symptom that would indicate a problem?" I asked.

"I would watch her temperature and her heart rate. Her heart may slow down considerably, and you don't want it to stop. Also, if she spikes a high fever, cool her down with wet towels and ice."

"Got it."

"I'll be back in another thirty-six hours. She should be awake by then."

I made myself responsible for taking hourly measurements of Anita's temperature and heart rate, recording them on a pad I left next to her bed. Luckily, there was no spike in her fever, but her heart did slow down to less than twenty beats a minute. That was scary, but it came back up a couple of hours later. Anita woke up early in the morning on the last day.

I walked into the room all set to do my measurements, not paying attention.

"Lorita," said a silky voice.

"Anita, you're awake, good!"

I called everyone in and they all came running. We were standing around her bed, when my youngest entered and gasped at her appearance.

"What's wrong?" asked Anita.

"You look so young, Mama Anita!"

"I do?"

"Yes," I told her. "You look about thirty years younger. If I were to guess, it's you when you were in your late twenties."

"Impossible!" cried Anita.

"Si, Mama, you have de-aged," said Rick. "You are young again."

Minni brought her a hand mirror. When Anita looked in the mirror she gasped in surprise. She then grinned, pouted, and made all kinds of faces as she watched her reflection react, finally laughing at the improbability of it all.

"Oh my, I'll never be able to play cards with my friends again! They will run me out of the city!"

"Now you understand why we have to keep to ourselves and keep things secret," said Rick. "Unfortunately, this means you won't be able to see the people you used to see in Georgia."

"So what? I will just die, then?" asked Anita.

"That might be the easiest way to deal with it," I said.

"Ha, I'll get to see who goes to my funeral!"

"So, Anita, do you feel anything else?"

"I'm aching all over. It feels like I've run a marathon and carried one hundred concrete blocks around the yard. My back hurts most and my legs."

"How's your vision?"

"I can see just fine. Why?"

"You're not wearing your glasses."

"Oh!" Anita said as her hands flew to her face and felt all around. "I'm not, and I didn't even notice. I can see perfectly, now that you mention it. Perhaps better than before."

"Your body will develop new skills and abilities, but we'll talk about them as they appear. I'll bet you are hungry."

"I am starving."

"Minni, take the boys and go get Anita some breakfast, please."

"Yes, Mom. Come on guys, let's get Anita a nice breakfast," she said to her brothers.

"Mama, we are going to do a test on you that involves cutting your hand," said Rick. He brought out the small pen knife again and flipped it open. Taking Anita's hand, he ran the blade across her palm. We watched a welling of bright red dots turn into a small stream, then break down and disappear with the cut in her skin.

"Wow," said Anita.

"It's freaky, eh?" I said.

"Welcome to immortality, Mama," said Rick.

"*Oh mi Dios misericordioso*," said Anita. *Oh my merciful God!*

Just then, the kids returned carrying a tray, with toast, bacon, and eggs, plus juice and coffee.

"We'll let you eat in peace. Abeo will be back later this afternoon. When you are finished eating, just holler and we'll come get your dishes."

"*Muchas gracias, mis hijas*," said Anita. *Many thanks, my children.*

"*De nada*," replied Minni. *It's nothing*. Anita smiled and dug into her food.

Abeo gave her a clean bill of health when he came back. He then advised Anita to change her name, and get registered as a new person who just arrived from somewhere. He told us that he had people who handled this sort of thing for him and he'd be happy to get Anita a whole new identity if she wanted.

"Let me think about it, Abeo," said Anita. "I look so different that no one will recognize me here. I'm not known here yet."

"Still, a new identity is better, just in case something happens," said Abeo. "I can make sure it's Spanish or similar. We will come up with the identity, you come up with the name. I don't believe you need another injection either."

"Mom?"

"Yes, Minni?"

"When can I get turned?"

"Hmm, Rick and I haven't discussed that yet. Technically, you can be turned now, but I'm not sure it will change you. Abeo, what do you think?"

"Because she is a child, turning will not change her child appearance, but it will change her adult outcome. Her body should age as normal and then stabilize in her late twenties."

"So I could start now?" asked Minni.

"I don't suppose there is any reason why not," I said. "You're an adult legally. Now, I want you to speak to Gwen about all the female things you need to know first. There may be something you don't want to change."

"Okay, but I am pretty sure I want to be like you and Rick."

"There are some advantages," said Rick.

"Like what?" I asked.

"Like not needing condoms for one thing. As an immortal, we don't catch human diseases, and she won't likely get pregnant either."

"Hmm, worth considering," I said.

"What do you mean I won't get pregnant?" asked Minni.

"Once your body has changed, your reproductive system changes," said Rick. "You won't have periods anymore. You won't easily get pregnant from a human boy either."

"Bonus!" cried Minni. "I love it already!"

"Not so fast, young lady. It's not an all-access pass to all-the-sex-you-can-do show."

"Umm," said Rick quietly.

"You! Don't say a word!" I said, sternly pointing a finger at Rick. "I'll not have my daughter going around having sex with every boy she can find because she thinks she cannot get pregnant."

"Mom, I wouldn't do that," said Minni, a little horrified.

"You're right, you won't do that. Let me and Rick discuss this and we will let you know at dinner tonight."

"Thanks, Mom."

3—Investigation

Rick

Two days after the bombing at L'Escalade, the police and fire department were investigating and information was trickling out of the news. It was frustrating to not know what happened, or why. The fact that the following day was a holiday wasn't helping. It was impossible to reach businesses because everyone was off. The police were not being entirely forthcoming about what they were finding.

I guess I should have expected that. Justin and I were foreigners here. They might not feel any duty to help us. Certainly, if the tables were turned, and this was Atlanta and I was Canadian, they wouldn't be working too hard, especially because I was Cuban-born. Lora kept telling me it didn't work like that here, so I hoped so.

Yesterday, I spent hours at the main police station asking questions. Do they have leads on who did this? Do they have a motive? Was the cook who was fired involved? Where is Justin?

The police had no answers for me. They had not found the cook; apparently the address he gave us on his application was false. They had not found anyone by his name in the city either, so that might have been false too. He was a suspect now at least.

As for the other cook who called in sick? The police spoke to him and he had an alibi for New Year's Eve. He spent most of the night in Emergency waiting for a doctor. So far that had checked out. It didn't absolve him of any responsibility, but if he was involved, it was in the background.

I was watching the news at lunch, hoping for a kernel of new information about Justin. They were still pulling bodies out of the wreckage. There was still debris to deal with as well. As rescuers brought down sections that were dangerous, they would find someone else. For instance, a bystander who had been walking on the sidewalk outside the restaurant had been buried by the rubble.

We were very lucky that the surrounding office buildings that were damaged by the blast were empty that night, and that the smaller stores and apartments nearby were also empty. It was only because it was New Year's Eve, but I was still grateful. The death toll would have been much higher if it had happened on a regular day. People would have been home, or shopping, or at the office. The buildings would have had people in them, and they would have all been seriously injured or killed in the blast.

As it was, there were too many dead. Many of my staff and firefighters lost their lives in the explosion and subsequent collapse of the building.

My insurance contacted me quickly, likely due to all the media coverage. They called on the first, which was a surprise. They assured me that because the fire or explosion was not caused by the normal business of our restaurant, they would cover us completely. They'd be working with the insurance companies of the other properties that were damaged, and everyone would get covered. I was very thankful for that. I had nightmares that we would be held responsible. I was a rich man, but my wealth was limited.

The city reached out to me as well. Because we were located in Old Montreal, the repairs to the buildings had to be in keeping with the area's heritage architecture and must be approved in advance. This I already knew, because we renovated the building once. However, the city assured me that they would be able to help with the cost of repairing the building again. That was wonderful news, because I would have to hire companies who specialized in heritage restoration.

I also had to hire building engineers to look at the damage and assess the best way to fix it without tearing the whole building down. We were somewhat lucky that only one side of the bottom of the building was blown out completely. We had a construction crew there the very next day to shore up the exterior so it wouldn't fall down on investigators. That saved the building's exterior too, because it put an end to the cracking.

There wasn't anything they could do about the ceilings, or the floors of the second floor. They would have to be rebuilt. At least the elevator in the back of the building was undamaged, as was the staircase adjacent to the elevator shaft. This let the tenants on the top two floors evacuate their belongings quickly. These were all good things. The extent of the damage reached the second floor only.

But I still had to wait for the engineering report for final decisions.

All of these thoughts were going through my head as I watched the continuing news coverage on TV. My attention was caught by the newscast switching to a live reporter standing in front of the bombed area. I increased the volume as the reporter started speaking.

> *"I'm standing here just outside the terrible explosion that happened on New Year's Eve at the brand-new restaurant, L'Escalade. This event was to be their grand opening event, and it was meant to mirror their very successful event in Atlanta a couple of years ago.*
>
> *"As you can see, there is still glass and brick debris everywhere. The fire investigators are still trying to determine why the bomb went off. Before*

it did, one of the bomb techs on the scene had said that it could safely be defused. Tragically, that was said only a moment before that bomb tech himself was killed along with many other victims when the device exploded.

"Investigators have cleared both the owners of any wrongdoing, saying this device was brought in by an unknown subject and likely detonated offsite somehow. One person of interest is a cook who had been fired the day before the blast. Investigators have found that his name and address were fake. A photo of the person is on screen now. If you see this man, call the police immediately. Do not approach him.

"The question facing fire investigators now is how was the bomb detonated? I have learned that the bomb tech said there was no remote access on the bomb during his initial sweep of the device. To be safe, the police even jammed all cell signals in L'Escalade's vicinity as well, to minimize the risk of someone blowing it up remotely.

"The body count is currently up to seventeen. Most of the victims were staff, both kitchen and waiters. It appears that one head chef was lost. The other managed to leave by the back door. One of the owners, Justin Madera of Atlanta, Georgia, is currently missing. He was last seen just before the blast evacuating kitchen staff out the front door. Why he didn't evacuate them out the back is unknown."

"He was told to, you jerk!" I yelled at the television. "The firefighter that was in charge there told him to bring the kitchen staff out and give him their cell phones as they exited. No one expected the device to detonate."

"This is Stéphanie Rousseau for Channel 12 news."

I was pacing back and forth in front of the TV. I was so agitated, I was vibrating with anger.

"Hun, come and sit down with me in the meditation room," said Lora. "You need to decompress."

"I need to find Justin."

"We'll find him. Right now, come here. Let me take care of you."

I succumbed to her voice and followed her into her meditation room, which was where she had all her magical tools and books. It was a room imbued with calm. When you walked into it, you immediately felt like sighing and letting it all go.

She made me lie down on the pillows. She took off my shirt and gently rubbed an oil into my skin. I felt the tension ease away as her nimble fingers massaged my body. Everywhere she touched me, I could feel the muscles relax and let go. It didn't take long before I felt like putty in her hands. Lora was sitting behind my head and had placed my head in her lap. She was using two fingers to repetitively make light tracings on my forehead and around my eyes and across my face. With each tracing, I fell deeper into a trance that felt like a bath of warm water. Soon I couldn't tell where my skin ended, I felt I was floating freely. No weight pressed my body down on the pillows.

"My love, you are floating freely now, weightless and worriless. Let your mind drift and be calm," said Lora in a quiet, soothing voice.

I sighed and felt heavier in the relaxation, but never stopped being weightless. I dimly heard a phone ring, but ignored it.

Lora got up and padded out of the meditation room and answered the phone.

"Hello?"

"Is this Lora O'Reilly?" asked a very loud voice on the other end.

"Yes, this is her. What can I do for you?"

"This is EMT Specialist Carnak, I think we have found your friend, Justin. Can you come and identify him?"

"Oh my! That doesn't sound good. Is he … dead?"

"No, but he is very severely injured and unconscious. An ambulance is taking him to MUHC right now. Can you meet us?"

"Yes, I can do that. What's your name?" asked Lora, not knowing if the voice was male or female.

"Trixie," said the voice. "Trixie Carnak."

"Okay, Trixie, please send him to the MUHC and we will meet him there."

Thirty-five minutes later we were running through the emergency doors at MUHC. Rick ran up to the desk and asked about Justin.

"Yes, he was brought in about fifteen minutes ago. He's being looked at right now by a doctor. Please wait and we'll come and get you when we have information."

I went back to Lora in the waiting area and sat down.

"They have him. He's currently with a doctor. We have to wait."

"We'll wait. We found him. The worst is over."

Over two hours later, a doctor came out to the waiting area.

"Is there a Rick Benal here?"

"Yes, it's me and my wife. How is Justin?"

"Mr. Benal, please come with me." The doctor took us through the emergency ward and out through some sliding doors and down a hallway, until we came to a small conference room. "Come in here and we can have a talk."

Lora and I sat down, both anxious about this cloak and dagger routine. "Mr. Benal, Justin has suffered a very serious traumatic brain injury. We have to surgically remove some shrapnel in his head that is currently pressing on his memory center. As a result, he has no idea who he is. We only identified him because he was wearing his wallet and all his ID was intact."

"What's in his head?"

"A long metal pole penetrated his temple and went nearly all the way to his brainstem. When he arrived, he still had the pole in his head, thankfully. Had someone pulled it out, he would have died instantly. We have treated his other wounds for now, but the surgery has us very worried."

"What other wounds?"

"Well, it appears Justin was crushed by something. He has several broken ribs, and one of his hands was crushed. The worst injury was to his hips. They were also crushed. The EMT reported that he was found under a slab of concrete. We have an orthopedic surgeon coming in to make an assessment. However, if he doesn't survive the head surgery, there's no real point to further surgeries to rebuild his body. If you know what I mean."

"Yes," I said. "Is he in pain?"

"No, he's on morphine right now. We need to keep him calm and nearly comatose. This is going to be a very long road of recovery. Is there anyone else that should be notified? I would do that. Especially any close members of the family. They may want to say their goodbyes, just in case."

Lora gulped beside me and squeezed my hand. Justin was like a brother to me. I knew his parents and he was an only child. They were long dead though. There was no one to call. I was the only family he had.

"Mr. Benal, I have to get back, but may I have a phone number where I can reach you if things change?"

"Of course," I gave him both of our numbers. We then sat in the car outside the hospital for twenty minutes. Tears were running down my face silently. I didn't want to leave, but the surgeon said there was nothing we could do at this time.

But there was.

"Lora, what about giving Justin venom?"

"What do you mean?"

"Well, when we were trapped in the explosion, I found you with a grievous injury. A piece of shrapnel had cut your neck nearly clean through. You were bleeding out. I panicked. I couldn't have you die, so I bit you. I don't know why, except my instinct told me to—that it would save your life. And it did."

"How? Why haven't you told me this before?"

"It healed you, well mostly. There was still an injury when the EMTs found us, but it was no longer life-threatening. By the time you got to the hospital, it was mostly healed. I hadn't told you, because I didn't think it was necessary."

"But I'm immortal. Won't giving Justin venom turn him?"

"Only if I give him enough to do that. But a little may help his recovery. We have that last syringe we never used for Anita, and it's pure. It should help him recover."

"It also may start his transformation. Do you want to do that while he's unconscious? Doesn't he need to be consulted on something like that? It would be wrong."

"I can't let him die. He's like a brother to me," I wailed.

While we sat there in the parking lot, Lora called Falon and Andrews from the car. Gwen suggested calling Abeo, in case he had any ideas. I don't know what about, Justin was human.

"Rick, Gwen suggested calling Abeo. Do you want me to call?"

"Sure."

Lora put her phone on speaker.

"Abeo speaking. Oh, hi, Lora, what can I do for you?"

"I don't really know. Our very good friend Justin has been found buried under rubble after the bomb. He's in very bad shape and has a metal pole in his head. They're not sure if he'll live. For some reason, Gwen suggested calling you."

"Hmmm, probably because our blood can heal a human. But it's difficult to administer. We can't have humans seeing us do it, or we'll be hunted to the ends of the Earth."

"So, we could heal Justin's injuries with our blood?" she asked.

"Yup."

"How?"

"Well, he'll have to either ingest the blood, or we would give him transfusions."

"Won't a transfusion change him?" I asked.

"No, it will get absorbed by his body. More likely is his blood will fight our blood. But the healing properties will still work. He won't change without venom."

"He won't change?" she asked.

"He'd live healthier. He may get a little aggressive, but the effects will wear off in a few months."

"Justin aggressive?" I asked. "That will be the day. Catty, maybe."

"Rick, he really should be given a choice before you do anything," said Abeo.

"I understand."

I had to think about this. I told Lora to go home, while I got out and walked around for a while.

When I started back to the hospital, I made a decision. When I got to Justin's room, I discovered a small crowd around his bed. He was surrounded by interns and doctors. It looked like a scene from a TV medical program.

“This patient has a very unusual injury and will require some very delicate surgery,” said one doctor.

“I know, Doctor. However, it needs to be asked whether it is worth it. An injury like this almost certainly ends with death, and if not, a vegetative state. His family may not want to put him through that.”

“Hi there,” I interrupted from the edge of the curtain. “I’m as close to family as he has. He’s an orphan, and we’ve been best friends most of our lives. I have his power of attorney. What are you talking about?”

“Ah, Mr.…?” asked the doctor.

“Benal, Rick Benal. I’m his business partner as well.”

“Mr. Benal, your friend has a very difficult injury. The metal shrapnel has gone through two areas of the brain, and we do not expect him to survive with his sense of self intact. There is just too much damage. We were just trying to figure out what the best course of action was for the patient.”

“Can you remove the shrapnel?”

“Yes we can, but we won’t know what damage it’s done until he wakes up—if he wakes up.”

“Has the injury removed any part of his brain?”

“We don’t think so, but we’re fairly certain that there is damage, and the brain does not regenerate.”

“Will he die if you try to remove the metal?”

“Death is always a risk.”

“I know that Justin wouldn’t want to live as a vegetable. But neither would he not try to survive.”

“We can take him into the OR this afternoon. Before that, we want to give him a blood transfusion.”

“Oh, wonderful, I can help with that. We’re the same blood type,” I told them, adding, “You won’t need to test us, because we’ve done this before,” with a light compulsion.

The doctor stared at me and repeated what I said: "You can give blood and we won't need to test you."

The nurse looked at the surgeon with a question in her eye, but went ahead and prepared me for giving blood. They took one bag of blood from me and told me they would start infusing it into Justin after they did some CT scans on his head.

"I'll wait here for him, then," I said. They didn't like that, but I didn't give them a choice. Compulsion is handy that way.

Calling Lora, I sat down on the chair in Justin's room.

"Hi, hun, I've just spoken to the doctors. They were hedging their bets on surgery, but I kind of insisted. When they told me they wanted to give him a transfusion, it played right into my hand. They took the blood from me, and they'll give it to him before the surgery."

"Good work. Hopefully that will help him," said Lora. "I'll pass on the good news. What are you going to do now?"

"I'm going to wait here at the hospital. I may make some calls to the police and see what's happening with the investigation. Has Andrews turned up anything yet?"

"I don't know, I'll ask when I call them."

"Okay, love you."

"Love you too."

When I got off the phone, I tried to think of the name of the detective I had spoken to a day ago. I couldn't, so I went through the switchboard.

"MUC, how can I direct your call?"

"Hello, my name is Rick Benal. I am the co-owner of the restaurant that was bombed on New Year's Eve."

"Yes, sir, what can I do for you?"

"I'm trying to reach the detective who is investigating, but I have forgotten his name."

“That would be Detective Meunier, sir. One moment please while I connect you.”

“*Detective Meunier ici, puis ce-que vous aidez*?” *May I help you?*

“Hello, Detective, this is Rick Benal.”

“*Ah, oui, Monsieur Benal, bonjour*. How are you today?”

“I’m doing better, thanks. We have found my business partner, and he’s in the hospital right now.”

“Ah excellent! What can I do for you?”

“I was just wondering if you have any leads on who the bomber was.”

“We have some leads. We have located the source of the materials. It was a small parts store in Repentigny. We are now trying to match records to a name on purchases.”

“Repentigny? Isn’t that a town on the South Shore?”

“*En fait, non*, it’s on the north shore, on the way to Québec City. It’s just outside of Montréal.”

“I will look through our records to see if anyone who worked for us came from that town.”

“That would be good, Monsieur Bénal. Merci.”

“Is there anything else I can do?”

“We have the list of employees you had, and we have a list of the patrons for the evening,” said Meunier. “We are very lucky that it was a special event. You had everyone pre-pay and register. That saved us so much work. So thank you for that. Do you have a list of suppliers for the food that day?”

“I can assemble that for you, yes.”

“Let’s start with that and see where it goes. In the meantime, check with the fire chief, Chief LaChapelle, on the status of your building. I’m sure you want to get in there and rebuild.”

"Yes, I do and I don't. If Justin doesn't make it, I'm not sure I want to run the restaurant on my own."

"I hear you. Good day to you, sir."

"Thank you, Detective, and to you too."

I got off the phone not really feeling reassured they were making progress, but what could I do? I could call Andrews. Perhaps his company could make better progress.

Still in the waiting room, a doctor came and let me know that the transfusion had been delivered and they were about to take Justin into the OR. It would be a minimum of twelve hours before he was out. The doctor suggested I go home; the hospital would call us to let us know how Justin was. I called Lora and let her know I was coming home for a while.

"Let me know when he's out of surgery and I'll Uber into the hospital," I told the doctor as I left.

When I got home, I placed that call to Andrews. He said he would start an investigation for us. Not knowing what else to do at the moment, I lay down on the sofa because I was exhausted. I must have fallen asleep, because I woke up to Lora shaking my shoulders.

"Sleepyhead, wake up. The hospital called. Justin is out of surgery."

"Alright, love. Thanks," I said. "By the way, how are you doing? With everything that has been going on, how are you? I've been rather insensitive to you."

"No you haven't. There has been a lot to deal with. I'm fine. My wounds are all gone and the baby is fine too. No one even noticed I was pregnant because it's so new."

I touched my wife's belly tenderly, then kissed her lovingly. She responded as always with passion and heat. I didn't want to leave her arms, but I needed to be with Justin. So, regretfully, I broke us apart and left. Five seconds later, she came barreling through the door and ran up to the car holding the syringe of venom.

“Just in case you feel you need to use this.”

“Thanks.”

Back at the hospital, I discovered they had moved Justin up to the surgical floor, so I went up immediately. He was just out of the OR when I arrived. A doctor came looking for me.

“Monsieur Benal?”

“Yes, that’s me.”

“Your brother, Justin, has made it through the first surgery. We experienced no problems, which was a miracle, and his brain seems to have been spared any serious trauma. When we opened him up, the tissue was swollen but not damaged. He may yet recover fully intact. I am extremely hopeful, and I wouldn’t have believed that to be possible before the surgery.”

“What’s next?” I asked, letting out my breath in relief. I felt a huge weight lifted off my shoulders, telling me I had made the right decision. Justin would survive.

“We will wait for him to wake up—because I now believe he will—and see what condition he’s in. You can go and wait in his room if you want.”

“Thank you. Which one is it?”

“Room 4213.”

“Got it.” That was on this floor, but in another wing. It took me a while to decipher the floor plan and figure out which way to go. Why were hospitals so confusing?

When I got there, Justin was propped up in bed but still out. I sat in the chair beside him and called Lora.

“Is he out of surgery?” she asked.

“Yes, they just brought him to a room. He’s on the fourth floor. Room 4213.”

“I’m on my way.”

4—Remembering a Tsunami

Gwen

We had all just lived through another tragedy. Why did it seem this time of year was a trap for tragedies? My life seemed like an unending list of horrible events at this time of year—the year end. The anniversary date of my first disaster was January—the year the tsunami that wiped out my family. I could not help reliving it.

Every year I slump into a depression because I end up remembering all the disasters that have happened at this time of year, notably the Haitian earthquake, the Japanese earthquake and tsunami, and the Indian Ocean tsunami. Hundreds of them with countless lives lost or destroyed.

My own disaster happened just a month after the Winter Solstice that year, in 1700.

When I was a girl, my family lived with the Haida indigenous people for three summers. We arrived on the coast after leaving the underground city my parents grew up in, on an overcast day. There was very little sunshine on this coast.

There were all kinds of small islands dotting the water up and down the mainland. My parents had decided to live on one of them and stay there isolated from the humans. However, we hadn't counted on the Haida. They were persistent people and didn't want us to be alone. In fact, they adopted us into their village and helped my parents build a home close by. Fortunately, learning their language was easy for us.

The Haida were smart people, and listened to nature carefully, paying attention to its warnings. That's why it was a surprise they had no forewarning of the disaster to happen on that day.

January 26th, 1700 started out as any other day. Partially overcast. My friends and I were skipping stones on the beach. Our mornings were filled with chores, but the afternoon was ours until dinnertime. Then we were expected to help prepare the meal.

The adults were sitting around the fire talking, drumming, and swapping stories. The children were dancing. When the little ones started falling asleep, everyone went to their separate homes to bed.

My family was all asleep except for me. I couldn't sleep, so I got up and walked down to the water's edge.

I was sitting on the beach staring at the moon. It was a very quiet night, with a few sea birds squawking. The waves weren't being pushed by wind offshore, they were sneaking onto shore with tiny ripples. Until the strangest thing happened: all the water disappeared, leaving the ocean floor bare to the sky.

One of the Haida was walking down the beach and saw this happen as well. Suddenly he became very animated, shouting at me to move fast.

"Gwenolin, go wake up your family quick and make your way up the cliff as high as you can go! Now!" he yelled at me.

I got up and ran to do what he said. He ran into the village and started banging on the big drum that acted as a warning system for all the villages nearby. It made a deep booming bass noise that traveled great distances. In a split second, I heard another drum make the same noise, then another, and another. All the drums within hearing distance were sending out a warning, but I had no idea of what.

By the time I reached my family's hut, everyone else was awake in the village. I yelled at my parents to wake them up. My groggy father got angry and told me to go back to sleep. But my mother heard the drums and shook my father awake as I reached for my little brother and sister. Picking them up, I ran to the trail that went up the mountain. Many others were trying to reach the cliff too. The way up was treacherous.

My parents were behind me when I heard the roar. I stopped dead and turned around. My siblings jumped from my arms and ran to my parents and were picked up by them. I watched in horror as a massive wall of water rushed into the bay and over the beach, over the huts, over the boats, and just kept going. The waves tore everything down in its path.

When the roiling water hit the bottom of the trail, it didn't stop. The water climbed higher and higher as it got deeper and deeper. I watched huts on the hill across the village from us get washed away from their platforms as the water swept through the village.

I turned back to look at my parents but they weren't there. They were gone from the trail—and now the water was coming for me and it was moving fast.

I turned back up the hill and ran as quickly as I could. But the water was faster. As it grabbed my feet, it made the ground slushy and impassable. So I fell down on my face and clung onto a small tree to stop myself from being washed away into the sea.

Using that small tree, once the water started receding I could stand up.

I was looking for my family in the wreckage when another wave came crashing in, bigger than the first.

My little tree wasn't going to help this time, so I ran farther up the hill and tried to climb a big tree to get off the ground. The water caught up to me again, swirling around my knees.

I waited for the water to recede again. Looking toward the sea, the forest down to the beach had been washed away. The water left huge trees lying on their sides among the wreckage of buildings and boats.

Then a third wave came rushing in, even bigger again. This time I didn't stop until I reached the top of the hill overlooking the beach. It was a very tall cliff and rock, so hopefully it wouldn't get washed away.

On the top of the cliff I found some of the Haida had managed to make it to safety. They were all clinging to each other and howling with sorrow at the loss they were witnessing. So many of their people were gone. A community of 1,500 was reduced to about a dozen. It was then that I noticed the drums weren't talking anymore. What had happened? Had all the villages been wiped out?

The third wave had pushed even farther into the bay, saturating the land with seawater for nearly as far as we could see. It had traveled up the river valley. All the newly planted crops were destroyed. Their food stores from last year were gone, the storage hut had been destroyed by the water. All their furs, shelter, boats, and their lives had been taken away by the water. Oh my, what were we going to do?

I could not find my family among the survivors on the top of the cliff, so I did the unthinkable: I started searching through the forest, what was left of it. The shoreline, which had moved inland about fifty paces, was inaccessible. It was clogged with the remains of our village.

When the water started receding, it still covered the spot where our hut had been located. What beach was left lay covered with broken trees and branches, boats and pieces of the village buildings. Occasionally, you saw a flash of color indicating a piece of clothing, which meant a person was buried there.

The adults who were left got together and sent one of their men to the next village to see if they had survived, and another man inland to a cousin village. Several hours later, the braves returned with men in tow. They organized a search party, looking for people who were alive first. Digging out the debris, the women sorted the pieces in case anything could be salvaged. The men dug under the debris looking for people who may have been able to shelter. A few people were found alive and they were carried to the top of the cliff, where the elder women cared for them. All told, about twenty people were found in the wreckage of the village.

The rest were gone.

The whole village—people who were able, including the children—worked until it was dark looking for survivors. Each one found was taken up the cliff to be tended by the elder women.

Some of the older men created a large fire on the top of the cliff so everyone could get warm and dry out. Everything was soaked with seawater. A couple of braves went hunting up the mountain so they could feed everyone. But they were all focused on their own people, and I had slipped through the cracks.

I was wandering through the forest calling for my family, trying to find them. I found my sister's shirt but not her. I found my father's shoe, but it was under a very large tree, and I could not move it. I ran back to the Haida and asked if someone could help me move the tree. They sent two braves back with me.

We tried and tried, but we could not move the tree more than a hand's width.

I sat down on the wet ground and cried. My whole world was gone. I didn't know what to do. The braves told me to come with them. When I didn't react, one of them picked me up and carried me back to the fire on top of the cliff. One of the Haida women took charge of me. She sat me down and made sure I ate, then put me with the other children to lie on a pallet of dry evergreen branches to sleep.

Who knew what the next day would bring?

That next day, the remnants of the village were brought together and a discussion took place. It was decided that the remaining people would travel inland to find other villages that could take them in.

The difficult journey started a few days later. The elders chose to stay behind and forage for whatever they could find. The journey overland would be too grueling for them. The braves hunted a buck for them, and we left them some shelter and blankets and bid them goodbye. Going across the mountains the second time was more brutal than when I crossed with my parents. We were all weakened from lack of food and water.

Many moons came and went before we found another village, and it was only by luck. A hunting party came upon us resting by a river. Hearing our story, they invited everyone back. But when they saw me, they almost blocked my way. I didn't look like Haida. I had blond hair and blue eyes. I was clearly of different descent. The Haida stood up for me, saying that my family had lived with their village, and that I had lost them all. So the new tribe took pity on me and let me stay with them too. The First Nations people had a very generous spirit, and a compassionate point of view.

I stayed with them until my early thirties. I had taken a husband according to their customs, but we had not created life. The shaman blamed my spirit, saying that it could not be taken by my husband's spirit, and therefore I was barren. Mother Creator had made me too strong, and I was destined to be barren until I found a man whose spirit was strong enough to conquer mine.

An entire group of people disappeared that night. There was no time for the villagers to save themselves. Everyone and everything was lost, swept out to sea. Modern science says there were two earthquakes off the coast, in the Cascadia fault line, one an 8.7 on the Richter Scale, and the other 9.5.

According to the oral history of surviving First Nations, the ground shook for five minutes. Then a wave thirty meters high—that is five storeys—hit land at Pachena Bay. The Raven clan of the Haida Gwaii people were all but wiped out. Those were the people who had taken us in and adopted us as family.

The tsunami flooded so far inland that it created a ghost forest. All the trees died where they stood without falling down; their leaves were all gone, only skeletons left, as far as the eye could see. Closer to shore, the forests had been flattened. Even up the cliffs, the trees had been flattened and nothing was left. All up and down the West Coast, devastation was found, people lost, cultures lost.

The Hakai area had been lived on by the Haida Gwaii continuously for 14,000 years. Artifacts from their culture were found as deep as seven meters underground. Those people cared for me, for my family. And then they were gone.

How strange it now seems, to have the words of that shaman echo back to me after three hundred years. Those people were right, and wrong. Mother Creator had made me too strong and I had remained barren—until I met Andrews, a man whose spirit was so strong he could tame me, conquer me, and give me a child.

This time of year had suddenly changed meaning for me. I'd been given a second chance. Long ago, I had been told my future, one that I had doubted vociferously. But now it has come to pass. I could now look back on that time without so much sadness, and a little bit of happiness.

While I personally felt something good had happened now, my thoughts returned to Rick and Justin and the disaster they'd just been through.

This time of year …

5—Looks Can be Deceiving

Falon

Mark and I had a date night planned—something we hadn't done in a long while. I spent extra time and care preparing myself. It seemed like forever since we'd had time to be relaxed and intimate. My body was missing him.

For some reason I was excited and nervous. When I drew a bath and added some lovely scents and bubbles, I sank into the water and just soaked for a while. David Arkenstone was playing on my Bluetooth speaker, and I just stretched out and let myself drift on the music in the warmth. My hand absently caressed the baby bump I was starting to show. I was excited about being a mom.

Our lives were pretty human. I mean, I didn't know what I expected my life to be after agreeing to become immortal, but it really hadn't changed that much. Not in any paranormal way. We had to be so vigilant about giving ourselves away, we were almost too human in public. It didn't help that Mark and I had made ourselves public figures with the charity. At the time, it seemed like a very clever idea, and it satisfied something in me to solve one of our society's problems. But it painted a bull's eye on our backs for the media and for anyone who might not like what we were doing. We had to be extra careful that neither of us showed any immortal characteristics. To that end, I promoted skin care, setting up the questions that would inevitably come about "not aging." If Jennifer Aniston could get away with looking the same for more than two decades, then so could I.

Men just naturally get away with it. All they need is a little gray in their hair and they're good. Not that Mark would age, but he'd always be perfect. Sigh. He was perfect. I closed my eyes and sank under the surface for a moment so that I was completely surrounded with the heat of the water. Touching myself, pretending it was his fingers, didn't bring me much satisfaction. I needed him.

Exhaling bubbles as I surfaced, I got busy shaving my legs so they were baby smooth, then shaved a little design into my pussy, just to surprise him. I washed my hair and let it flow down my back in the sudsy water. I'd always thought my hair was one of my best traits, long and lustrous with nice natural waves. Some women spent money to get what I had, so I didn't take it for granted. Showering off the suds and the soap out of my hair, I gave myself a masque treatment so my hair would be soft and silky.

Wrapped in a couple of towels, I walked into the closet to decide what to wear. We were going to dinner, then dancing. Something sexy, except he'd seen everything. I didn't have time to go shopping.

"Lora, I need your help," I said when she answered the phone.

"What's up, dear?"

"I have a date with Mark tonight and I don't have anything to wear!"

"That's ridiculous. I'll be over in a jiffy."

True to her word, the doorbell rang a few minutes later. I answered in my towels.

"You could always wear that," she said, carrying some clothes. "Let's go take a look at this tragedy."

Lora dumped the clothes she had brought on the bed, then walked into my closet and started going through all the clothes. When she found a piece she liked, she threw it on the bed. When she was finished, she sat on the bed.

"Rule number one: no underwear."

"No?"

"Uh uh."

"But my boobs need support."

"We'll give them support, don't worry."

She pulled out a very tight, stretchy, sequined, tube top and a short black skirt.

"Start with this."

The top squashed my boobs at first, until she reached inside and pulled them up so that the nipples were almost at the top edge. The compression of the top kept them there. I pulled the top up just a bit more to make sure my nipples stayed undercover.

The skirt was short, very short. It hugged my hips too. It was so tight, it would have been difficult to walk if it had been any longer. Instead, I was concerned that my ass would be hanging out.

"Lora, I look like a working girl!"

"Nope, this is the style today—tight and short. Now we will dress it up with a gold shirt."

The shirt was designed to be like a jacket, long, almost mid-thigh, but it was sheer and it had gold thread woven through it. It looked smashing with the black sequins. The shirt was a couple of inches longer than the skirt too.

"Are you sure this isn't a throwback to the '80s?"

"It is, but the kids are wearing this today. It's like the '80s, but more extreme and with lots of glitter. Today it's all about curves and sheer fabrics. If you can wear something that looks naked but technically isn't, you're in style."

"What ever happened to leaving something to the imagination?"

"Gone. Now it's 'put your goods on display.'"

"Ugh."

"Big hoop earrings to complete the look. Oh, and leave your hair down."

"It gets hot dancing."

"Yeah, but leave your hair down. It looks sexy. Come, let's do your makeup."

I sat for her while she did my makeup. It seemed more like costume makeup than wearing makeup. My eyes were made to look huge, with long wings coming from the corners. She used dark purple and black for the shadow. The effect was striking. She put on lashes, which tickled like crazy, but they swept back and forth.

"I can certainly bat these lashes!"

"Shh! I'm not finished."

Lora added little gems at the corners of my eyes too. She finished up by sculpting my face with deep tones that brought out the auburn in my brown hair. Deep red lips finished the picture.

When I looked at myself in the mirror, I barely recognized myself.

"Wow. That's a transformation."

"Good. Now have fun!" With that, the whirlwind that was Lora left, leaving me to think about the night ahead. I had about thirty minutes before I needed to leave to meet Mark. The kernel of excitement in my gut started jumping up and down wildly with my imagining his face when he saw me. At the last minute, I put on a thong. I couldn't go out without some kind of underwear.

I decided to Uber into town so I didn't have to worry about parking. When the car dropped me off in my four-inch heels, the driver gave me an appreciative wink. "Honey, you look hawt tonight. If your date is not there, call me back. I'd be honored to be your date."

"Thank you," I said, closing the door. Not necessary, really.

As I walked into the building, I got plenty of stares. I wasn't used to this attention. I couldn't help but feel self-conscious. Even wearing a coat over the outfit didn't hide my face, and the four-inch heels were obvious. I was alone in the elevator at least, and when the doors opened there was no one else on the floor, so I walked to his office quietly. I knocked, and waited until I heard him say, "Come."

I removed my coat and walked in dragging it behind me. He wasn't looking up, so when he did his face jumped back to being Zisis for a split second. He was speechless for a minute or so, just drinking in my appearance. He swallowed heavily.

"Falon, you are, wow … stunning. It's the only word I have at the moment because my brain stopped working."

I chuckled. "I'll take that." I took a step closer. "I kinda like the face change."

"My what?" he asked, confused. "Oh, my face changed?"

"I saw Zisis for a moment."

"Oh, sorry. I didn't mean to. I was just so shocked and surprised, in a wonderful way."

"I didn't mind. Do it again. Please."

His face relaxed into the Greek god visage of Zisis. My loins tightened significantly. I growled out loud as the lust shot through me.

His response was a growl of his own as he leapt over the desk and took me into his arms.

"I hope you brought your lipstick, because it is not going to stay this way for long." He kissed me hard then, a kiss like I hadn't had in a long time, demanding and sweet, impassioned and filled with longing, lustful and hot as hell. It demanded submission and I was happy to comply. One of his hands went under my skirt to my heat, and the groan that escaped from his throat was delicious. His fingers gently lifted my thong and probed my folds. He felt my excitement, took my sex, and turned me into gelatin very quickly. It's a good thing his other arm was around my waist.

"You're barely wearing underwear," he said, breathlessly, his face returning to Mark.

"I am." I kissed him again, deeply reaching into his mouth and rubbing my tongue on his fangs. "Wait," I said, panting. "Let's try something new."

"What would that be?"

"Take me as Zisis again."

"As you command." His face changed into Zisis. I was looking at the man I initially fell so hard for. Everything about this was a massive turn-on. It was like having an affair with an old boyfriend without cheating.

He spun around and sat me down on his desk, pulling off my thong, unzipping his trousers and stepping between my thighs.

"I need you right now," he said quietly. His rock-hard cock pointed directly to where he wanted to go. In one thrust, he impaled himself deeply.

"Fuck! Zisis! Oh my God. Fuck me."

He grabbed my ass and pulled me against him, pushing himself deeper inside me. As his thrusts became deeper, my screams became louder and the closer I got to a climax. Locking my ankles behind him, I leaned backward to push even further.

"Falon, my God, I'm going to climax! Ah! God, Fuck! He sped up and the orgasm took both of us together.

I collapsed against his chest as my body shuddered in the throes of climax. He was throbbing inside me like he needed to go again.

"That's one way to finish a workday," he said, chuckling. "It's a good thing we're alone here right now." At that moment, someone walked past his open door and called out "goodnight!" without looking up and walking by quickly.

We both burst out laughing, clinging to each other. Considering we hadn't removed any outer clothing, we both still looked like we were dressed, except for the fact that his cock was inside me. Of course, the way I was sitting, you couldn't see that. However, the noise we made surely made it quite clear what we were doing. I hoped that person wouldn't be too embarrassed to come into work tomorrow.

"How are you doing?" he asked me.

"I'm still hungry." I realized I was so horny still that it surprised me. Zisis kissed my neck and sucked on my ear, sending shivers throughout my body again. He lay me down on the desk and squeezed and kneaded my breasts, which were getting larger and firmer because of the pregnancy. When he started pulling down the tube top to expose my nipples, I got all excited again. He took a nipple in his teeth and gently tugged on it, licking around it and then sucking deeply on it. After what seemed like ten minutes, my head was dizzy, and I was flushed with heat throughout my body. He carefully lapped up the beads of sweat dripping between my breasts that set off the perfume I had applied there—Goddess Oil.

Discovering the Goddess Oil, Zisis groaned and his nose dove between my breasts and inhaled the scent deeply. He stood up, lifted me off the desk, then flipped me over so that I was bent over the edge of it. My ass was nicely exposed now and he didn't need to remove my skirt. His fingers found my vagina and one found my ass. He applied pressure to both sensitive areas at the same time, making me buck and scream some more. Just when I didn't think I could take more, he pressed his cock into my vagina just a little, teasing me, moving in and out, slicking me up and making me pant.

I was now so horny, I needed more.

"Let's go to the sofa," I suggested. He stopped what he was doing and helped me stand. I looked at that face again, and pushed him backwards to the sofa on the back wall of his office. He fell down into the pillows. His cock was standing up so I straddled him, finally understanding the dress code for clubbing today—easy access—and took his amazing cock into my hands. He'd always been well-endowed, but he was beautifully shaped as well, long and thick, with a light curve upward. That curve was very useful to hit all the best spots inside. His cock was harder than usual, and already producing lubricant, which was completely unnecessary. I rubbed him on my clit, making my own breath catch as the sensation nearly overwhelmed me. Positioning him at my vagina, he placed his hands on my hips and lifted himself to take me at the same time I pushed down on him. In one motion, he was fully inside me, tipping me, pressing against that innermost sensitive spot, the spot that made me lose all control.

For a moment, I held him there, gently squeezing him, feeling him there in all his length.

"Oh God, Falon, I needed you so much. It seems like we've lost touch, this … this here … is my ultimate happy spot with you."

"Zisis, I missed you so much." I started to rock back and forth, feeling him rub me inside, feeling him move in and out with delicious hardness. Every time I pulled him out, as I drove him back inside he would gasp. I drew out the sense of connection as long as I could, until I needed release, and him to take control.

"Zisis, fuck me hard."

"Then get on your knees," he answered me.

I didn't think the sofa would be too comfortable for that position, so my idea was to bend over a chair. His guest chair was nicely padded, so I bent over, bracing my arms on the handrests. He smiled and licked his lips. He stepped behind me and bent his body over me so that his cock was pushing between my legs. He licked my shoulder, my neck, my earlobe, nipped and licked and kissed, while his cock gently moved back and forth between my legs.

I was so horny now, I needed him to take me.

"Enough teasing, take me!" I bit his bicep, delivering my own venom. I counted in my head one … two … and he thrust hard as the drug hit his blood. I felt him gasp suddenly and his cock slid into place suddenly.

He took hold of my waist to gain some control and drove into me, each thrust hitting the end of my channel and my deep touchstone, sending waves of pleasure and pain through me, building higher and higher as he slapped against me. He hardened and lengthened, indicating he was about to climax, while I felt my own wave come to a crest. I was riding on the top of it, and the moment he released he bit down, flooding my body with his venom. My mind crashed, and I was set free as I hit higher than I had in a while.

His seed pumped into me as his last thrusts finished him off. As the shuddering calmed in both of us, we stretched out together, still connected. We had to stay there like that, bent over the chair until he could pull out. He couldn't separate until he got softer. He was such a perfect fit, it caused a suction until he got smaller. That often took an hour.

"This was not a good position to get locked in," he said with chagrin.

"It could be worse."

"How?"

"We would have to call 9-1-1 to separate us."

"Ugh!"

"Oh, Mark, I love you so much, and that was so much fun."

"Who is this Mark?"

I turned my head to look at his face. I grinned, saying, "Oh, he's just another lover I have."

"You're stepping out on me, woman?"

"Not often, although I've missed you." I realized I had completely processed the duality of Mark/Zisis now. I didn't care which face he wore. In private, I kind of liked seeing Zisis. The differences were so subtle and yet distinct. One didn't look like the other, and yet they did. They had the same body, even though Zisis showed his off and Mark was always wearing suits so you didn't see what was underneath.

I felt him pull out, so I stood up and turned to face him.

"You know, I love any face you care to give me," I said, touching his face. These were the features that drew me in the first time, the perfection of his face. I realized I had never lost Zisis at all. How special was it that my man could be anyone? Talk about variety. But I didn't want variety, I just wanted him.

"So where are you taking me on our date, Zisis?"

"I have a special evening planned, and then more of this," he replied.

"Mmm," I said. "Can we play a little game?"

"What kind of game?"

"Switching up who we are."

"That could be interesting. I'll have to teach you how we do that. It will take practice."

"I love practicing!"

6—Back to Consciousness

Justin

Pain was slowly creeping into my dreams, and it was affecting what I was dreaming about. At first, it was an endless parade of decorators who brought samples to me to choose from for the new restaurant. There were so many things to decide on: color of the chairs, fabric, drapery, wallpaper, paint colors, light fixtures. Normally, I adored this aspect of building, but for some reason my temper was short and I was yelling at everyone. Just not like me. Okay, I was bossy in the kitchen, but I had to be to make sure everything was done to perfection. I had a reputation to uphold after all.

As the different decorators were coming into the office and leaving, each time one left I felt another stab of pain somewhere in my legs. I was having trouble moving and realized I was tied to my chair behind this huge, ugly Victorian desk. Who uses Victorian decor today? Really! My legs were tied down and I couldn't move them. I bent over to untie them and hit my head on the desk. A dull throb from the back started to hurt, which was very strange indeed. When Rick came in and opened up the heavy drapes—again, who uses heavy velvet drapes today?—the light stung my eyes and made them water terribly. Rick was bending over me, crooning like a little old lady and making sounds like a mourner at a funeral.

I lifted my head in spite of the throbbing and asked him what was wrong.

"Justin?" asked Rick. "Are you waking up? Come on, buddy, come back to me."

"What do you mean *come back*?" I managed to get out of my very dry mouth. It ended in a fit of coughs, which prompted Rick to insert a straw into my mouth. I thankfully took a few pulls on the straw, filling my mouth with delicious cool water before it was taken away. "More," I croaked out.

"No, the doctor said little bits at a time." Rick sat down in a chair beside the bed.

"Why?"

"Because you've been through an ordeal and nearly died, that's why."

"Died?"

"Very nearly. Do you remember the New Year's Eve party?"

"No."

"What's the last thing you remember?"

I thought, and the last thing that was clear to me was the night I had drinks. "Greggory."

"What about Greggory?"

"Date."

"When was that?"

"Christmas."

"So you don't remember anything about New Year's, the opening, the bombing?"

"Bombing?" I asked, alarmed.

"The restaurant was attacked. Somehow, someone planted a bomb on one of our dessert carts and it went off just after midnight. We managed to get all the customers out, and some of the staff, but you were caught in it, along with me and Lora and about fifteen other kitchen staff and two firemen."

"Oh my God."

"Yes. The worst was you disappeared. We couldn't find you in the wreckage. We were afraid you were lost. They eventually found you buried under the rubble, badly injured and unconscious. You were brought to the hospital."

"Disappeared?"

"Well, we couldn't find you in the wreckage of the restaurant. Oh, Justin, it's gone. The whole thing is gone."

"Gone?"

"The building has been tagged unsafe by the city until we get engineers to assess the whole damage and see whether it can be rebuilt or whether we have to tear it down. All the tenants had to move out. I've put them up in a hotel for now, and hopefully they'll be able to get back in to pack their things."

"Geez."

"How are you feeling?"

"Not good. Woozy, headache. And my legs, I can't feel my legs."

"They're still there, for now."

"For now?"

"Well, your legs and lower torso were so damaged they were afraid they may have to amputate."

"Now?"

"Now we're waiting to see how you heal."

"How would I heal from that?"

"Well, that's a complicated explanation. It's kinda weird and scary. Right now, we're waiting to see how your head injury heals."

"What happened to my head?"

"A piece of pipe impaled your head. They just removed it."

"How did I survive that?"

"You were lucky."

"I'll say, who gets luck like that?"

"I gave you blood."

"Thank you—but hey wait a minute, you're not my type. I'm type B."

"Correct. But I'm a universal donor."

"Oh, thank you. How would that have helped me survive a pipe through my head again?"

"My blood has curative properties."

"Curative, as in healing, as in … what?"

"My blood can heal someone."

"What? No! It does? What gibberish are you speaking! Speak plainly, Rick!"

"Okay. Here goes." Rick got out of the chair, made sure the door was closed, then came back to the bed.

"I'm immortal."

"Rick, stop talking crazy."

"I'm not crazy, I'm immortal. Watch." Before I could stop him, he pulled out a pocketknife and sliced open his wrist in front of me. I shrieked and then watched it heal, like nothing was there in three seconds."

"Oh. My. God."

"Yes, well, my blood helped you through the surgery. It repaired the damage before they got in so they only had to remove the pipe and close you up."

"Oh my God, oh my God."

"Do you have anything else you can say?"

"Oh my fucking God."

"Well, that's different at least."

"You're not shitting me, are you?" It was more of a statement than a question.

"Nope."

"How long have you known this juicy tidbit without telling me, hun?"

"As long as I've known you, I've known there was something different about me since I was a kid. However, it wasn't until I met Lora and her friends that I was able to know just what that 'difference' was. Lora, Falon, and Mark are the same. So are Gwen and Andrews, Margaret and Abeo. We now have this little community together."

"Wait, okay, there is just too much to absorb right now. Let's come back to that. What about me?"

"Because I gave you my blood, it will heal your injuries. It should even heal your leg injuries, but it will take time."

"How much time?"

"I'd say weeks, perhaps a couple of months at most."

"That seems fast. Is that fast?"

"It's fast for a human, yes. So somehow we have to get you out of the hospital, before they notice that you're healing."

"What about going home for medical care?"

"You mean like to Atlanta?"

"Yeah. Then not actually going. But I don't have anywhere to stay right now if the building is ruined."

"Don't worry about that, we can find you a place to convalesce."

"I'll pay anything. I'm good for the money. Even a hotel would suffice."

"It's not about the money."

"Then what?"

"It has to do with secrecy. I will have to get back to you—I have to speak to someone first. I'll see you later this afternoon."

"Wait, what day is it? How long have I been here?"

"It's January 5th. It took a couple days to clear the restaurant site before we realized you were missing. The next day, you were found and brought here, and it took a day for them to decide how to proceed."

"A week?"

"Yes, almost," I said. "Look, I've got to go, but I'll be back, and I will let everyone know you're awake now. They all want to come visit."

After Rick left, I lay there thinking about all he had just told me. *I've lost a week!* What would we do about L'Escalade? Who would bomb the restaurant? *Why? A bomb!* Thank goodness most of the people got out. I needed to send condolences to those families who lost someone. I needed to speak to insurance and the fire department. *I need to get out of here!* Greggory! *Oh my, I wonder how he is.* He was there that night. Did he get out? Rick didn't say anything. Surely he would say something if one in our circle had been injured.

Who else had been there that night? Mark and Falon had been to the early sitting. That hunky Andrews and Gwen were there too, but which sitting? I could not remember. My head was too fuzzy. I closed my eyes, which were hurting, to block out the light. I heard the door open quietly and close, and footsteps approaching the bed.

I was drifting at this point, because the walls had taken on a watery look. The meds they were giving me made it difficult to focus.

"Justin?" asked a quiet voice. "Are you awake?" I felt a hand take one of mine and cover it with another, and then someone sat on the edge of the bed. I cracked open an eye and peered out.

I wanted it to be Greggory. I was worried about him. I couldn't tell who it was though. Do I know you?

"Are you okay? Are you able to speak?'

No, I can't speak, my throat feels like the Sahara and I can't even think straight! What do you think? I had a pipe in my fucking head!

"Hello, you are Justin Medera, right?"

What does it say on my tag, honey? Who the fuck are you? I wanted to scream but my lips wouldn't move.

"My name is Robin Walker. I'm with the Montreal Gazette. I'd like to ask you some questions if you feel up to it."

What do you think? I managed to move my head side to side. Go the fuck away!

"Please? I won't take long."

Oh gawd, please save me from some stupid girl who won't take no for an answer.

I nodded my head once.

"I can work with that. First question: As the co-owner of L'Escalade, will you be rebuilding in Montreal?"

I nodded my head.

"Can you elaborate?"

I shook my head.

"Okay, second question: Can you think of who would want to destroy your restaurant? Is it tied to the one in Atlanta?"

I shook my head.

"One more? Do you think the target was you, the restaurant, or some attending customer?"

I tried to shrug my shoulders, but couldn't.

"May I reserve the chance to come back when you're feeling better?"

I shook my head.

"Was that a gentleman who left your room before?"

I nodded my head.

"Is he your partner?"

I nodded my head.

"You were listed as one of the most eligible bachelors just before Christmas. Has that changed?" asked Walker.

"Are you gay or straight? Your fashion sense says gay," she fired another question at me.

I managed to let a scream out of my mouth, and the reporter scurried out of my room.

What the fuck is wrong with people? Why does it always come down to who the hell I want to fuck? Why is it anyone's goddamn business? She wouldn't have pressed those questions on a straight guy. They wouldn't come out and ask a guy if he prefers men or women. They assume he's straight until they're given the news. But why does it have to be news? For fuck's sake, let us just love who the hell we want and fuck off!

I was so goddamn tired of this shit. Why the hell is there this endless game of asking is he gay or is he not? Even television programs now have to have their token gay, not always played by gay actors either. Or if the program is about gay life, they have a token straight guy who's everyone's friend. Fuck! Life isn't like that. We don't go around and ask each other who the other is fucking!

Orientation and skin color; gotta have your token black dude; now it's a Latino and you have to have a token lez or homo in the cast too. Or else you take two female characters and suddenly make them interested in fucking each other, with no chemistry at all. You know, why don't they hire the right actors for those roles?

Society hasn't improved. The LGBTQ community fights so hard to be treated equally, but first people have to stop making distinctions so people stop asking questions, like it's important who the hell I want to fuck.

This had my blood pressure pumping again. My head was throbbing and I needed a drink. I just wanted to be Justin Madera, master chef, co-owner of Escalata and L'Escalade. That's it. It shouldn't matter who adorns my arm at an award ceremony, just that I am there to win.

Well, that managed to waste a bunch of time. Hopefully, Rick would come back soon. I needed answers.

7—An Outing

Lora

It had been almost two years since we brought the witches back to this world from the pocket dimension. Gwen had a baby, we met Abeo and Margaret, they had triplets, and some of us moved into new homes. And just recently, we had a bombing to get past. It had been a busy two years.

I had left the witches we rescued with Amarlyis for reintegration into the twenty-first century. I figured they could stay on the ark ship, go to school, catch up on education and history, and learn some twenty-first century skills.

Within a few months of them being rescued, we assigned one of the crew quarters to each of the witches as a residence. At first, it was like they were living in the Stone Abut we though. There was no power. Thankfully I knew someone who knew the ships. I asked Abeo how to turn the power on, and he came with me to start the ship's systems and left me with instructions on bringing the ship back to life. The ship was a living entity. It could generate its own power, and it could dispose of waste.

A year later, Amarlyis was supposed to be teaching them basic math, reading, and writing, as well as how to cope with general life. They were supposed to be learning about shopping, banking, where to get food, clothing, and everything else. But when I visited them, that's not what was happening. They were all happy, but basically still living like it was 1795.

Now that Justin seemed to be on the mend, I felt I had to take some leadership and make sure they were progressing. I had been negligent in monitoring what they were being taught.

The last time I spoke to Amarlyis and asked about our thirteen guests, she had told me that most were learning very well, and a couple of them felt they were ready to integrate into modern life. So I decided to book a day and take Falon with me for a visit to the coven's location. We arrived at the occult store and Innogen transferred us to the ship without comment.

"That was a little uncharacteristic of her, wasn't it?" asked Falon.

"Being quiet, yes a little. I hope we aren't walking into something."

We started down the extremely long tunnel leading to the launch room we had performed the ritual in. As we got closer, we heard voices echoing up the walls, so we knew people were in that main room. Exiting the tunnel, we saw that they had managed to learn quite a bit about the cavern, how the machinery worked, and we saw ample lighting—in fact, it was almost daylight inside.

"Greetings, visitors," said one of the men on the platform. "Who shall I announce to Amarlyis has arrived?"

"Wow, that's formal," said Falon.

"Hello, I'm Lora O'Reilly. I was the one who organized your rescue from the pocket dimension."

"Oh! Indeed, Amarlyis has spoken of you and your power."

"I didn't get your name," I said, hoping he would let me know.

"Of course, I am known as Dubh. However, I would like to choose a modern name."

"Oh, that's fun. We can help," said Falon.

"We're here to speak to all of you, to find out who is interested in a foray into the modern city."

"Lora, when is now?"

"Some of you are aware, you are now in the twenty-first century," I answered. That got some gasps. They had leaped ahead by almost five hundred years.

"I shall collect all of us here," said Dubh.

Falon and I walked up to the platform, went up the steps, and walked around looking at everything they were doing. Apparently, Amarlyis had the witches doing exercises to get them limber again.

A large group of people was approaching through a different tunnel. We turned to face the rest of the witches coming into the platform room. Amarlyis was among them.

"Greetings, Lora," said Amarlyis. "It is good to see you again."

"Likewise," I said.

"You're here to take them to the city?"

"I heard from Innogen that a few thought they may be ready to."

"Ah, yes, I see. Innogen is correct. Some do feel ready. They are all very eager. Could we arrange a field trip for them all at once? It could be a good learning experience and they could share their feelings about it when they get back."

"I think we could do that. How about doing something like going for lunch?"

"That's a wonderful idea!" said Amarlyis. "How would you do it?"

"I'd tell the staff the group was from a foreign country, and they were exchange students."

"But they aren't all kids."

"Well, what about from a foreign religious order that has granted them an excursion?"

"That seems silly. Why not just a vacation group from a foreign country?"

"Much better," I said. I hadn't expected to take them all, so I hadn't planned on some group explanation for their awkwardness.

"Okay, everyone, please listen for a moment." I raised my voice. "Falon and I are going to take you to a common place to get a meal. You will see modern life at work. You will get to order what you like from their menu and I will be paying."

"Amarlyis, what type of food have you been giving them?"

"They have been introduced to modern beverages like coffee and tea, as well as sandwiches. I've explained the monetary system we use now in most countries, including debit and credit cards. They have been taught that women do for themselves now, and that men don't own them anymore."

"That sounds like good progress."

"Who thinks they're ready?"

"These three," she motioned toward a small group of three standing apart from the rest. A male and two females. "Their names are Cailleach Dhé, and Ailbhe for the women, and Artúr for the man."

"We'll need to get them to choose modern names. People won't be able to pronounce them today."

"I know," said Amarlyis. "Where are you taking them?"

"McDonald's," Falon said. "You cannot get more modern than that."

"Indeed."

"Okay, everyone, please gather around us. We're going to use the portal to get to the occult store first, then we'll exit in Montreal, Canada."

There were murmurs of excitement as the group of people gathered. All told, thirteen men and women with magical ability could be difficult to handle.

"Oh, folks, no use of magic once we're outside on the street please. The modern world still does not believe, and they are very suspicious of things they don't understand."

"So humanity has not made any progress since we were last alive?" asked a man.

"Legitimate question," said Falon. "In many ways, no, no progress whatsoever. In other ways, huge leaps in progress. In the ways that truly count, none at all. Humans are still suspicious, greedy, and aggressive."

"So we need to keep you a secret," said Falon. "The less noticeable you are, the better. A group of fifteen people walking into one restaurant will cause enough notice. So let's be really calm and invisible, okay?"

"You said to not use magic."

"Yes, don't use magic. Invisible was a figure of speech," I said.

"Figure of speech?"

"Oh this is going to be fun," I murmured to Falon.

"I think it would be easier if we took three at a time. Less noticeable, and less risk of discovery."

"I think so too," I said. "But Amarlyis promised them all … so let's try it."

The first step was to get to the occult store, and that was accomplished without any problems. Lora had an idea but she needed to speak to Innogen about it.

"Innogen, is it possible to open a doorway into a McDonald's restaurant so that we can see but they cannot see us?

"Yes, I should be able to do that for you, kind of like a one-way mirror?"

"Yes, exactly."

"I'll need you to go to the restaurant and stand there as a grounding rod," said Innogen.

"Will do. Give me five minutes to get there."

Five minutes later, I was standing inside a McDonald's store looking at the counter and menu. I felt a wave of magical power wash over me, and felt Innogen's presence. Falon was probably explaining to them what they saw. A few minutes later, the magical power was gone and I knew that the "window" had been closed.

I could hear Falon speaking outside the restaurant. I exited and walked around the corner and found them all standing in the parking lot. Glancing around, I only saw one security camera and it wasn't pointed this way, but at the drive-through.

"Okay, everyone, let's go over what we saw again," said Falon, taking over. "Walk up to the counter at the front. That's where you stand and place your order for food. You will wait your turn in the line between the bars. Lora will meet you at the counter.

"Choose the food from the menu displayed above the counter. It is divided up into several categories like breakfast, fish, chicken, burgers, dessert, beverages. I recommend you select a meal of either fish, chicken, or burgers, with a small order of fries, and a beverage of your choice. Once they have your order, move down the counter and they will hand it to you. After you have your food, you can go and sit at a table. Choose one that is clean, and where no one else is sitting if possible. Others from our group will join you."

"Any questions?"

Several hands went up. "Yes?"

"What if you don't want any of those things?"

"You don't have to order anything. All restaurants have a limited menu. They don't offer everything."

"Any other questions?" asked Falon. "No, okay, we can start going inside. Let's move toward the front of the building. There is a doorway you can use."

Falon got them to walk in pairs and we marched around the corner. She then had them enter the restaurant two and a time and line up. So far so good.

"You've done this before, haven't you?" I asked her as they lined up.

"I spent a summer as a camp counselor as a teenager."

I went and stood at the counter beside one of the two cashiers, explaining our situation.

"You see, we are a group of fifteen. However, they have never been to a restaurant before. They're from a remote location. I will pay for everyone, but they'll all come up and order individually. Is that alright?"

"Yes, of course. I'll put that order on this register."

As the different customers came up, I signaled the girl which ones were mine and she ordered their food on one cash register, while doing everyone else's order on another register. It went very smoothly until one of the men didn't want to order anything before trying.

"I'm sorry, sir, we don't give out samples," said the cashier.

"Then how do I know what I would like?" he asked.

"Well, do you feel like having meat?" asked the cashier.

"Yes, I think so. I like meat."

"Then I would recommend a burger. How hungry are you?" asked the cashier.

"I'm very hungry."

“Then I would recommend a larger burger, perhaps a double 1/4 lb. Would you like that?”

“Okay, I’ll try that.”

“Would you like to try cheese slices on it, or bacon?”

“Yes please, I like both those things.”

“And what would you like to drink?”

“Mead.”

“Ah, we don’t have mead. If you see our beverage menu there, you can choose something from there.”

“What is a milkshake?”

“Oh, you’ll love one of those. Vanilla, chocolate, or strawberry?”

“Strawberry?”

“And I’ll add fries to that to make a meal. Thank you, sir.”

“Thank you for your help.”

The last of our group went through and Falon and I ordered something too. The total was almost $160. The most I’d ever spent at McDonald’s.

We turned around and discovered they were all seated at four tables. We went and joined them after grabbing lots of napkins and some ketchup cups. They were all surprised that they enjoyed the food, and happily ate it all up. When everyone was finished, we asked them how many would like a treat for dessert. They all said yes, so we went and ordered fifteen sundaes of various flavors. The girls behind the counter were busy with that order, and then the machine broke down. Only five of the sundaes were delivered.

So our group shared. Each was given a spoon, and they got to taste each of the sundaes. Of course the question, “Why would the machine stop?” was asked.

"Lora, do they no longer need cows for milk? Do machines provide milk now?" asked one of the group.

"No, milk still comes from cows, but the machines turn milk into ice cream, and they're often broken, unfortunately."

"I'm going to the ladies' room. Does anyone else need to go?" asked Falon.

"Go?" asked one of the women. "Go where?"

"To the bathroom, to urinate," I clarified.

Several raised their hands. "Okay, follow Falon and she'll help you. What about you guys?"

"I would like to as well."

"Well, you cannot use the same room, but I will take you to the men's room. I just cannot go in," I explained. "The rest of you stay here until we are all back." *This isa lot like being a camp counselor,* I thought as I collected the guys and walked them to the washroom.

While I was directing the guys, some young men in the restaurant decided they were going to sweet talk the younger girls still sitting at the table. I could see one particularly dressed dude was chatting up a girl and she was blushing bright red. I tuned in on their conversation.

"I think you're pretty. I'd like to take you out, to—you know—hook up tonight."

"I don't know what you mean, but I have to go back home anyway."

"Ah come on, you can go out for a little while," he said. "I'll bet you've got a sweet pussy."

"I don't have a cat," she said, confused. He laughed.

"I'm not talking about that pussy," he said, as he leaned toward her, rubbing the back of her head. "I'm talking about the one between your legs, sweet thing."

Okay, time for me to interrupt. "I'm sorry, but my baby sister is not interested in going anywhere with you."

"Hey, no harm no foul," he said. "I could warm your bed, beautiful," he said, trying to charm me.

"Ah, no. You don't have the right equipment," I said. I shouldn't have, but I did.

"Maman, I have the right equipment, it's right here!" he said, grabbing himself and rubbing himself to an erection.

I got all the witches to stand up and file out of the restaurant, and wait for me just outside the door while we waited for the rest of the group inside. It didn't take long, but it was long enough to endure the leers and suggestive comments coming from the clearly loser teens. I wanted to get my group as far away from them as possible. Unfortunately, we couldn't walk to the alley behind the restaurant again, as it would be an effective trap.

Once we had all the witches outside, we walked down the street and around the corner. I was looking for a different private place to open the portal to the occult store. Finding another rear access alley, I quickly created the exit and they all went inside. Safely on the other side, the girl the boy had bothered had something to ask.

"Lora, what does the pussy between my legs mean?" she asked.

"What's your name, hun?" I asked her.

"Ailbhe," she said. She was one of them who was "ready" to enter modern life. *Hmmm.*

"Well, Ailbhe, it refers to your sex."

Ailbhe turned bright red again. "Oh."

"Before you enter modern life, we need to educate you a little bit more, I think."

"Yes, it seems so."

Opening another portal, I got everyone back to the launch bay. Amarlyis was waiting.

"How did it go?" she asked.

"Not badly at all. I think they all enjoyed the outing. However, there are some modern-day issues we need to teach them before we let them free."

"What are those?"

"Well, sexuality for one. Today, people are forward, especially the boys. We need to teach the girls especially how to behave, how to defend themselves, and above all about their sexuality. I'm not convinced they know." *I'd love to teach those boys how to be more respectful, but that I have no control over. ARGH!*

"They're all very aware of sex and how procreation happens."

"That's not what I'm talking about. I mean casual sex, hook-ups, dating, things like that."

"Oh. I have not explained anything about that. I'm afraid I'm not the one who can, because I've been sequestered from modern life to some extent."

"Alright, that will be my job, then. I will work with small groups though."

8—Escaping the Hospital

Rick

My biggest concern was getting Justin out of the hospital before the doctors noticed that his body was healing at an alarming rate for a human. How was I going to accomplish that?

My first thought was to have Justin pull a hissy fit and scream about going home and getting discharged to Atlanta. That might work. He could put in an Oscar-winning performance too. But then how would we explain to him about not leaving Montreal?

Maybe we don't. He just needed to stay hidden until he was healed. He would realize that humans don't heal from the injuries he had. That meant I'd have to explain immortality to him. I needed to be very careful. This was opening the immortals up to more people, and as the circle of those in the know widened, so did our exposure and risk.

Do we offer Justin immortality? Is that how we swear him to secrecy?

I needed to ask the rest of our group first.

I decided to call Mark first because he was the "leader," or at least the first of our group.

"Mark, it's Rick."

"How's Justin?"

"That's why I'm calling. I made a hasty decision based on emotion, and now I've painted myself into a corner."

"What happened?"

"When the doctors were describing his injuries and how fatal they were, they expressed severe reservations that he would pull through. The only solution was to double-amputate his legs. I panicked a bit. Well, I panicked a lot, really. So, when they said he would need a transfusion, I told them to use my blood. Abeo said our blood would heal him without turning him. I wanted him to have the best chance of surviving the first surgery, which was removing a pipe from his brain."

"Oh, wow. I see. I would probably have done the same thing as you. Of course, the blood transfusion would start to heal him quickly. So now he's healing, and we have to get him out of the hospital before they notice it, right?"

"Yes. Exactly. So my question is, should I offer him immortality?"

"He'll surely realize that his injuries are healing too quickly, so we have no choice but to explain why. He's part of our circle, I don't see a problem bringing him in."

"Thank you. I didn't want to unless I had agreement from the rest."

"Then perhaps we should have a quick Zoom meeting."

"Good idea. I'll get on that now."

After Mark hung up, I set up and invited our circle of immortal friends to a twenty-minute Zoom meeting in thirty minutes. They all accepted.

When all eight were connected and displayed on my phone, I started.

"Friends, I have a question to ask all of you, and I need a unanimous decision to proceed."

"This sounds grave," said Abeo.

I explained to them as I had to Mark about Justin. When I finished, some were nodding.

"I think you did what you thought was best. I don't think there is anyone in our group that would begrudge you that," said Gwen.

"No, but it does open the question, should we be giving our blood to just anyone?" asked Abeo. "We need to have that discussion."

"I agree, and no, not just anyone," said Mark. "But close friends, those within our circle, those we would otherwise have to leave and they would notice, yes. They can be given knowledge and options. Otherwise, what sort of lives would we have?"

"My brother is soft," said Gwen. "But I agree with close circle friends and perhaps family."

"I agree," said Lora and Falon.

"Agreed," said Andrews.

"I'm not one to object," said Margaret.

"Abeo? What's your opinion?"

"Justin is a close friend. So I say yes. But where does it stop? With him? Greggory?" asked Abeo.

"We'll have to make that decision when we cross that road," I answered.

"I have an idea for getting Justin out of the hospital," said Mark. "We'll tell the hospital that I have a specialist that can help him, and that we'll be taking him out of their care."

"That sounds much better than having Justin have a hissy-fit," I said.

With a decision by the group in my pocket, I returned to the hospital to see Justin. I found him asleep, so I sat in the chair to wait for him to wake up. Nurses came in regularly to check on him, write down his stats, and leave. He was asleep for about six hours when he started to move around in bed. I leaned over and took his hand, startling him, and his eyes popped open.

"Rick, you're back. Thank you. I feel like I was hit by a train."

"Basically you were. Listen, Justin, I have to explain something to you and it's a secret. But you need to know this now."

"Oh so cryptic. Go on, I'm listening."

"Before your surgery, I convinced the doctors I was the person to provide your blood for transfusion."

"Yes, I vaguely remember you saying something about that. But wait, that can't be, we don't have the same blood type."

"Remember I also told you I'm a universal donor. But there is another reason."

"I don't remember. I was on some pretty powerful pain meds. I plead the fifth."

"My blood heals you because I'm immortal. It will continue to heal all your injuries quickly. Which is why we need to get you out of the hospital before the doctors notice."

"Immortal?"

"Yes. Mark is going to tell them that he has a specialist that will take over your case from here, and get you discharged. Rich people can do that easily. We'll have an ambulance pick you up and bring you to another location where you will be able to heal."

"When?"

"Soon. Everything is in play now."

"You're going to give me a doozy of an explanation when this is over, Ricardo. How long have you been sitting on this little tidbit of information?"

"I only found out about myself a few years ago when I met Mark, Falon, and Lora."

"Are they…?"

"Yes, they are. Our circle is eight wide at the moment."

"Hmm, eight you say. So basically all your close friends?"

"I can hear you say, 'But not me' in that statement. There is a reason. Each of the couples has an immortal and a human. Well, a former human."

"Former human? Am I to believe that the status of humans can be altered?"

"Yes, it can."

"Hun, you've been holding out on me. We'll talk. Right now, what am I supposed to be feeling that I'm not?"

"That's a very good question. The injuries you sustained were severe, fatal even. Remember, they were going to amputate your legs."

"Amputate! Oh my God, no!"

"Calm down. That won't happen now. But for now, you cannot feel anything from your waist down, understand?"

"Oh, yes I understand. That means I cannot move either, right?"

"Right."

"What about taking a pee?"

“I believe you have a bag hooked up to you for that. There was a pipe impaled in your head. They’ve removed that. They’re already surprised there was no serious damage caused from that. So I would be a little forgetful when they ask you questions.”

“Alright.”

At that moment, a group of people in white coats walked in the room.

“Mr. Madera, you’re awake. That’s good to see. How are you feeling?” asked one of the doctors.

“Fuzzy,” said Justin. “I can’t feel my feet!”

“That’s expected, Mr. Madera. You’ve sustained a serious injury to your spine. We will try to fix that, but the outlook isn’t good. In all likelihood, we will need to take a more aggressive action.”

“Aggressive?”

“Your legs and hips have been crushed. X-rays showed many fragments, and we may not be able to put them back together.”

Thank God they haven’t taken any more X-rays since the first ones! I thought.

“Excuse me,” said Mark, entering the room behind the doctors. “I have a specialist that will take over Mr. Madera’s case from this point. He’s in Switzerland and he specializes in crush injuries. I’d like to have his discharge papers completed now please.”

“And who are you?” asked the doctor.

“Ah, he’s one of my best and closest friends,” said Justin. “Mark Chisholm. He’s cute, isn’t he?”

“Mr. Chisholm, this is highly irregular.”

“I realize this. But Justin is an internationally recognized master chef, and we want to save his legs.”

“Very well. But I’ll need to speak with this specialist of yours first.”

“That won’t be necessary,” said Mark, adding a little compulsion to his voice. “You will trust my judgment.”

“Well, I guess that won’t be necessary after all. I’ll trust your judgment,” said the doctor. “Nurse, please get Mr. Madera’s discharge started.”

The white coats exited Justin’s room and I let out my breath, not realizing I’d been holding it.

“Compulsion?” I asked.

“Yes, I hate doing it, but sometimes you just have no choice.”

“Compulsion?” asked Justin.

“We have the ability to compel people to do things.”

“Oh, Ricky, you have a lot of ‘splaining to do!”

It took me a few days to arrange everything. Duffy was to move into Andrews’ condo, so when Justin got there, he would not be alone. Duffy was an old army buddy of Andrews’ who now wanted to live in Montreal part-time. Duffy’s business was recently purchased by Mark’s enterprise and now fell under their umbrella.

The night before Justin was to leave the hospital, Andrews and I met Duffy at the condo and showed him the suite on the second floor. He would have a view of the mountain and the west side of the island.

“This is all mine?” asked Duffy. “Wow! I love the view. Thanks, Andrews.”

“Yes, will it be okay for you?” I asked.

“Yes, it is the size of my entire apartment in Florida. But there is no furniture.”

"No, you will have to go shopping and have what you like delivered. Duffy, here's my card," said Andrews, handing him a black credit card.

"Oh, fancy schmancy."

"Try to keep to a budget of $10,000, please," said Andrews.

"No problem, boss."

Ambulance drivers hired by Mark arrived at the hospital to transfer Justin. Mark arranged for Andrews to be in the ambulance. They would be delivering Justin to Andrews' old condominium for convalescence.

After moving Justin to a bed in the condo, Lora came to play nurse for the first shift. Mark figured it would be at least three or four weeks before ninety percent of the injuries were healed, based on the amount of blood they had transfused. We told Justin we would tell him the whole story once he was completely healed.

9— Listening for News

PI Adams

It was a hot, sticky evening in New Orleans even though it was the middle of January. Normally, it got a little cooler this time of year, but not this year. It was downright unbearable without air conditioning, so I was thankful my office had it.

As a private investigator, I looked into things the police didn't want to take on. Working for the private sector, I usually had crap jobs like following a spouse. However, my current client was a young woman. I was searching for her father. She didn't want to be associated with looking for him because she was a lawyer, hence hiring me.

Turns out her daddy wasn't such a nice person. He ran a cult here in the NOLA region that attracted some weird teens. They believed in vampires or monsters. They also believed they were hunters of said monsters. They had a clubhouse down in Ward 9, in an old building by the docks that had been destroyed by Katrina and never really reoccupied. It was an industrial building, perhaps used for fish processing. Difficult to tell. Some of the walls were gone, and what was left looked like it should be demolished.

Putting aside the spooky part of his life, I discovered that her daddy had been tracking a man called Mark Chisholm. He had followed this man, who it turned out was a filthy rich dude, all the way to Montreal, Canada. I still wasn't sure why, but the last known location I had for her daddy was in Montreal.

I uncovered his connection to a group in Switzerland early on, with the same silly objectives, just not teens. But it took a long time to find Mark Chisholm and his connection.

What broke my investigation open was an incidental news item buried on page six of the local NOLA paper about a local businessman being found dead. The article quoted a Canadian paper as saying:

> *Last night, a body was found in the woods behind the sleepy community of Hudson. The body was well decomposed, so it was in the ground a minimum of two years. So far, identification has not been released. Police suspect foul play, but there are no suspects yet and no cause of death.*

It had taken me over two years to find something on Derek Staung. He was a very secretive person, covered his tracks well, and left virtually no trace. Normally, I found my targets within a few months. This was a lead that might connect with what I found: that he was last seen in the Montreal area about the time that body was killed. Maybe I'd found him.

When I inquired at the paper, they were able to tell me the identity was Derek Staung, even though they couldn't print it. Their reporter was following the investigation. So having found him dead it was now a matter of finding out where he had been killed, and why and when he died.

10— Witches

Lora

It was clear I needed to spend time with the witches. Since I was the one who initiated this whole situation when I decided to rescue them, I felt it was my responsibility—duty? obligation?—to see it through. I couldn't leave it to Amarlyis to decide who would be suitable to start integrating into the twenty-first century. I traveled down to the ark ship and spent a week there. After meeting with all of them, spending time talking to them, it was evident that Amarlyis was not introducing them to modern life.

Human reproduction was covered, but modern sexuality was completely ignored. They had learned a little about monetary systems and commerce, but nothing practical. I decided to have a general gathering and speak to them all directly.

As the group came into the large platform room, they were chatting quietly. Interestingly, the acoustics in the room were such that I could pick up everyone's conversation and listen in. Of course, my immortal hearing helped.

"Hello, ladies and gentlemen, thank you for coming today," I said. "I hope to discuss with you what you need to learn in order to integrate into modern life. After spending time with each of you individually, I think I have an understanding of what you have learned, and where the holes are. I'm here to help. First, does anyone have any questions?"

A number of people put up their hands.

"Will we need new clothes?" asked one.

"Yes. If that has not been provided yet, I will give you each an allowance to go shopping for clothes."

"Shopping? What is shopping?" asked another.

"It's like going to the market. Today, we buy our clothes ready-made instead of making them. There are different kinds of stores for clothing."

"Where will we live?" asked a man.

"We are working on a large plan to integrate all of you gradually. The first step will be to foster you with a modern family, until you get used to modern living."

"Will we still be able to practice our craft?"

"Yes, but not in public. As a coven, you can meet here anytime and do what you want as long as it doesn't break any laws."

"How will we know what the laws are?"

"Well, that is pretty straightforward. Don't hurt anyone, don't kill anyone, don't steal. Those kinds of things. Don't change anyone into something that isn't human."

"What if we are not human now?"

"Who asked that one?" I asked.

"I did," said a tall man, who stepped forward. "I am not human. I'm immortal."

"Are there any other immortals among you?"

A couple of hands went up. “Could all of you come to the front please.” Three people, two women and a man, walked up to the front where I was.

“Hello, are all of you immortal?” They nodded.

“Do you know who turned you?” I asked. One nodded, two didn’t.

“Okay, you were turned?” I asked the women who nodded.

“Yes, an immortal man turned me about a hundred and thirty-two years ago. Well, before we were trapped.”

“Do you know that man’s name?” I asked.

“Yes. It was Samuel Druggins.”

“Okay, you two shook your heads. You were not changed, so that means you were born?”

“Yes, this one is my daughter by Samuel,” said the woman, pointing at her daughter. “She was only sixteen when we were trapped.”

“Oh, I see. So did Samuel and you have a long relationship?”

“It would have been, if we had not been trapped.”

“Was your daughter turned by someone?” I asked.

“No, we were in suspended animation in that dimension. So nothing happened.”

“Where did you last see Samuel?”

“At the ritual site where we were trapped.”

“Where was that exactly?”

“Carlow, Ireland.”

“Huh, I wonder if he’s still there with the coven, I’ll have to ask Amarlyis. What’s your name? Why do you think you’re immortal?” I asked the man.

“Because I heal too fast to be a human,” he answered.

"Well, let's test that." I pulled out a pocket knife and asked for a hand from each of them. A small cut in each hand healed quickly, indicating that they were potentially immortal.

"Do you have fangs yet?" I asked the man.

"Fangs?" he asked. "No, I don't have fangs."

"So you haven't fully turned yet, and neither has your daughter. I presume you have your fangs?" I asked the mom.

"Yes, I have fangs."

"You do, Mom? I've never seen them!" said the daughter.

"Okay, folks, your names please."

"Siobhan is my daughter, and I'm Mary."

"I'm Seamus, Seamus O'Sullivan."

"If you three stand to one side for me, I'll have a separate conversation with you later. Right now, I need to address the whole group, some of which will apply to you, some won't."

"Everyone, let's get back to the main reason we're here right now. I need to find out what skills you have so that I can make sure you will learn enough to survive. So let's go down a list and we'll see where everyone is. First, everyone line up in a straight line on this side of me. Every time I mention a skill you have, take a step forward, okay? The first one is math. Who can do basic math like adding and subtracting?"

About half of the people stepped forward.

"Next is reading." Another stepped forward with the ones who did math. On it went through writing, geography, and money. And that's where the progress stopped. "Okay, since many of you don't read and write, we will start there. The basics, reading, writing, and math just about everyone in this time can do. While you're learning that, we will show you other things. But I have a question: how did you order food at McDonald's?"

“We listened to people around us and looked at the pictures. The pictures on the menu were very helpful,” said one of the witches.

“And that answers that.”

I was very disappointed in Amarlyis in that she had not made any headway on their integration into our life. “Everyone, you can go back to what you were doing. You three, come with me please.”

I brought the three immortals with me home. Once I got there, I called Margaret.

“Margaret, how would you feel about a live-in babysitter?”

“Why?”

“I’ve got an immortal mom and her daughter here who have to start learning about our century. I was hoping I could place them with you and they could earn their keep babysitting and housekeeping.”

“Bring them over and let’s check them out.”

“Be right there,” I said. Then I turned to the two in question and said, “We’re going to walk over to their house. On the way, you’ll see part of where we live.” I pointed out the Chisholm’s house, Gwen and Andrews’ house, and of course Margaret and Abeo’s house.

“You’re all so close together,” remarked Seamus.

“Yes, it just happened, but it’s ideal to keep all of us together too.” I walked up and rang the bell.

“Come in please,” said Margaret.

“Margaret, this is Mary and Siobhan. Mary was turned by her mate, and Siobhan has not yet finished.”

“Hello, you two. Can you cook and clean? I have five babies, and another on the way, so it’s very busy here, and I could really use some help, especially help that knows who and what we are, if you know what I mean.”

"I'd be honored to serve you, mum," said Mary. "My daughter is a right fine cook too, and she would be good at helping with the babes."

"Wonderful. We have rooms for you upstairs. You can go pick out whichever one you want. The babies are still sharing for now."

The two women went upstairs to select a room. "Mum, can we have the room at the end of the hall?" asked Mary.

"That is the one that is all blue?" asked Margaret. "Yes that one can be yours."

"Excellent, mum, we'll both sleep here, then."

"What is next is to get them their own modern clothes. Can you do that, Margaret?" I asked.

"Yes, we'll have fun shopping online," she said. "And what, pray tell, are you doing with this one?"

"I'm going to see if Andrews can find him a spot in his business, and perhaps in their house."

"That's a good idea. Let me know. I can always use a man around here," she added with a smile.

"Come on, Seamus, we'll go back to my place. I need to call Andrews to see where he is first."

———

"Andrews, it's Lora. Hey, can you stop by the house on your way home today. I have something I want to run by you and someone for you to meet."

"Sure, I'll be there around 4:30."

"Seamus, you have until then to relax and wander around the house."

"Thank you."

11— Seamus Gets a Home

Andrews

Stopping by Lora's house was perfect, because I wanted to ask her about Duffy and hooking him up with an immortal woman. Duffy's wife left him, and he was really on the decline. He needed someone to take care of, and since there were all kinds of witches who would need integrating into our century, maybe one of them would hit it off with Duffy. She might not be immortal, but that wasn't as important.

Ringing the doorbell, I was startled when a strange man answered it.

"Hello? Who are you?" asked Andrews.

"Hello, I'm Seamus, pleased to meet you. Lora is a little indisposed at the moment. Please come in."

"Where are you from, Seamus?"

"Ireland, but five hundred years ago," he answered. "Lora is helping me settle into this century."

"Great! You two met!" Lora said, as she walked into the room.

"Yes, we did," I said.

"Andrews, Seamus here is immortal, but not fully. He's also a trained witch. Do you think you could find him a position in your company to work? He needs to learn everything, but his skills may be beneficial to you. The other thing is, he needs a place to live until he's capable of getting a place of his own."

"What sort of skills do you have, Seamus?"

"I have a broad range of skills. But for your work, I can see through walls, find things, and cover things up. I'm not a spellcaster, which means I don't need to perform a spell to do something, rather I have inherent talents such as this." He created a ball of light out of thin air in his hand.

"Hmm, yes, I may be able to use someone like you, Seamus, so we can definitely set you up with a job. At least, you can help with the mundane work we do too. Once that is done, we can help you get your life started too. I have an extra room in my condo that you can use—my condo was empty, but now Duffy and Justin are there. It has three bedrooms on two floors."

"That's a good solution, because I didn't want him alone," said Lora.

"Duffy needed a place. As I said, his wife left him and he's crashing. So I brought him up here to Montreal and he can work for us out of my office during the winter. He still wants to keep his business open in Florida, but his staff there can handle that end for now."

"Oh, that is another good idea."

"I was hoping to introduce Duffy to some of the ladies…"

"Too soon for that," said Lora. "But Duffy can help teach Seamus all about modern conveniences."

"Yes, remember, Duffy is fully briefed. His crew and staff are not," I said. "Let me make a call."

"Duffy? Hi, it's Andrews. I'm calling to let you know we're bringing another guy over to stay at the condo. He's one of the witches that was rescued. He's also immortal."

"Oh, that sounds cool," said Duffy. "We can have some fun. Absolutely. I'm in. I'm not there at the moment, so I'll make my way over and meet you guys there."

"Great, no rush though. We'll be there around eight this evening. I'm taking him home for dinner first and then driving back into the city."

"Gotcha."

Turning back to Lora, I said, "Seamus, come with me. I'll take you home to meet my wife and have some dinner."

"I'm very grateful. Terribly grateful," said Seamus. "Is it far?"

"No, it's just around the corner." Arriving there five minutes later, I opened the door and called for Gwen. She walked around the corner of the hallway a moment later carrying a baby.

"Gwen, this is Seamus. He's nearly immortal. I'm going to find a spot for him on the payroll because his skills will be useful. He's going to move in with Duffy into the condo downtown so he can learn twenty-first century things."

"Hello, Seamus, I'm Gwen, and this is Terrence Liam Andrews."

"He's adorable. Pleased to meet you, little one. Looking at your daddy, you're going to be a big strong fella when you grow up."

"Yes, I expect he will be," said Gwen. "Seamus, Andrews said *nearly* immortal. Can you please clarify?"

"I'll try. You see, I heal very quickly but I don't have fangs. So I think I've been partially changed. Is that possible?"

"Not to my knowledge. The only thing would be if you were born immortal but not yet finished. Do you know your parentage?"

"No, I don't. I was orphaned and taken in by the coven. How do I 'get finished?' What does that involve?" asked Seamus.

"An injection of venom. Then the rest of your immortal characteristics will develop."

"Can I arrange to have that done?"

"Yes, I'll make the arrangements for you."

"Thank you."

After dinner, Seamus and I helped clear the dishes and get the kitchen cleaned up. I showed Seamus the dishwasher and the modern convenience of having it do the dishes.

"Now that is progress!" said Seamus.

"Gwen, Seamus and I are going to get going."

"Okay, hun, we'll see you later," answered Gwen.

"I will introduce you to Duffy and Justin," I said, once we were in the car. "Both are human. Duffy knows about us, Justin just found out. He's a little fragile at the moment. He was injured very badly in a bombing, and he's recovering at the condo."

"Wouldn't that be better to do at a hospital?" asked Seamus.

"Well, yes, normally, but Rick, who's one of us, gave him immortal blood to make sure he wouldn't die. Then we had to get him out of the hospital quickly before the human doctors noticed he was healing from injuries that he shouldn't be healing from."

"Tricky."

"Indeed."

It was a quiet ride downtown to the condo building and up the elevator. I wondered if Seamus was uneasy.

“Seamus, are you nervous?” I asked.

“A little. This is all so strange to me. The conveyances, the machines that lift us up, these tall buildings, I feel like I’m walking around in a dream.”

“Ah, I’m sorry. Yes, this would all be strange and I haven’t given you a shred of information.”

“No worries, I figure that’s what I have to learn, right?”

“Yes. First, these tall buildings are a fact of life in modern times. Both residences and offices occupy tall skyscrapers, as they’re called today. From a convenience point-of-view, they are pretty much self-contained, often with shopping levels built into the lower floors. Here in Montreal, we have blocks and blocks of the city that are all connected underground by retail and transportation hubs. It’s a convenience for us during the winter. I can walk all the way from the McCord Museum on Sherbrooke Street to the Place Bonaventure Hotel on de la Gauchetière underground. That’s at least eight city blocks.

“Residential buildings like this one have tight security. This building uses a keycard instead of a metal key. The card unlocks the doors like a key.”

We approached the front door. “To use the card, hold it in front of these boxes like this,” I said, showing him which way to hold the card. “This light will turn green when it has read the card correctly. You can then open the door. If it doesn’t work the first time, simply move it away and place it again. There are security points like this at all the exterior doors, by the elevators, another to access my floor, and finally to open my door. Do you understand?”

“As best I can,” he replied.

I unlocked the outside door, handed Seamus a keycard, and we walked into the building. I showed him where the elevators are.

“Place your card here. When it turns green, press this button,” I said. “When an elevator arrives, it will ding and the doors will open. Only this elevator goes to my floor.”

Inside the elevator was another scanner. I let him do that one, then press PH for our floor. Finally, we made our way down the hall. The last security pad was outside my door. I let him do that one too, and we walked inside the condo.

“Anyone here?” I called out.

“I am,” said Justin from upstairs.

“Justin, it’s me, Andrews. I bring you a new roommate.”

“Excellent!”

“So I use this card to get in at all times. Do I need it to get out?” asked Seamus.

“No, just to get inside.”

“Got it. Keep it with me at all times.”

“Let me give you a tour,” I said. I led him around the main area of the condo. “This is the living room. None of the windows open, a security feature at this height, but this door does. It slides open like this and you have access to my patio.”

“Wow, what a view. How far up are we?” asked Seamus as he walked out onto the wide, fenced patio.

“We’re twenty-five storeys up. If every storey is fourteen feet, then it’s about 350 feet. Now, it can get very windy out here, so don’t leave anything outside.”

“Got it.”

“Next is the dining room. You don’t have to eat here. There’s the kitchen, and it has an eat-in counter.”

“Wow, this looks very fancy.”

“It has the basic appliances you’ll find in most homes today. This is the fridge. It will keep things cold and fresh on this side, and frozen on the other side. This is the stove and oven, where you can cook. Sink of course, and this is the dishwasher."

"What's that?" asked Seamus pointing to a squat appliance sitting on the counter.

"My favorite machine. It's a coffee maker."

"Amazing. And the other smaller machines?"

"They all have specific purposes. I'll let Duffy teach you how to use them in order of importance. Come on, I'll show you the bathroom. There are three and a half bathrooms in this condo. This is the half—a small one, with just a toilet and sink. The three full bathrooms are upstairs attached to the bedrooms. I'll show you your room."

We walked up an open staircase as Seamus rubbernecked around the apartment. Half a flight up there was a landing.

"Your bedroom is down there," I said, turning to the left.

We walked into the ensuite and I said, "It has a separate bathtub and shower, a bidet, a toilet, and two sinks. There is a heat lamp in the ceiling and an air shower for drying. Here are the switches."

I also showed him how to use the shower taps and the toilet.

"This place is amazing, Andrews. Thank you for letting me stay here. Where is Duffy's room?"

"His room is down the hall from you, on the same landing as your bedroom. You'll like the view of the port. Justin is upstairs in the master suite."

"So many new things to learn."

"It will become second nature. Once you're comfortable with this, we'll get you started on a job. My office is only a few blocks from this building. You can walk there easily in ten minutes."

"About the injection to turn me...?" he asked.

"Yeah?"

"Do you know what it is?"

"Yes, I went through it."

"What happens?"

"Gwen will have you take an oath, and then we'll inject you with venom."

"That's all? What's the oath for?"

"Yup, unless you want to do it the old-fashioned way and fight one of us. The injection will likely cause you to sleep during some of the transition, but after that you'll have fangs and develop some other skills. The oath is a promise to keep the secret of our existence. We all take it."

"Um, no, I don't want to fight, thanks."

There was a knock on the door, and we heard the door open and close.

"Anybody here?" came Duffy's voice up the stairs.

"We're upstairs, Duffy. I'm showing Seamus around."

"Be right up."

"Seamus, this is Duffy. He's a longtime and very good friend of mine. We also work together for Mark. Duffy, this is Seamus, a witch from the sixteenth century and born immortal, but not fully turned."

"Sixteenth century? Um, wow! This must be a confusing place for you. Pleased to meet you there," said Duffy. "So, you'll be taking the last room?"

"It seems so," said Seamus. "Nice to meet you. I plan on being your shadow to learn all about this life."

"Yeah, well, don't get me wrong, but most people don't live this Well, in this century. This place is a bloody palace!"

"I don't know about that," I said, slightly embarrassed. "Let me show you your room, Seamus."

They each walked into the room on the left end of the hallway.

"Seamus, Duffy will take you shopping so you can buy furniture and stuff for your room. Just have it delivered."

"Yup, I have his black card," said Duffy, brandishing the card like a sword.

"What form of payment is that?" asked Seamus.

"It's called a credit card," I explained. "It links to a line of credit that our boss has and automatically gets paid off from his business. It allows us to purchase what we need without the need of carrying actual money."

"Interesting."

"You have a $10,000 budget to get everything you need. Try not to exceed that."

"That's a lot of money!" exclaimed Seamus.

"It goes fast when you're purchasing large items," said Duffy.

"I'll introduce you to Justin," I said.

We went upstairs to the master suite and I knocked on the door.

"Enter at your own risk!" came a voice from inside.

"Justin, you've met Duffy, but this is Seamus, your new roommate."

Hi, boys, it will be fun having our little trio together!" said Justin.

"I leave you three to it—have fun nesting," I said, and left.

12— Anita Meets Seamus

Anita

My life changed three months ago. I would not have imagined it so, but it is the truth. I was no longer a human being. Just saying that out loud made me cringe. Imagine! *Not being a human being!*

The obvious change was my appearance. Suddenly over the course of just a few days, I went from being a nearly senior-aged housekeeper who was heavy-set, gray-haired, wrinkled, and weathered, with arthritis, to a young-looking woman again. I had to admit, I missed being twenty-nine. I was no J. Lo but I had my moments. I grew up with Chita Rivera as a role model. She was saucy, smart, and sexy. Now, I was delighted to have my long, thick, dark brown hair back. I loved my hair. I had always thought it my best feature.

Standing in front of my mirror was like being at a carnival. I was looking into a fantasy mirror that showed me how I would look in some other world. It still didn't feel real. But I had my hair back. And my figure. I gazed at myself—I had a waistline again! And a bust that didn't sag, and hips that were smooth. But my face! Oh my God, my face was smooth; hardly any lines creased the skin except for laugh lines, and I didn't mind those.

My skin glowed with health and didn't look like the weathered leather it had been. I barely recognized myself. But I could tell it was me, because it was still my eyes.

And my hands! There was no pain, my knuckles were slim and not stiff so I could move them with great dexterity. I might be able to play the piano again. Not that I was a great musician, but I learned as a young girl to play a few tunes. I moved my limbs and realized there was no pain anywhere. I was completely hale.

———

Growing up in Cuba, I met Rick's parents when they were on vacation. I was dirt poor, and they were coming to Cuba to adopt a child. I was a volunteer at the hospital and saw a lot of girls come in pregnant and leave without their child. The business of adoption was big business. Some women got $5,000 to give up their child. That was a year's wages for some of us. I had overheard numbers in the hundred thousand range for adoptive parents, so they had to have money.

When Ricardo's parents came to the nursery, I was playing with their intended baby, and they were so struck by our connection they offered me a job on the spot as a nanny. Being a domestic in America was a foot in the door to a better life. So the answer was an easy yes for me. They even helped me do the legal paperwork, which I felt privileged about. My friends who were also going to be domestics didn't have such generous employers. Most had to hide as illegals. In the early years, other domestics were living in fear of being deported at any moment. I felt for them, but I was helpless to do anything.

Mr. Benal was a big shot in something and they frequently had large parties. I would get my friends to help with the serving and food prep so they could earn a little extra money. Most didn't get paid for their services beyond food and lodging. A few were given an allowance for shopping for clothes and such. But Mr. Benal was generous. He paid me more than a fair wage. When the girls came to help, he paid them too.

I got very good at catering the Benals' parties, and soon was in demand for my services. Their friends expected to get me for free, but the Benals insisted I was paid, and to that end dealt with the business end of the catering. They paid me out of the money they took in. I wasn't getting rich, but it was my money, and it was separated in a bank account of my own.

By the time Rick was a teenager my job was no longer caring for Rick, but exclusively running the household. The Benals had three additional people working for them over the past ten years: a driver, a housekeeper, and a gardener.

Mr. Benal approached me one day and asked me if I wanted to leave their employ.

"No, sir, I love working for you. Is there a problem?" Suddenly, I was very nervous.

"No, Anita, not at all. We love you, you are family. But without a baby to care for, we, Mrs. Benal and I, thought perhaps you would want to live your own life now."

"I see no reason, sir," I said. "I still have you and the missus to take care of."

"Ah, that's just it. We will be leaving on a long trip—one I have long promised to Mrs. Benal—to see the whole world. We may not be back for years. I am letting the other three go with large severance checks so they can buy their own houses. We are offering you the same deal."

After thinking for a moment, I answered, "Mr. Benal, if you don't mind, I would rather live here. I can be here when Rick needs to come home, and take care of the property in your stead. It would not be good to leave it unattended."

"Are you absolutely sure, Anita?"

"Si! Mr. Benal."

"So be it, then."

There was a cast-off party for the Benals a few weeks later as they started their trip around the world. They planned on traveling for the next five years: visiting the capital city of as many countries as they could, each for a few days. As it would happen, they died in a plane crash a few months later in some remote region of China above the Himalayas. They were on their way to visit the historic city of Kathmandu. We never saw them again.

On the reading of their will, the entire estate was left to Rick of course, but they had left me one million dollars as well. When the money came into my hands, I immediately sent half of it down to my family in Cuba, and for the first time in their lives they could purchase a house of their own.

———

All these memories came flooding back in as I gazed at my reflection, the reflection of a woman who was young again and had just inherited a fortune. Now, I got to start my life over for a third time. How lucky was that? I picked up my brush and ran it through the thick dark brown hair and plaited it into a braid that fell down one shoulder to my waist.

I was glad Lora had taken me shopping to get some new clothes. All my clothes were too big or too old for me now. It was amazing to have a whole new wardrobe.

There were new friends in our circle of people, and I wanted to welcome them into the fold. Two of them, Duffy and Seamus, were staying at Andrews' condo. Justin was staying there too temporarily until he healed. I had prepared lunch for the three men and was going to pay them a visit.

I selected one of my new pretty printed dresses that accentuated my waist and showed my cleavage. I slipped on some pretty shoes and checked my reflection. I applied a little lipstick and some blush and checked myself one more time. I was finally ready to leave. Why was I nervous? Perhaps because it was the first time I was leaving the safety of Rick's house looking like this. What would the neighbors think? *I'm making something out of nothing, they probably won't even notice me.*

After calling an Uber, I waited on the front porch. There were several people out on the street. None of them noticed me. Even the next-door neighbor drove right past me without a glance. Margaret walked by with a stroller and waved. But she knew who I was. Finally, when the Uber arrived, I hurried to the car and got in. The driver smiled at me and said hello before pulling out of the driveway.

Andrews' condo was close to downtown, so it was about thirty minutes before we arrived. The driver watched me in his mirror as I struggled with my basket.

"Mademoiselle, would you like me to help you inside with your basket?"

"I'm okay, thanks."

"Perhaps, we can go have a drink?" he asked, which surprised me.

"Ah, no thanks," I said. "Maybe another time."

I managed to extricate myself from the car and get to the lobby. But I must admit my heart was racing, and I was jittery, nervous. It had been a long time since someone had asked me out for a drink. Taking a deep breath, I rang the bell for Andrews' place and a deep accented voice answered.

"Aye?"

"Oh, hello! This is Anita. I was bringing a care package for Justin." *That voice gave me shivers!*

"Come on in, miss." The door buzzed and I pulled it open.

Andrews' condo was a penthouse, and when I pressed the floor button it rang their condo again. They had to allow it to come up. When the doors opened, the windows at the end of the hall showed a spectacular view of the whole city at your feet. I found Andrews' door. It was one of four on the floor, and knocked.

A very handsome ginger man around forty answered. He had a kind face and a scruffy beard. He towered over me, but then I was only five-foot.

"You would be Anita?" he asked, taking my hand. "My name is Seamus, pleased to meet you. Please come in."

"Hello, Seamus, pleased to meet you too." *Oh my, that voice! It was like a siren song.*

"I wasn't expecting such a pretty young thing, to be honest."

"Oh, what were you expecting?"

"Well, Rick had said you have been the family keeper since he was a child, so I was expecting someone in their fifties at least."

"I'm sixty-two, actually." *He is still holding my hand and I'm starting to overheat. Oh my!*

Seamus grinned from ear to ear and his blue eyes sparkled with the light of a leprechaun. "So you'd be an immortal, then."

"I am now. It's a recent change." *I was having difficulty not panting with that accent.*

He drew me inside and let go of my hand, holding out the other hand, and asked, "May I unburden you, milady?"

I stupidly gawked at him for a moment before I realized he was offering to take the basket. I handed him the basket, he nodded at me graciously, and then carried it into the kitchen. That gave me a moment to glance around the place.

Oh dear. Bachelors lived here, you could tell. There were things not put away, dust bunnies were rolling in the corners, food take-out containers were left out, and dishes not washed. It looked like it hadn't seen a vacuum in months. *Sigh*. Well, I had my work cut out for me.

"Thank you, Seamus. I'd better get busy with what I came for."

"Will you be staying a while?" he asked.

"It seems I will be," I said, with a smile. I walked into the kitchen and prepared the tray for Justin and delivered that first.

Going upstairs, I found the room Justin was in and knocked.

"I'm not naked," came the reply.

"That's a good thing," I said, walking in. "How are you feeling, Justin?"

"Oh, Anita, you look amazing! It is you, no?"

"Yes, it's me. Do you like my new look?"

"Girl, you've got it going on! I love your hair, it's luxurious. What's this?" he asked, taking the tray from my hands.

"I've brought you some real food, because I doubt you bachelors are eating properly."

"Mama, you're right on that. Oh, I can't call you Mama anymore. You're too gorgeous. Believe me, if I were into petite Latina women, you'd be my first call."

"You're too kind."

"So tell me, what was transitioning like?"

"Well, not much of anything really. They gave me an injection, I went to sleep, and woke up with a fever. They gave me a second one and I slept two days and woke up with no fever. I was sore all over, like I was growing again for weeks, and my jaw was sore, but other than that it's been pretty easy."

"What changes have you felt?"

"I feel stronger, more vital, like I was at this age. No pain! Nothing that hurt before like my hands, shoulders, and knees. And I've got complete flexibility again. I don't need glasses anymore, and I can hear much better. I haven't yet noticed anything else. The cut test was freaky though."

"Cut test?"

"They make a small incision in your hand to see if it heals quickly. If it does, you're immortal."

"Are you happy you made the decision?"

"Absolutely. I would not change anything. I have no regrets," I said. "Oh, and I have these now." I extended my fangs and smiled at him.

"Cool! Do they work?"

"I hope so, I haven't had the opportunity to try them out yet," I said, feeling the heat creep up my cheeks as I thought of Seamus holding my hand.

"What about your family and friends? Have you said anything to them?"

"Well, that's just it. I left my family more than forty years ago. Friends? Well, I haven't really made any beyond you guys here in Montreal, and the ones I had in Georgia I'll never see again. So I'm good with that. I had an easy decision. I had nothing to lose."

"Hmmm, you read my mind."

"The way I look at it, you're either going to be here or there. If you're here, well, who cares who's left there? If you're there, then you leave behind what's here. I believe they can remove memories. But enough of me, how are your legs doing?"

"I can move them now. Look!" Justin wiggled his toes for me. "And I can feel them too."

"That's very good progress. Have you tried standing?"

"No, I'm scared to."

"Come on, let's get you up to the edge of the bed and try." I flipped back the covers and pulled his feet to the side of the bed. I looked at him as if to ask him to move them now himself. I could see him try, so I helped him. I took his hands and he pulled himself up to a sitting position, and then his feet landed on the floor.

"Yippee! I can touch the floor." Duffy and Seamus burst into his room at that moment.

"Come on, boys, help him stand." They each took a shoulder and helped him to stand.

"Oh my God, I'm standing again," cried Justin, the tears in his eyes spilling down gently illustrating how momentous this was.

"Boys, walk him around the room once and then get him back to bed. We're going to do this every day now."

"You're used to orders being followed, aren't you?" asked Seamus, smiling.

"Yes, I suppose I am. I've raised a lot of kids."

"I have to go out, do you need help with anything else?" asked Duffy.

"Nope, I've got it under control," I said. I tucked Justin back in, and gave him his tray.

"Justin, there is a whole lot of gym equipment downstairs in the exercise room. As soon as you can, I want you using that equipment to build up your muscle mass again.

"Yes, Mama."

"I thought you couldn't call me Mama anymore."

"Well, that was before you became a sergeant!" he teased.

I left his room with Seamus following me. By the time we got downstairs, Duffy was gone.

"Seamus, you and Duffy can make sure he gets up every day and walks, right?"

"Of course."

"I want him to start doing stairs too. Let's start with three, and add two stairs every day."

"Okay. We can do that too."

"Excellent. Well, I will stop by every day and check on your condo, tidy up, and cook."

"You don't have to do that."

"By the looks of this place, yes I do. It was very nice meeting you, Seamus." I picked up my bag and started walking to the door.

"Wait. Would you come and sit for a while?" asked Seamus, taking my hand again.

"I'd like that."

"You brought us enough food, we could have lunch together."

"I'd love that," I said. After I laid out the food, I sat in a chair next to him and went to serve him. Seamus stopped my hand. "There'll be none of that. You're my guest, not my maid," he said.

His voice sent shivers down my back as I let him serve me. I inhaled his scent as he leaned over me. He was all male, pleasantly musk, with a hint of mint. That was an interesting combination. When he sat back down beside me, our shoulders were touching, and our hips too. I could feel the heat of his skin through my thin dress.

How am I ever going to get through lunch?

We chatted about inane things, small talk about life. Neither of us offered anything of substance. When I had finished eating, I was about to jump up. "That was nice, thank you. Just let me put these things away and clean up before I leave." I went to stand and he caught my hand.

"That can wait. Please stay with me. I'd like to get to know you better. You intrigue me."

Nodding and blushing a little, he led me to the living room, where there was a huge leather L-shaped couch. He sat on one side of the corner and I sat beside him.

"Anita, I've been locked away from life for a very long time. So I'm going to be direct. I am very attracted to you. I feel there is a connection there and I would like to have … I want to … be intimate with you."

I looked into his deep blue eyes and saw a man, a man with a great deal of passion. I felt that connection, it was already giving me tingles. I'd had my share of partners over the years, but I never found anyone I was attracted to this fast. My job hadn't allowed for that anyway. So I remained single, but not a virgin. I could feel the passion and lust radiating off this man. It matched my own and that was astounding. *Why is he so interested in me?* I touched my cheek with my fingers and remembered I wasn't an old woman anymore.

I'm pretty again. Dare I?

"Seamus, I feel it as well. I have not had a partner in a very long time, and I've not had a partner since becoming this." I motioned to myself. "I don't know how this body works yet."

"Would you like to learn?" he asked. "I can teach you what it's like to be with an immortal man."

I licked my lips, which had suddenly become very dry like my throat. A tightness in my gut, which wasn't unpleasant, was happening, and a flush up my spine to my neck. The changes, which were happening so quickly, seemed to indicate my body was up for this, even if my mind couldn't wrap itself around it.

"Alright. When?"

"No time like the present."

"I'll follow, you lead," I said.

He led me to his bedroom on the second floor. "Let's do this one step at a time. First, bodies," he said, undoing his shirt and placing it over the back of a chair.

I looked at him. A physique that was athletic, wide shoulders, Well, defined chest muscles, formed biceps, no hair—huh! He had a six-pack as they call it, right down to the slim waist above the belt of his pants. The cut of his body formed a V that tempted me to follow its direction. He turned around for me to look at. That was nice. His broad back was straight and strong.

"Do you want to touch me?"

"Not yet." But in my turn unzipped the back of my dress, and let the shoulders slip off. I watched his eyes drink in my skin, caress my shoulders, lay bare my breasts and tickle my nipples.

"May I?" he asked, motioning me to turn around. He undid my bra and slipped the straps down my arms, laying delicate kisses where they had sat. His fingertips brushed every so lightly across the skin of my back, causing shivers to travel down my spine and arms. When his hand closed on my shoulder, the warmth of it soaked into my skin as it slipped down my arm. I was caught by surprise as his fingertips, which were traveling down my arm, moved to cup my breast in his hand. He held my ample breast like a dove, feeling its weight and heft. His thumb caressed my nipple until it was erect and wanting.

I turned around and raised a hand to his chest. I let my fingertips play across the muscles of his chest, outlining the contour of one breast, then the other. Since his nipples were at the same height as my head, it was easy to lean into his body and take one into my mouth. I felt the gasp as he sucked in air quickly, and then the groan as he let the air back out in pleasure. His hand came up under my plait and cupped the back of my head, pressing me against his breast, urging me to do more. I did—I sucked on the nipple, hard. He started breathing faster and pressing me more. I played with his nipple using my tongue and teeth, then nipped him and felt him shudder in pleasure.

His hand still held my breast, lovingly holding and caressing it. But now he pinched the erect nipple. It was my turn to gasp. When I let go of his nipple, he knelt down so that he was level with mine and gave me my own treatment. I felt a heat rising inside me. A heat I hadn't felt since my early twenties when I thought I was in love. That heat spread between my legs.

Seamus' nose twitched, and he inhaled deeply. When he looked at me, his eyes were swirling, the blue of them now green and rotating like a hurricane.

"You're aroused," he said simply. "I can smell your arousal."

"Really?" I asked. "How?"

"It's a skill we acquire as immortals. You will get it too. Do you want to go further?"

"Yes," I murmured breathlessly.

He undid his belt, pulled it out, and then slid his trousers off his slim hips. His briefs were strained by his swollen cock fighting to get out. He pulled the elastic waistband out and over it, letting it spring free. Free indeed, as thick as a cucumber, and just as long. I had never seen a cock that large in my life. I had to touch it. It didn't seem real.

He stood up and stood there, completely naked, unashamed and waiting for me. First, I let my dress drop to the floor, and dropped my panties too and stepped out of them. We stood there, both of us, looking at each other. The difference in height was in our legs.

I wanted to take hold of his cock so much it almost hurt. His bottom was adorable, nice and tight. I stepped up to him first. I placed one of my hands under his cock until it was resting in my hand. Seamus was smiling and his eyes were closed. He was just waiting for whatever would happen next.

While my hand was holding his cock, it gently jumped and wiggled, as if it were eager to play too. I enclosed my second hand around him and with two hands felt him from end to end. I knelt down this time and took his cock in my mouth. Seamus groaned and his cock pushed more. I slowed him down by stroking him slowly.

"Anita, this will bring me to climax quickly," he said. "If you want me to pleasure you, let me do that first."

"Okay, lead."

He stood me up and took both hands and brought me to the bed. After pulling the covers down, he indicated to get up so I scrambled to the top center of the king size bed. He crawled on his hands and knees after me. Opening my legs, he lay between them with his face right there. I didn't know what was going to happen next, this had never been my experience. So when he buried his nose in my slit, I was shocked, but the pleasure rocked my body. He rubbed his nose and inhaled my scent, then took my clitoris into his mouth and nearly brought me to tears, stopping just before I would have exploded. He repeated that with his tongue in my vagina, showing me things about my body I didn't know about, sensitive spots I was unaware of, again stimulating me until I nearly exploded. Coming down this time was a little painful though, and I was still half high.

When he added fingers to his tongue ministrations, I did lose it. I screamed and screamed in release as wave after wave of my orgasm took over my body, leaving me weak and shuddering.

"Oh my God, I feel like I'm a bowl of liquid. How did you do that?" I asked with a wobbly voice.

"Was that good for you?"

"Good? Oh my God, yes! Amazing. But you haven't climaxed yet."

"Don't worry, we've got lots more to do."

"Really?" I thought back and didn't remember ever having more than one orgasm, ever. Sometimes not even getting one. "I don't know, Seamus. It may be difficult."

"Ah no, your new body will have no trouble at all." And to prove that, he simply inserted a couple of fingers inside my vagina and all of a sudden I was nearly there again, panting like I'd run ten miles. Only this time Seamus crawled up my body to find my breasts, and was gently tugging on them, building up my wave. He pulled my knees up and wide apart so that his hips lay between them, and I could feel his cock at my door. It felt hot and hard, and not likely to fit. He slid his hand down to my vagina and spread my secretion all over his cock, adding to the lubrication he already was providing. He slipped himself up to my opening and gently pressed until the tip of him was inside.

"Oh my God!" I cried loudly.

"Did that hurt you?" he asked with concern.

"No." I heard the surprise in my own voice. "No, it doesn't hurt, quite the opposite. I thought it would hurt but it feels right."

Seamus started pushing gently, to a chorus of ahs and ohs, and oh mys. My body was loving this. I heard myself making all kinds of noises as that wonderful cock stroked me inside all around. He slid in and out like he was made for me. It didn't take long before he said something strange.

"Anita, I may tip you. Let me know if it hurts, okay?"

"Tip me?"

"Hit the end of you."

"Really?" Then it happened on his next thrust. His penis pulled out completely and thrust in with such force he hit the very end of my channel.

"Ahhh, oh my."

"Are you hurt?"

"No, I feel pressure, but not pain." Ah, ah, ah, ah, oh, there was the pain. And then it was gone.

He thrust again, and again, and again. Each time harder, and it seemed deeper. He started going faster, until we were both frantic and pounding against each other, wanting to consume the other, and be inside, become one, and then we climaxed. With a huge release, I felt his seed spill like a hose. My climax was epic. I felt myself detach from my body as the orgasm left me feeling like liquid again. My body was shuddering with pleasure, leaving me feeling like I was floating in the air above a field of fluff.

It all went black after that. When I opened my eyes, Seamus was lying on top of me, still inside me.

"Did I black out?" I asked.

"For a few minutes," he said. "How do you feel?"

"I can't describe it. Euphoric, energized, sated like never before. Is this normal for sex with an immortal?"

"Yes. I'm afraid I cannot disconnect quite yet."

"Why not?"

"Our cocks stay hard for a long time, blocking the semen from leaving to provide a higher chance of getting pregnant."

"Pregnant? Oh, I didn't even think of that. I'm too old for pregnancy."

"Ah, no, not anymore. But as an immortal, you won't be able to get pregnant easily, so don't worry. That aside, how did you enjoy yourself?"

"Seamus, thank you, that was the best sex I've ever had."

"My pleasure, milady. Really. Anytime you want to scratch an itch … perhaps the next time, I'll have my fangs."

"Fangs? Oh, that's right. I don't have fangs yet either."

"Not yet, but you'll get them."

"Hmm, that'll be interesting."

"Don't use them on humans though."

"Of course."

I felt Seamus' cock suddenly let go and slide out. It's not like it was soft, it just wasn't as hard.

"Does your cock remain at the ready all the time?"

"I wish. No, but it takes a great deal to make them small."

"Ah, I see." But I didn't—

13—Justin Hears the Tale

Rick

Justin's recovery proceeded well. He got daily exercise, and was soon able to walk on his own again and navigate the stairs. He impatiently took over the task of cooking for the three guys living at the condo because he was sick and tired of takeout food. But they had to help him down the stairs to do so. Not that the food was bad, it was the same thing every time.

With cooking went shopping, and Justin was never happier than shopping for food. He was doing that online because he wasn't strong enough yet to go to all the open-air markets and farmers' markets. He loved finding new and exotic ingredients to use. Cooking was an obsession with him, and he started working on new recipes for the restaurant that he was determined to get back. But that would be a while yet. We were still waiting for the insurance money.

Every time I was over there, he had me tasting yet another new creation he had come up with. It was going to be an awesome menu. That meant I should be working with him to come up with new desserts too. But I'd become too distracted by life to do much culinary exploration. It was a good thing Justin worked at it all the time.

When I arrived on this day in March, Justin was in the kitchen working, Seamus was in his room, and Duffy had just returned from some stakeout he was doing.

"Hey, Justin, now that you're Well, on the road to full recovery, I thought we could have that extended conversation about immortals and you can ask your questions."

"'Bout time. Let me put this in the oven and pour us some drinks. I think this is going to need alcohol to hear." When he settled on the sofa opposite me, he said, "Okay, lay it on me."

"Alright. As I have said, I'm an immortal. I didn't know at first, and it wasn't until I met Lora and her friends, Mark and Falon, that we discovered who and what I was. Since then, we've pieced together my story.

"I was born in Cuba, but I was conceived on an island in the East Caribbean by a couple of people who descended from beings that came to Earth before the last Ice Age ended."

"Came to Earth? What do you mean, you're aliens?"

"To this world, yes. Our people escaped a dying planet, traveled across the universe, and found this planet. At the time it was covered in ice—Well, half of it was, and there were only a few pseudo-intelligent life forms."

"You mean humans, don't you?" he asked, then smiled. "Okay, I get the pseudo-intelligent. Go on."

"On this planet, our people are long-lived. So much so that humans consider us immortal. We can live thousands of years, but we can still be killed by a catastrophic injury. Our blood can heal humans, as you now understand, and our venom can turn a human into one of us."

"So, why did you give me your blood?"

"While I was standing there listening to the doctors explain your injuries, I realized you weren't likely to make it. I panicked. I didn't want to lose you—you're my best friend."

My voice broke. Tears were forming in Justin's eyes, and I felt them well in mine too.

I took a deep breath. "As the doctors described the trauma to your head, I knew there was only a slim chance you'd make it off the table. It was severe enough that they said if you lived, you'd be a vegetable."

"Oh. I wouldn't want that," he said, somberly shaking his head.

"I knew that. Then they told me that the crush injuries to your legs were irreparable. They would need to remove both legs. I knew you'd rather be dead than live like that."

"You got that right. Go on."

"So the only solution I could think of was to give you my venom and turn you. But I stalled for time so that I could ask the group and get their opinions. Abeo gave me an alternative. He told me a transfusion of my blood would heal you quickly. So this is what I decided to do, and the responsibility to make sure you understood the need for keeping it a secret fell to me too."

"There are several words in that explanation that require explanation. First, what secret?"

"Of us. No one can know about us, our blood, who we are, anything."

"So how did you manage to get me a transfusion?"

"When the doctors said they would need to give you one before the surgery, I told them we were a match and to use my blood. I had to use what we call compulsion to make sure they followed my instructions."

"Compulsion?"

"It's a skill some of us learn. We can add a layer to our voice that compels the person listening to us to follow our will. They have no choice. We use it very judiciously."

"Well, that makes sense. If someone found out, you'd be thrown inside a cage so quickly and experimented on, your head would spin. I get that. I won't say or do anything to give you away. And don't tell me who the others are. I'd rather be ignorant."

"Well, there is a little more."

"More?"

"We can turn people."

"You mentioned that word before. Turn people? Into what?"

"One of us. You could become immortal with us. Become one of our circle. There are some amazing advantages to it."

"And I can imagine the cons too. Always hiding. Always on guard. Watching people you love die."

"Yes, those are the cons. But the pros outweigh them, I think."

"What are the pros?"

"Other than the obvious? Getting to have unlimited time to be with the love of your life, having unlimited time to try everything you ever wanted to try. Imagine how many 'careers' you could have, if you could start over? Never getting sick, healing from injuries quickly, and the sex, that's the best perk."

"Sex is better?" asked Justin. "How?"

"We immortals are a very lusty species. We love sex, every way you can think of, and often, and long."

"Hmm. And just how do you turn humans into you?"

"Now, all it takes is a couple of injections."

"Of what?"

"Our venom."

"There's another word. Venom? As in a snake?"

"No, not as in snake. However, we are predators. On our home world, our race produced venom as a defensive and offensive weapon, delivered through fangs, similar to a vampire."

Laughing uproariously, Justin said, "Okay, you almost had me believing you—right up until the word 'vampire.' Okay now, give it up for what's really going on."

Seeing that Justin was now firmly in the don't believe column, I had to show him. I slowly let my fangs elongate. Justin stared—his eyes widening like saucers—a mixture of horror and curiosity plain on his face. Before the fangs retracted, he reached over to touch them.

"Oh my God! They're not props," he screeched.

I took his hand and bit the edge of it just a little—enough to give him a small dose of venom. I watched his eyes dilate and he squinted at me, his mouth formed an "O" as the venom rushed through his blood.

"Oh my God, that's a rush!" he said, looking at his hand and watching the puncture holes vanish before his eyes.

"I gave you some of my venom. It has many properties, hallucinogenic, aphrodisiac, and in large doses would create an immortal from a human or kill our enemy. I can force it, but normally these physical changes occur whenever we get aroused or agitated." I let my eyes return to normal and my fangs retract.

"That's a nice party trick. I'll bet all the girls love it."

"The boys do too."

"Really? Can girls do that?"

"Yes they can."

"What about a man biting another man?"

"Same thing. The emotional state of the person determines what it does to our body."

"So if I were one of you, could I give someone that feeling?"

"Yes, but we advise against doing that, because eventually you'll have to have this conversation with them."

"I see. What if it was someone already within our circle of friends?"

"Who?"

"Greggory. He and I started dating casually before the bombing."

"Again, any new members to the club have to be considered by everyone. The more people we have, the greater our risk to exposure."

"That makes sense. May I know who's a member now?"

"Yes. Mark, Gwen, Abeo, and I are not human. Falon, Andrews, Margaret, Lora, and Anita are turned humans. Plus, we have included Lora's children. Any children born to us carry the DNA of an immortal, and their development gets finished at puberty. Some of the witches are also immortal, like Seamus, Siobhan, and Mary."

"Duffy isn't?"

"No, but he's read in like you because of the nature of the work he does for Mark, but he's not turned. We tend to want to wait till there's a good reason—like a true-love mate."

"Are there gays among your species?"

"Why wouldn't there be? Love is love is love. In fact, from the research I have done, my species believed there were many more genders than just male and female. Gender was fluid and sexuality was too. When we met the group in the Caribbean, they were all sorts of genders."

"That's good to know, that makes me happy. Clearly, yours is an enlightened species. I think I'd rather be part of your species than a member of the human race."

"Yeah, well, we still have to live here."

"Pity."

"Do you have any more questions?" I asked.

"How long and how soon can I be turned?"

"It takes about three days, and you can do it whenever you're ready."

"Alrighty, then. In the meantime, what's happening with the restaurant? That is what has been keeping me up at night."

14— Cooks are Found

Andrews

Within days of the bombing, both Rick and Mark asked me to run our own investigation into the bombing at L'Escalade in case it led to a supernatural suspect. There weren't many other reasons the new restaurant would be targeted. Neither Rick nor Justin had any enemies themselves. That left their association with the rest of us. That left a few enemies on a list.

The top of that list was Mark's family, and the next one was the Brotherhood. We thought the head of that particular snake had been cut off, but you can't be too sure. Derek might still be alive, or a member of his group was continuing his work. We thought that Staung was taken care of, but if he has a second, that could be a motive.

One of the things that came out of the Zoom meeting was a question of where did we draw the line on telling humans who and what we are? I had thought the line was directly around the six of us, until we met Margaret and Abeo. When our circle expanded to take them in, it also needed to expand to bring in our children, and that left an even larger question. How would the kids be educated?

All this was muddling around in the back of my head while I was looking into theories for the bombing. It became clear to me: we needed a secure place to live. When we needed to collectively disappear in ten to fifteen years, we needed somewhere we could go. I couldn't help shake the idea of an island, like Group 32.

Meanwhile, running down human things was mundane, simple, and reasonably easy to do. Grisham found the cook who was fired and brought him into our offices.

———

"Hello, Josh is it? My name is Robert Andrews. I'm investigating the bombing of L'Escalade. Can you please tell me your full name."

"Joshua Spencer."

"Josh? You were fired from L'Escalade the day before the bombing. Do you know why?"

"Um, yeah, the bitch fired me because I was late a third time. My mom doesn't have daycare for my youngest brother and I had to take the kid to a babysitter before my shift."

"The bitch? Who was that?"

"The sous-chef."

"Did you explain that to the sous-chef?"

"Yeah, and she didn't care. 'There are no exceptions,' she told me."

"Where were you on Dec 31st?" I asked.

"I went out with my homies to party."

"Can anyone vouch for you?"

"I have a parking ticket for the lot I used when we went to the bar."

"May I see it?"

"I gave it to the police."

"Okay. What time did you get home?"

"We dragged in about 2:30 a.m. My mom was home and up, she'll tell you."

"Okay. Do you know the other cook who called in sick on the 31st?"

"Who was it?" asked Josh.

"His name is listed as Eugene Brent."

"Gene, yeah I sorta know him. At least the time I worked at the restaurant."

"What did you think of him?"

"He didn't talk to anyone in the kitchen. He was always there too, doing everything he could."

"Did he like his job?"

"I guess. I don't know."

"Did you like your job?"

"Yeah, I did. I want to learn how to cook for real. But as long as my little brother needs a sitter, I'm kinda on the hook."

"If I could get you your job back, would you take it?"

"Oh man, yes! I want to learn there."

"Thanks, Josh, you can go now. If I have any more questions, may I call you?"

"Of course."

So Eugene was a loner. That could be an indicator of something or nothing. I needed to speak to him next.

"Hello, is Eugene there please?"

"Who's askin'?" answered a female voice.

"My name is Robert Andrews, I'm investigating the bombing of L'Escalade restaurant."

"Are you police?"

"No, ma'am. Private investigator."

"Just a moment."

"Hello?" came a voice a few minutes later.

"Eugene?"

"Yeah, call me Gene."

"Okay, Gene, would you mind coming into my office? I need to ask you some questions about the restaurant."

"Sure, when?"

"Anytime today is great."

"I'll be there in an hour."

"Thank you."

By the time Gene arrived, I had a copy of the parking receipt for Josh from the police and confirmed his alibi with the mother. Josh, it seems, was in the clear. The police were no closer to a suspect either.

Gene walked into my office roughly an hour later. He was a scruffy looking dude, with long hair and an odor to him you couldn't quite place.

I invited him to take a seat. A distant seat.

"Hello, Gene. I'm Andrews. Nice to meet you. Thank you for coming in today."

"No problem."

"Gene, how are you feeling today?"

"Fine, I guess," he answered, with a little surprise in his voice.

"I ask, because you called in sick to work a couple of nights ago. Can you tell me why?"

"I was sick."

"Sick enough to go to a doctor?"

"No."

"Sick enough to stay home?"

"For a while."

"Did you go out?"

"No."

"So how long were you home, then?"

"Till around midnight I guess."

"Where did you go?"

"Why does it matter?"

"Because there was a bombing at the restaurant that you were supposed to be working at that night, that's why."

"I wasn't there."

"Where were you?"

"Nowhere."

"But you said you went out."

"Yeah."

"So where did you go?"

"I dunno."

"That's not an answer, son."

"I'm not your son."

"That's right. So where were you?"

"I told you I dunno."

"That's not an answer. Did you drive?"

"Yeah."

"What year is your car?"

"2016."

"So it has a nav system?"

"Yeah, built in."

"Good. We can find out where you went from the GPS system."

"It's broken."

"Oh yeah, since when?"

"December."

"Really? It just broke. Why don't you show me?"

"I didn't use the car today."

"How did you get here?"

"Uber."

"Where is your car?"

"Mom has it."

"The woman I spoke to at your house?"

"Yes."

I picked up the phone and called the house again. "Hello, Mrs. Brent? Is Gene's car parked at the house right now?"

"Lemme look. I heard her walk. "Nope, it's not here. He must have taken it."

"Thank you, Mrs. Brent. Goodbye," I said, hanging up the phone. "Gene, may I have your keys please?"

"You can't take them. You have no right."

“No, but I can call the police and they can. So we can do this the easy way, or the hard way. Which do you prefer?”

Gene handed me his keys.

“Okay, stand up and take me to your car.” We walked out of the building and around the corner. He had parked on the street. I unlocked the car and the trunk and looked in the trunk first. I wasn’t that surprised to find wires, tools, a box, and other things that could be used to make a bomb. There was no explosive in the trunk though. Inside, the car was a mess. Empty cups, empty bags from take-out, dirty clothes—quite a pigsty. There was that strange smell again, only stronger.

“Gene, have you been sleeping in your car?”

“Some days, yes.”

“Other days?”

“I’d go home to my mom’s but she doesn't want me there, so the best I can get is a night here or there. It lets me shower at least.”

“And when was the last night you slept at your mother’s house?”

“A week ago.”

“Were you actually sleeping at your mother’s on the 31st?”

“No.”

“Where did you sleep?”

“At a friend’s.”

“What’s the name of this friend?”

“Steve Bushing.”

“The address?”

“It’s 901 East 43rd Street.”

"Okay, I'm going to interview your friend, and I may have some more questions for you. So don't leave town, Gene." *I hope he doesn't realize that I don't really have any authority here.*

"No, sir."

I handed him back his keys and walked back to my office. I called Grisham and asked him to do a rundown on Steve Bushing for the address I was given. In the meantime, I needed a coffee and to call Gwen.

15— Fostering

Rick

I hadn't realized that when Lora told me she wanted to foster, she meant two of the witches. I felt I needed to ask her about it.

"Lora, are you sure you want to foster two girls while going through a pregnancy?"

"It's not like they're babies," she said. "They're teens, and they'll fit in with my kids just fine. In fact, we can bunk the girls together. We have six bedrooms. If we put Anita in the guesthouse, we can put them in Anita's old bedroom, and then they'll have the whole suite to themselves and our kids won't have to bunk."

"That's a good idea. That would give Anita more privacy, and that will be important now for her gentlemen callers."

"Wait, Anita has gentlemen callers?" asked Lora.

"She will have," I said. "She told me she and Seamus hit it off."

"You're an old gossip, Rick!" Lora teased. "But you're right. It will give her privacy."

"So the kids don't have to move, and the baby still has her own room."

"Yes, and putting the two fosters in Anita's suite will give them some privacy as well," said Lora.

"Are you sure you're not biting off more than you can handle?" I asked.

"I'm not. I'll let you know when I have, okay?" said Lora. I could see she was getting angry with me for doubting her. "One of the two witches is a fifteen-year-old girl, and the other is nineteen. They both need an education in modern life from a young person's point of view. I think Minni is a good candidate to help with that."

———

When the doorbell rang, there were three people standing outside. I only remembered one of them.

"Amarlyis, nice to see you again," I said.

"Rick, yes, and thank you for fostering these two ladies."

"No problem, happy to help. They'll get along with our oldest daughter," I said. "Come on in, ladies. What are your names?"

"I'm Cailleach Dhé, and she's Ailbhe," said the older one.

"Anita, come and meet our guests," I called. "Anita is my longtime housekeeper. If you need anything, let her know. Anything at all."

Anita came walking around the corner from the kitchen carrying a large tray of refreshments.

"Come, señoritas, sit in the parlor and have some lemonade and cookies. I'll go and get Lora from the back for you."

I took the three of them into the parlor, where Anita left the tray and then left. Amarlyis whispered to me on the way: "Is Anita an immortal?"

I nodded, and directed them to have a seat. All three women sat on the edge of their chairs nervously. I left to go fetch another chair from the kitchen.

"Please take a glass and help yourself. No one is going to object," Anita told them. "We don't stand on ceremony here."

"How could you be a long time housekeeper? You barely look more than twenty-five," asked the older girl.

"Gracias, señorita, I was turned into an immortal recently, and I no longer look as old as I am. I'm actually sixty-two," answered Anita.

"Oh!" said all three witches quietly. The teens glanced at Amarlyis nervously and then back at Anita.

"They are nervous, because they know you are immortal with power, and they are a little afraid of you," explained Amarlyis.

"Who said that?" asked Lora, coming into the room. "There is no reason to be afraid of us, whatever someone says."

Lora looked pointedly at Amarlyis. "Disregard such statements. We're not some all-powerful beings who will keep you imprisoned."

"What's this about prisons?" I asked, walking into the parlor carrying the chair.

"The girls are apparently afraid of us, me, because I'm an immortal," said Lora. We both burst out laughing. Lora found her voice first. "This puffball?" she crowed. "He's a pastry chef! He makes pies and cakes and cookies for a living. He's not some overlord with slaves."

It took a few extra moments for me to catch my breath. "Lora is not a scary immortal either. Her goal, our goal, is to teach you about modern life so eventually you can live on your own and find your way in this world. Just like *our* kids."

"Oh my, I needed a good laugh!" said Lora. "Amarlyis, I'd thank you not to put silly notions in their heads."

"Fine," said Amarlyis. "I'll be on my way, then, since you have everything under control."

"Thank you for dropping them off for me," said Lora, as Amarlyis reached the front door.

"How did she bring you girls?"

"We drove in a taxi," said the younger one.

"Minni, boys, please come downstairs," called Lora. "I want you to meet our new houseguests."

When the kids got there, I introduced them as our kids. Minni gave me a secret smile of pleasure.

"Minni, will you take them upstairs? Show them around, and let them unpack what they brought. The girls will be sharing the spare room for a night until we can move Anita. We can take them shopping for clothes tomorrow."

"Okay, Mom. Ladies, follow me. Guys, do you want to show them your rooms?"

"Sure, we'll all go together." The five children ran upstairs chattering. Anita cleared her throat.

"Move me? Where are you moving me?" asked Anita, once the children were gone.

"Oh, we thought that the perfect place for you would be the guesthouse. You'd have your own space, free of children, and privacy in case you want gentlemen callers," said Lora.

"Really? I can have the guesthouse?" asked Anita.

"Yes, it's a perfect solution, really," said Rick. "Go take a look and see what you need. We'll move your things over tomorrow."

"Thank you!"

"Can you imagine Amarlyis making them afraid of us?" I asked Lora after we were alone.

"Unfortunately, yes I can imagine. Amarlyis wanted power over them, so anything she can do to shake their confidence in us, she will use."

"Hey, Mom, what time is dinner?" asked Minni from upstairs.

"I don't know. Why?"

"I thought we could go swimming until then."

"Good idea. Do you have two extra swimsuits for the girls?"

"Yeah, I can manage with a bikini and give them one-piece suits."

"Perfect."

Ten minutes later, the five kids were running downstairs with their towels and out to the pool.

"Don't run in the house!" yelled Anita after them. "*Ah Dios*!" we heard her say under her breath, but she was smiling broadly.

We looked at each other and chuckled quietly. Off to a good start.

"Anita really does love having a full house, doesn't she?" Lora asked. "Why don't we go swimming too?"

"Yes, she does and yes, let's go swimming too."

"Race you!" called Lora as she took off up the stairs.

"That's where the kids get that!" I called after her. I ran past her at immortal speed.

"Hey! No fair!"

"All's fair in love and war!" I sang to her as I caught her in my arms and hugged her to me, inhaling her hair and scent at the nape of her neck. She was uniquely Lora. A mix of sandalwood, ginger, and Goddess Oil. "Oh, you smell so good!"

"None of that or we won't get to the pool."

"Hmm, there are more fun things we could do inside."

Turning around to face him, I kissed those wonderful soft lips until I felt my own fangs drop a little with desire. I licked the seam of his lips until he let me in, and groaned as I explored my way around. Finding his fangs elongating too, I pricked my tongue on them and got a tiny drop of venom to rev up my engine.

"It's a point of no return," I said. "Either we go or we stay, but more of this will tip the scale in favor of staying. Just saying."

"Then I will take a rain check, my husband. Let's go spend some time with the new girls. The only way they won't be afraid of us is by getting used to us."

"You're right," I said. "I hate it when you're right and it means no sex."

She laughed at me, dropping her clothes on the floor and displaying her gorgeous body to me. Another groan escaped my lips as I feasted my eyes slowly down her body, from the dainty collarbones and slim arms with surprisingly strong biceps, to the full breasts of a mature woman, the slim waist and the soft belly proving she had children. Right down to the soft pussy she kept perfectly manicured.

"Mamacita, you are a sight to behold. I love everything about you," I said. "But now I cannot go down to the pool without embarrassing myself."

Lora slipped into an adorable tiger print string bikini that hugged her curves and accentuated her assets. Then she walked to me to tie up the strings behind her back. While she was standing there, she pressed herself against my hard shaft and rubbed me slowly.

"That's definitely not fair!" I said. "Now I'll have to wear a Speedo under my shorts just to keep him contained."

"Oh, poor baby. I'll make it up to you later when the kids are in bed. We can have a private swim."

"Oh, I like that." Grabbing some big towels and carrying them in front of my erection, I led the way down the stairs to the pool. Lora put on a matching beach coverup over her bikini.

We listened to the kids having a ball in the pool. This was going very well! When we got outside, all five were in the water. The new girls were in the shallow end.

"Hey, girls, do you know how to swim?" asked Rick.

"No," they answered together. "It was not something we did," said Cailleach Dhé. "The only time we were fully immersed in water was to bathe, and then we were naked."

"Swimming is a gift that nature gives us. We learn to swim so that we can do more things around the water safely. Besides, it's fun," I said. I threw down my towels on a lounge chair and dove into the deep end of the pool quickly. I was hoping the cold water would shrink a certain appendage and put the genie back in the bottle. It worked.

Lora sat on the side of the pool with just her feet and calves in the water.

"Do you know how to swim, Lora?" asked Cailleach Dhé.

"Yes I do, I just take a long time to get in the water," she said. "I'm not a fan of cold water."

"It's not too cold. We've been in rivers that are much colder than this. This is almost like bathwater."

"Brrrrrr," said Lora. "I don't want a bath this cold. Girls, welcome to the twenty-first century. Hot water for bathing, *inside* the house."

Pascal got out of the water, grabbed one of the balls, and jumped back into the pool. He started throwing the ball back and forth between the five of them until Cailleach Dhé almost missed it and used magic to trap it in a bubble.

"Oh cool!" cried Pascal. "I want to learn how to do that!"

"May I teach them, Lora?" asked Cailleach Dhé.

"You know, if you can, go for it. I'm still learning myself because I was never taught. So I'd like to listen in on that lesson too. I hadn't thought of that benefit of having you here. You can teach us as well!"

"We should schedule regular practice sessions, then," said Cailleach Dhé.

"Practice?" asked Pascal.

"Well, you didn't think you'd learn and master it the first time, did you?" asked Cailleach Dhé.

"I guess not."

"Benal family, dinner is ready," called Anita. "In the dining room please."

We all got out of the pool, wrapped towels around ourselves, and dried off as best we could. When we got to the dining room, Anita shook her head.

"*Oh mi, sin modales mis dulces hoodlums*," said Anita. "Go and put shirts and pants on for dinner! *Ah mon Dios*!

We all ran upstairs giggling and threw on clothes quickly and returned to a feast like we saw at the wedding. All kinds of Cuban dishes, homemade tortillas and soft tacos. Boy, was I hungry.

"Mama, you've outdone yourself!" I told her, kissing her cheek."

"Ricardo, we are welcoming to the family two lovely ladies. They need a proper party."

It was a very good thing I bought a huge house for my Lora, because I had a feeling it was always going to be filled with the laughter of lots of children. Our table could seat twenty, so we had lots of room. My heart was filled with love for this woman, and for her children who were now mine as much as if I had created them. Now there were two more souls to add to our family, not including the one in Lora's tummy. I felt blessed, and realized she was very right. It was all going to work out.

After we got all the kids to bed and Anita had retired to her suite, I had Lora to myself.

"*Mi amor*, come and sit with me," I said. She came over and sat on the sofa with her legs draped over mine and leaned back into the pillows with a sigh. I started rubbing her feet and earned a deep, happy groan from her as the tension left her body.

"Oh, that feels so good," she said.

"I won't stop." Continuing to pay attention to her toes, I lifted one to my lips and casually nibbled on the big toe. She giggled and opened her eyes to watch me.

"That tickles."

"Oh?"

Then I licked her toe and drew it into my mouth.

"Oh!"

"Do you like that?" I asked, after thoroughly sucking on her toe.

"Mmm, it was stimulating."

I put her foot down, reached over to her hips and pulled her closer to me. Then I got up and leaned over her and planted a sensual kiss on her sweet lips. Lora wrapped her arms around my neck, which let me lift her up and sit her down on my lap.

She planted a kiss on me this time, deep and open, exploring my mouth, finding my fangs. I kept my tongue still, letting her have the lead. When she stopped, I pounced on her, pushing into her mouth, finding her fangs too. That kiss made me forget we had bodies. It took over my mind as I got lost in the passion.

A quiet *ahem* behind me stopped me cold, and I looked around to see Cailleah Dhé standing behind me.

"Excuse me, but are we allowed to take food to our room?" she asked.

"Yes, of course. Just bring down any scraps and the dishes please," I answered.

Lora had her head leaning on my chest, her shoulders shaking from silent laughter she couldn't hold back.

"It's like getting caught by our parents," I said with a smile.

"I know, eh? The condemnation on her face was hysterical."

"Shall we take this to the hot tub?"

"I think that would be nice. Let me grab some towels." Lora ran upstairs and came down with big beach towels, a couple for each of us.

I was waiting in the hot tub. When she approached, her eyes gleamed and she fanned her face. Quickly disrobing, she joined me in the water. A long, contented sigh escaped her lips as her shoulders settled beneath the surface.

"I cannot imagine how I ever did without a hot tub."

"Me neither." She snuggled close to me, laying her head on my chest, and closed her eyes, almost purring like a cat. I ran my finger up and down her back under the water, enjoying the heat, the closeness, and the happiness that filled me. People might not understand what happiness is and question whether or not they were ever happy in their lives. Not me. I would remember this moment, etch it into my mind, curated with all the other moments I had saved, and keep it safe.

Happiness is a treasure to keep because it's sometimes fleeting. We cannot enjoy happiness without experiencing its opposite, sadness. You cannot recognize being happy unless you've had sadness in your life. I'm baffled by the people who claim they have never known happiness but have never really suffered either. Maybe it's the lack of extremes that clouds our ability to enjoy simple things, to find happiness in little things, to simply be happy.

16— Justin's decision

Justin

My convalescence went well. I had no signs of brain damage, nor any lingering effects from being crushed nearly to death. I would say I was lucky but that would be a lie. It was not luck that saved me but the blood of an alien. *How weird is that?* Better than the blood of a vampire, I supposed. I just wouldn't be able to live that one down.

It was almost spring and I was sick of being in the condo every day. However, it was agreed upon that I would remain behind walls until I was healed, then I could come back from the miracle of whatever fictional doctor Mark had arranged for. It had been a long five weeks. I hadn't spoken to Greggory once since the hospital. They didn't want any leaks.

Duffy and Seamus were good to me. Either Anita or one of them helped me with my exercises daily, getting me walking around, at first with their help, then eventually with a walker. Now, I could manage on my own without. Tackling the stairs was like back to square one, but again the guys really helped.

Once I was able to navigate the stairs on my own, they didn't have to bring food upstairs, and it meant that I could go down and spend time with them. As straight guys go, they were cool. But gay is cooler.

Seamus intrigued me. He was an immortal, but he only recently "finished" his transformation, he said. What the hell is finished? He was quite smitten by Anita, Rick's housekeeper. Who would have guessed she was such a looker as a young woman! Ai chihuahua!

Seamus and Anita had quite the tussle the first day she came over. She was coming by every day now to do some housework for us, cook meals, and check on my physical therapy. I had a feeling that she and Seamus were also having private sessions. Every now and then I would hear screams of pleasure from downstairs.

Don't ask, don't tell, was my policy.

Anita didn't come over on the weekends, and Seamus and Duffy were usually gone too, so I had the condo to myself. I called Andrews to talk about that offer he made me.

"Andrews speaking."

"It's Justin."

"How are you feeling, Justin?"

"Well, I believe I'm totally healed and I am ready to run some tests."

"What kind of tests?"

"The sexual kind."

"You want to try sex with an immortal to see how you like it?"

"Yes, please."

"Let me talk to Gwen and get back to you."

"Thanks."

———

In the meantime, I put together a meal for myself from the ingredients I could find and sat in front of the television to listen to the news.

> *"There is a new lead on the bombing of the restaurant L'Escalade last month," said the announcer. "Police and fire investigators are looking for a person associated with one of the cooks, who is known to them as an explosives expert. This man, whose photo is on screen now, may be living or working around the Ahuntsic area. Anyone with information on this individual should call the phone number on the screen."*

"Well, that is something. I should find out if Andrews has that information." The doorbell rang. I was not supposed to answer it, so I let it go. However, three minutes later, there was a knock on the door. I got up and looked through the peephole to see a face I didn't recognize. Picking up my phone, I placed the camera lens at the peephole and took a photo.

"Is anyone home?" came a voice from out in the hall. "Please answer if you're home."

Not on your life, I thought to myself. I watched and waited until it seemed he had left. Returning to the couch, I pulled up the photos and was happy to see something. I quickly composed a message to Andrews and attached the image of the person from the hallway.

An answer came back immediately. *"Stay inside and don't answer the door!"* it read.

In compliance there, I thought to myself.

"I have keys to the condo, so I will not be ringing. If this guy is still there, I will find him," said another message from Andrews.

Oh, he was coming over! "When will you be getting here?" I typed back.

"I should be there in five minutes," answered Andrews. *"Let me deal with this visitor before we get started."*

God, I'm all nervous. Should I get changed? This was more of a hookup than anything else. No romance. I went upstairs and decided to put on some silk pajamas and a matching robe, and made sure I was all clean. It looked sexy but not overt. I hoped.

Back downstairs, I heard voices in the hallway. I crept up behind the door and put my ear to it listening.

"Who are you?"

"My name is Jackson Perry."

"What are you doing here?"

"I heard you were looking for Steve Bushing. I know where he is."

"How did you get this address?"

"Around."

"Around where, exactly."

"I can't say."

"Well, if you have information for me, you can come to my office and give it to me there."

"I can't be seen going to your office."

"But you can be seen in my condo? Leave now, before I break your face and call the cops. Five … four … three … two…"

I then heard a key in the lock and jumped away from the door quickly as Andrews came inside quietly. He stopped dead when he saw me standing there.

"Did you hear that interchange?"

"Yes I did. Was I not supposed to?"

"Nothing like that. Just sorry for the threat."

"Honey, you can go and threaten anyone you like, it's sexy as hell. Just not me, okay?"

"Right. So, Justin, how would you like this to go?"

"Can we pretend it's a hookup?"

"Yes. Would you like a drink?"

"Please. For some reason, I'm nervous. I need to calm my nerves." I crossed over to the bar and took down two glasses. "Scotch?"

"Yup."

I brought over the glasses to the couch where Andrews was sitting and sat beside him. "Where do we start?"

"Let's start with bodies. How about I show you what an immortal male looks like?"

I swallowed and nodded. Andrews stripped for me, slowly. As he did, I felt the heat rise in my own blood unbidden. When I noticed his amber eyes swirling, I was captivated by them. As his clothes dropped to the floor, the exquisite sculpt of his body was displayed. I couldn't help myself, I ran my fingers over his pecs and the smooth hairless soft skin of his abdomen. Shivers laced up my arms, giving me gooseflesh as I felt myself harden in response. I looked back up at his face, and long teeth were protruding from his lips; his lower jaw was open just enough for his pink tongue to dart in and out. I wanted to kiss those lips, and bite that tongue. I closed the gap between us and reached for his head as I pressed my own lips against his and flicked my tongue inside his mouth and felt his fangs.

Andrews shuddered as I made contact with his fangs. *So that's an erogenous zone—noted.* When I made another pass, he grabbed me by the ass and pressed me in against his body. I felt my own erection get crushed against his, like two dueling swords. He deepened the kiss and I felt him slip my robe off. We were now skin to skin, chest to chest, belly to belly. The skin contact was exciting and it made me want more.

He was pushing me backwards gently, until my calves bumped up against the side of the sofa. The next thing I knew, I was falling down lengthwise and he was on top of me. My excitement ratcheted up two notches.

“Hello there,” I said. “Fancy meeting you here.” I don’t usually joke, but the tension was thick and I needed to cut it.

“Come here often?” he quipped back. “Or would you just like to?”

“Oh, I like you!”

He stopped the conversation by reaching into my pjs and stroking me. A groan escaped as his warm hands enveloped my head and the stroke became faster. When he pulled me out, and started licking me like an ice cream cone, I thought I would lose it. It had been so long. But I kept it contained.

“Do you want penetration?” he asked me.

“It would be nice. What about you? Are you good for that?”

“I came prepared. Do you want to go inside or outside?”

“I want you inside. We’ll need lube.”

“I have everything with me.” Andrews got up and went to his bag and pulled out strawberry flavored lube. He brought it back and the bag. I removed my pajamas and waited for him. He sat on the couch behind me, his cock sandwiched between us.

“I have lube, gloves, condoms, even some wipes,” he said.

“You’ve been with a man before.”

“Yes, I have. Do you want to be top or bottom?”

“I’ll be bottom this time. I douched before.”

“Thank you. I’m very large, so do you want toys or me?”

I pressed my body against the glorious cock between us. “You, definitely you.”

“Bend over.” I did what he asked. He lubed my ass thoroughly, then did something I hadn’t expected—he rimmed me expertly, teasing out sensations that quickly became arousing. *He's good—God, he's good.* Some pros won't even do that.

Adding more lube, he finger fucked me with two fingers. Feeling around and exploring my ass was great foreplay. However, when he reached around and started stroking my cock too, that was a double whammy. I couldn't resist this orgasm. I came all over the couch and was still screaming as he finished off the orgasm with his fingers.

"Oh fuck, that was good," I said, flopping down.

"I'm not finished yet."

"No?" I said, watching him. He knelt behind me, changed gloves, put on a condom, and lubed himself and me up some more.

"This may hurt a bit," he said.

"Honey, fuck me."

Andrews held on to my hips as he slowly pushed his cock inside, adding lube as he went, past the bend, way past anyone else, and filled me to the point I could feel him nudging my prostate.

"Ah, you've hit my p-spot." I said, between gasps and groans. "My God, you are big."

"Is it too much for you?" he asked. He was right behind me, stroking my cock while he was inching his way inside. I was feeling a little delirious.

"No, not too much … ah, ah, ah, oh my."

Andrews was now moving in an elongated oval motion, in and out, but side to side too. I had taken over stroking my own cock as his rhythm increased. He was holding me with his arms across my chest, pressing me into his chest while his cock continued its dominance.

I was losing my sense of place, suspended in this pleasurable ride, as the orgasm built and built, and just before I was about to climax I felt him lick my shoulder and bite down on my skin. The momentary pain set off the climax and the orgasm was beyond this world. I was flying.

It took several minutes for me to come down. Andrews held me the entire journey, until I was lying limp on the sofa.

"Wow, that was awesome. I've never had a climax like that before," I said.

"Glad to be of service," he said. "Do you want to talk about it?"

"Strangely, yes I do," I said. "You've clearly had gay sex before. Are you bi?"

"No, I'm fluid. I don't really think about gender. It's just about feeling good, and how to get there."

"Very enlightened. If I become immortal, do you think I will become fluid too?"

"I don't know. I was fluid before becoming immortal."

"Ah, I see. Andrews, you're a wonderful lover, thank you. Anytime you want a gay hookup, you come see me."

"Now that you've experienced this, and spoken to some humans who have been turned, do you have an idea of which direction you want to go?"

"Mmm, one. How do you watch people you love die?"

"You don't. Mark says the need to vanish every twenty years or so means we are not around when loved ones die."

"What about watching the world self-destruct? I mean, it's clear humans are killing themselves. What do you do about that?"

"That's more complex. I don't have an answer to that."

"Why can't we, you immortals, just change things?"

"Ah, that is an easy answer. The immortals have a moral imperative that governs them. They are not allowed to interfere with the natural evolution of humanity. We can perhaps improve something they were about to create, but we cannot interfere."

"Ah, sort of a *Star Trek* Prime Directive?"

"Yeah, sort of. If we chose to interfere, we would end up having to play God. We're not gods, and we should not have that power over any species."

"I like that answer. Okay, I'll do it. When can we schedule my transition?"

17— Afternoon Delight

Anita

Daydreaming while dusting, my thoughts became introspective.

Mi tiempo ha volado! My, has time flown by! It'd been nearly five months since I was turned into an immortal. The adjustment hadn't been too bad. Every time I looked in the mirror I was startled at the face looking back at me. That took some getting used to. As you get older, age creeps in, you don't see many of the changes, until one day… you ask yourself where did that come from? *Who is that old lady looking at me?*

Then you become immortal and the face you got used to over fifty years is gone! *Desapareció—vanished.* It's unnerving. It's not just the age that disappeared either. It was the puffiness, the extra skin, the fat, the body you became. I at least recognized the person in the mirror—it was me the way I looked when I was in my twenties.

I remembered that girl. She had fun. Getting the chance to be that girl again, without the same concerns, was truly a blessing. I wasn't sure my God would see it that way. That left me feeling strange. What would God think? He didn't give me this blessing—*or did He?* Perhaps He did. Maybe God brought me to this family so that I could become who I was now. Maybe He had a purpose for me to watch over these people, and to do that I must be one of them.

That thought settled me, gave me solace and made sense. Otherwise, why would He have put me into this situation? This must be a God-given blessing. After all, who created the immortals but God?

Feeling better about myself, I considered what I had to give up to live my new life. Other than my cousin, Carlos, I had no other family. Carlos hadn't said anything about my appearance. It was questionable if he even noticed, but perhaps he was just being a man and not saying anything for fear of insulting me. After all, how do you ask anyone why they suddenly look much younger? Bitchy people would answer, "Why did I look old before?" And of course that would start something. So perhaps he was just avoiding that discussion.

It was nice to not have the aches and pains of my age now. I woke up in the morning not sore! No arthritis and no stiffness. *Ah mon Dios!* It put a spring in my step. I felt up to the task of looking after all these children. Ricardo was having a new baby, and I could not wait to take care of that little one.

What did I give up? Not much. I didn't have friends here in Montreal yet. At least no one close that I couldn't do without, but I had made some acquaintances. My cover story if I ran into those people was I was Anita's niece. Outside of the family, I was using my maiden name now. My full name was Anita Teresa Juanita Mercanto.

Andrews was kind enough to get me a new set of documents with my name Teresa Juanito Mercanto. I was officially a landed immigrant and my job was an au pair. It felt good to be official. In the US, so many of my fellow Cubans were considered DACA or Dreamers. They could be deported at any moment. Ricardo was adopted by US citizens, so he was fine. He married a Canadian girl, so his citizenship in Canada was also no longer in question.

My phone rang, disrupting my reverie. I walked back into the kitchen to get it.

"*Hola soy Teresa,*" I answered.

"Anita? It's Seamus."

"Si, Seamus, how are you today?"

"I'm doing very well, thank you. You?"

"Oh, you know, lots of housework in a house this big, especially with children."

"I was wondering if you would have some time off this afternoon," he said.

"Hmm, before the kids get home, si."

"Would you like to have lunch with me?" he asked.

"Eat lunch or play lunch?"

"We could do both."

"Pick me up in an hour," I said.

In that hour, I got changed into something pretty and put on some lacy lingerie. Seamus and I had become a couple. He was good company, and the sex was pretty amazing. Considering I hadn't had sex in decades, it was a much different lifestyle.

The doorbell rang precisely one hour later. I like punctuality. Seamus walked in without needing me to get the door.

"Anita, I'm here," he called.

"I'm coming down,"

"Oh don't bother, I'll come up to you," he said. I heard him run up the stairs and down the hall to what used to be my bedroom suite. "Knock-knock," he said at my door.

"Do come in, *por favor*," I said.

"Ah, Anita, you look good enough to eat."

"Let's put that to the test, shall we?" I asked. "But first, let's go out to my guesthouse, where it's private."

He had dropped a basket on the table the girls used as a desk. I picked it up again and walked out of the room. He followed me outside and across the pool deck to the building at the back. The guesthouse was a one-bedroom suite with a small parlor, kitchen, and bathroom. It was perfect for one person.

Once we were inside, Seamus swept me off my feet and spun me around. His kiss was anything but chaste; he lit up my nerve endings. I dropped the basket on the coffee table once the dizziness stopped.

"Anita, you taste good."

"I borrowed Minni's strawberry lip gloss."

"Mmm, that's not what I mean."

"Oh," I blushed a little. "Let's eat in this room."

"Wonderful, I will pour the wine."

———

Lunch with Seamus was wonderful. He did romantic things like feed me grapes and cherries, and gave me long sultry looks from under his long eyelashes. When we finished eating, he helped me clean up the dishes, then we sat on the sofa and I curled up against him. Seamus was playing with my hair, which I chose to leave loose today, running his fingers through my tresses, sending pleasant little shivers across my scalp in waves. It was a relaxing sensation. I closed my eyes, content with the comfort of being in his arms.

My eyes popped open when I felt his lips against my neck. He was kissing me and leaving ripples in my flesh. The tiny nips sent microdoses of venom into my blood, heating me up and revving my libido. Since becoming immortal, I realized this new body wanted sex all the time. It was always in a state of being ready. I got turned on by the smallest things. But Seamus licking my neck wasn't small, and soon my body needed more.

"Why don't we go to my room?" I asked him.

"Lead the way."

As soon as I crossed the threshold, he kicked the door closed gently and pressed me up against it, lifting me so that our shoulders were level. I wrapped my legs around his waist so he didn't have to hold me, and his hands wandered under my dress and found my hot center.

Seamus groaned in pleasure as he discovered that I was ready for him, and wearing a garter belt instead of underwear.

"Oh, you sexy woman," he groaned into my ear. His fingers gently explored my body, making me shudder in pleasure.

His kisses were demanding and ardent as our tongues teased each other. When he rubbed my fangs, it shot exquisite sensations into me, and I felt my internal coil tighten, winding me up even more.

Seamus lifted me away from the door, walked over to the bed, and gently put me down. I unhooked my ankles and left my knees open for him. He slid my dress up my thighs slowly with his hands, kissing the inside and the back of my knee, which made me giggle a little.

"Funny? You think it's funny?" he teased me.

"No, the kisses behind my knees tickle."

"Really?" he asked, diving back to my knees and applying more kisses and raspberries behind them, sending me into fits of laughter. He only got serious when he resumed his trail of kisses on the inside of my thigh. The closer he got to my center, the hotter I got. He knelt down on the floor and looked at me between my legs. I was watching him as he bent forward and casually licked my mound.

"Ah, ah, oh my!" I gasped. He did it again, but this time his tongue probed between my folds. That made me do more than gasp. I yelped and squeaked.

"I love those noises," Seamus said. "I want to hear more."

He repeated what he did, and sure enough I was yelping and squeaking some more. The timbre of my noises deepened the more contact he made, the deeper I felt his tongue go. Before I knew it, I was moaning like the wind, and my hips were involuntarily moving as if to pump him. My groans and moans got louder still with the occasional squeak when he touched something new. I felt his tongue lick me from stem to stern, lapping up the fluids generated by my excitement.

"You are wonderfully wet, my love," he announced. He slid his pants down to the floor and stood between my legs, leaning over me. One arm supported him as the other stroked my vagina with his cock.

"Oh my God, oh my God, oh my God!" I screamed. I lifted myself to get him to enter me, but he kept teasing me, rubbing his cock all around, getting the head covered in my fluids.

When he did push in, it was not with a thrust, but with a gentle push—first just the tip, which made the both of us groan in relief, and then more until the ridge of his cock was inside. That made me sigh with pleasure, but made me hungrier than ever. Edging more and more of him inside me slowly built up a different kind of pressure. I felt like I was going to explode with anticipation.

Seamus had both of his arms supporting his upper body now as he leaned down to kiss me again. I wrapped my arms around his neck and helped pull him down to me. I felt his hips settle between my legs and his cock slide home completely. The connection was sublime, like it was always meant to be like that, he fit me so perfectly. He kept still a moment, busy kissing me. I nipped his bottom lip and was rewarded with watching his pupils dilate when the venom hit his blood.

"Oh my God, Anita, you feel so good." he murmured. "You were made for me."

"I feel the same way, Seamus. Funny how I had to wait my whole life before meeting you."

"I've been around for over two hundred years! But I was never interested in being with anyone before. Something about you is different."

Seamus slowly and gently started driving himself into me. Each push re-engaged the connection, sliding home like a key. He gradually got harder as his orgasm built, and the harder he got the faster he plunged himself into me. When he started hitting the end of my channel, I shrieked and keened and melted. The pressure was about to boil over when he did a megathrust and released his own seed, which sent me into my own orgasm. As the pressure released, my climax bubbled over, sending wave after wave of energy across my whole body.

Then Seamus gave me a delicious bite, making me climax again and again until my body was weak and everything felt like a puddle of viscous fluid. He collapsed on top of me, but rolled over to hold me on top of him so that we were fully lying on the bed.

I lay on top of him with my head nestled in the concave of his neck. I could hear his heartbeat thumping in his chest. I was listening to its happy rhythm when I realized it was in sync with my own heart. They were beating as if they were one.

His cock wiggled inside of me as if to say, 'Hey, I'm still here!' I giggled with the sensation, which didn't help, because he slid out of me. I felt a gush of semen run out of my body.

"Oops, sorry," I said.

"About what?"

"I just gushed on you."

"It was my mess, love. Roll off, and I'll go get some towels to clean us up."

What a considerate man. I rolled to the side and lay there spread-eagled. When he returned, he paused, gazing at me, and I suddenly felt like a goddess because of the look in his eyes.

"You are truly a spectacular woman, Anita. I feel fortunate and honored to love you."

"Love me?" I asked. "Do you mean make love or love me?"

"Both. I realized a few days ago that you have captured my heart. I don't need you to reciprocate if you don't feel it, just know that the seed is there. It's young and alive, and small, but I expect it will grow every time I'm with you."

"Seamus, I don't know if it's love yet, but I really care about you. I want to see where this goes too."

He sat on the bed beside me and carefully cleaned me, then himself, and then curled up behind me, spooning us. I sighed with contentment.

I hadn't felt contentment like that before.

I carefully took it in and held on to it.

18— Ready to Party

Minni

After Cailleach Dhé and Ailbhe moved in, life got interesting. I'd never had sisters before, only my little brothers. The eldest, Cailleach Dhé, was nineteen, and her sister, Ailbhe, was fifteen. They shared the in-law suite down the hall from me. Within a week of them moving in, I suggested that we find Canadian names for them because people wouldn't understand how to pronounce their Irish names. Cailleach Dhé chose Cally because it was close to the same sound. Ailbhe chose Alison, because she liked the name.

Cally came down the hall one afternoon and knocked on my door.

"Come in."

"Hi."

"Hi, what's up?"

"That means 'How are you?' Correct?" asked Cally.

"Yes, very good. How are you and what can I do for you?"

"I was wondering if I could go with you when you go out next time."

"With me... do you mean out at night?"

"Yes. I'm getting restless, and need to do something. I'll teach you some magic in exchange."

"You don't have to, but that would be cool. I'm meeting some girls who are sort of friends tomorrow night, if you want to come along. I'll help you dress appropriately."

"Thank you very much. What do you mean 'sort of friends?'"

"Well, they're school chums, but we don't hang out much. They invited me this week to go out with them. That's sort of unusual, but it's an opportunity. Actually, it'll be good to have someone with me that is there with me and not just there. Come on, let's take a look at clothes."

We went down to her closet. Mom had taken her shopping, so I was pretty sure she made sure Cally had some town clothes. Sure enough, there was a little black dress hanging there, as Well, as some nice black jeans and tops. Cally usually walked around in a long skirt and baggy blouse as if it were the 1960s, so I hadn't seen these clothes on her yet.

"Hey, look, you have some nice jeans and a pretty top. Let's try them on while I look for some shoes." I didn't find anything in her closet, so a quick glance at her feet told me they were close to my size, and I went to get some of mine. When I got back, Cally was struggling into the jeans.

"How do you wear such tight clothing?" she asked, panting with the effort.

"You get used to it. These stretch. Such an improvement over regular jeans. I'll help."

I showed her how to jump up and down to help slide the jeans over her hips. She wasn't a big girl but she had curves. I wished I had curves like her, but I was a straight board. Once the jeans were over her hips, they molded to her body beautifully.

"Gosh, you look fabulous in those!"

"Really?"

"Oh my God, yes! We're going to have trouble keeping the boys off."

She turned to look in the full-length mirror and saw herself in modern clothes for the first time: an average height woman with lustrous black hair, green eyes just like Mom, a tiny waist, curvy hips, and an ample bust. In fact, you'd think Mom and her were related somehow. I'd have to ask next time I saw her.

"Do guys like girls with curves?"

"Oh my yes. It's all about the curves right now. The curvier the better. Now you need a pretty bra. Did Mom get you a black one?"

"I don't know. I don't wear them. They're uncomfortable."

"I know, but the difference is amazing." I dug into her drawers and found a black demi-bra. It's an essential piece of equipment for women. It had lace cups, and a deep V neckline.

"Here put this on. Here's the trick." I showed her how to bend over and place the cups around her breasts before doing it up in the back. When she stood up, she choked on a gasp.

"Oh my, they stick out so far!" she cried. "How will I cover these up?"

"You don't, silly, you use them as bait," I answered with a grin.

"Bait?"

"Yup, use these bad girls to attract guys. Of course, you can't control who's attracted, but you can control who you speak to. It's a time-honored game between guys and girls. There are some difficult rules to remember though. Let's get back to the clothes first. You need a top, and I suggest that sheer black one hanging there."

Cally put on the sheer black blouse, doing up all the buttons. Considering the blouse was completely sheer, it looked pretty cool. You could see the bra underneath, so you didn't need to open the neck.

"Now that's a hot outfit!" I added some simple jewelry to the top of the blouse that would hang down at the right spot, drawing the eye.

"Here, put on these shoes," I said, handing her my red stilettos.

"How am I supposed to walk in these?" she asked.

"I'll teach you, and you can practice between now and tomorrow when we go out."

"Okay. But I think I'm going to break my neck!"

"You'll take to it like a duck to water, all girls do. It's the strut. It accentuates your ass when you walk." I showed her what I meant. It required walking a little like a model, by placing one foot right in front of the other. That made your hip drop on that side, and the other hip rise up. The result was a sexy sway back and forth as you stepped. It was the difference between walking and sashaying. Sexy women sashayed across the floor. We took turns walking down the hallway first in bare feet until she got the gist of it, then I put her in low heels. After a couple of stumbles because she was looking at her feet, I gave her some advice.

"You have to keep looking ahead and keep your back straight," I said. "Don't walk looking at your feet."

She tried again and had better success. Of course, my brothers were watching from across the stairs on the other landing, catcalling and making stupid boy noises. Alison was also watching, and trying out the technique with her sister. She mastered it faster, but I didn't tell Cally. Once Cally seemed comfortable in the low heels, I got her to put on the stilettos.

"Oh my God, I'm so tall!" she cried. "This is amazing!"

"I know, eh?" I asked. "I love wearing heels just so I can be tall and willow-like. I feel like a model when I wear them."

"What's a model?"

"I'll show you after we finish up here. So go ahead and try a few steps. Remember, keep looking ahead and don't look at your feet."

Holding on to the banister, she took a few wobbly steps. Soon, she could let go and still balance. Within a short time, she was walking.

"I can't walk normally."

"No, not really, but you need to put your foot down more toe first."

She tried that, and had better success. That step, plus the crossing, was making her hips sashay perfectly.

When her feet were tired, she took off her heels and went into my room and I showed them both runway models working in the fashion industry. We found a couple of shows on YouTube that they watched with fascination.

"Do you mean to tell me people actually wear clothes like this?" asked Alison.

"No, this is called haute couture."

"High sewing?" asked Cally. "That doesn't mean anything."

"Today, haute couture is what would have once been called bespoke. Rich people get a designer to create and sew a garment for them."

"Like royalty?"

"Yeah like royalty, except they aren't always royals. They're also celebrities or wealthy business people."

"Cel-e-brit-ies," Cally rolled the word off her tongue.

"Yeah, they are rich people who are actors, singers, professional athletes, that sort of thing."

"Actors and singers are rich?" asked Cally. "In our time, actors and singers were usually poor, and traveled from town to town looking for audiences and paid for their food with their craft."

"A lot has changed since then!" I said. "Successful actors are now some of the wealthiest people in the world."

"But how?"

"Movies. It's because of movies. We'll watch a movie tonight," I said. "But for now, I need to teach you about some of the rules about going out drinking."

"Okay. I'm listening."

"Rule #1: Never leave your drink unattended. Always keep it in front of you, in your hand, or covered. Ask for a cover if you have to."

"Okay."

"Rule #2: Never go anywhere alone. Always take someone—another girl—with you. Don't go to the bathroom, don't go outside, and don't go dancing, without another girl friend."

"Is there another?"

"Yes, Rule #3: Always keep your purse on your body. Even better, don't take a purse, but hide ID and money in places with difficult access. For example, your jeans have lots of pockets, but someone could steal from your pocket without you noticing. So we'll find a better place to hide money. I usually wear a pouch inside my pants, under my clothes."

"Why do you have rules?" asked Alison.

"Because there are a lot of mean people. There are people who will steal from you if they get a chance. There are people who would attack or harass you. And there are people who will drug you if they get an opportunity. So while we go to have fun, we also need to be careful and vigilant."

"That sounds too dangerous to bother," said Alison.

"Is that why you go out with friends?" asked Cally.

"Yup, always go out with another person," I answered. "I think we're done. It's just your makeup, but I'll do that tomorrow for you."

"Thanks, Minni, I really appreciate it," said Cally. "I cannot wait for tomorrow."

"Can I go with you?" asked Alison.

"No, my dear, you aren't old enough yet. You have to be eighteen to get into a bar."

"Rats!" My two "sisters" walked back down to their bedroom while I went back into my room to go to bed. It would be interesting tomorrow night. I'd better let my friends know I was bringing my guest sister with me.

19— Nightclub

Minni

So tonight was the night. I was taking my guest sister Cally out to a bar with the girls from school for the first time. She looked hot, which meant as soon as she walked into the place, all eyes would be on her. Rick drove us downtown, with instructions of calling him if we ran into difficulty.

We started at the Peel Pub, which had good cheap food and cheap beer. They catered to the university student crowd. They also had karaoke nights. It was a great place to meet friends and have some food before heading out to the clubs.

When we got to the door at 7:00, there was a bit of a wait for a table. I told the doorman that I was meeting friends, so he let me walk in to see if they were there. I found them in a booth toward the back by the stage, so we went through.

"Hey, girls, I'd like to introduce you to Cally. She's my guest-sister from Ireland. It's her first time out in this country, so help me keep an eye out for me!"

"Hi, everyone, pleased to meet you. Thanks for letting me come with you tonight," said Cally.

"Cally, this is Tamara, Lisa, and Kalisha, all girls from school I've known for years," I said, pointing to each girl.

There were "Hi, Callys" all around as they made room for us at the large round table. The table sat eight people, and we were only five, so there was lots of room. We put all the bags in the middle, the farthest from the edge of the table. My friends hadn't ordered anything other than a pitcher of beer so far, so we all dug into the menu and ordered food, and I ordered another pitcher of beer for Cally and I.

Within minutes, the food arrived and my stomach rumbled loudly and my mouth started watering.

"What was that noise?" asked one of the girls.

"My stomach." I dug into my spaghetti with verve, coiling it up on the spoon and slurping the last strand into my mouth. *Mmmm, that's good.* Cally ordered the same as me, so I showed her how to fork a few strands of noodles and twist the fork on a spoon to scoop them up. Giggling as the noodles dripped sauce, she slurped them up quickly and wiped her mouth.

The dish came with a baseball-sized meatball, so I showed her how to slice it into pieces without it rolling off the plate. It was a tradition with my friends and I to order pasta before going out to drink. It helped to prevent getting drunk. The other tradition was to not mix drinks. If you started with beer, you stayed with beer. Don't start on cocktails or wine. A shot or two was necessary, just for fun.

"So Cally, how do you like Canada?" asked Kalisha.

"It is pretty, but I haven't had much chance to get out yet. This is my first time."

"Oh wow. What kind of things did you do in Ireland?"

"We would go to pubs—not like this though, they were small local places. Maybe fifty people inside and we all knew each other. I served in a pub. Beer or mead was the only thing we drank, really. Well, wealthy people got wine too. The water wasna fit to drink."

“What kind of music do you like?”

“I don’t know yet. Again, it’s so different here. We were rather isolated at home. Music, other than cultural, didn’t get played often.”

I was really proud of Cally. She was answering these questions like a pro! Nothing out of the ordinary or strange. Good work!

“Hey, we should play our game!” said Lisa.

“Start, and I’ll explain it to Cally,” I said. I leaned over to Cally and said into her ear, “We like to critique some of the strange behavior and clothing choices we see here.”

“Why?” she asked me.

“Because … well, you’ll see.”

“Look at that guy over there,” said Lisa, indicating with her nod a guy that was standing on a chair with his pants halfway down his ass.

“Oh my, he’s so drunk!” I said. “He’s going to fall over any second now.”

“What’s up with the pants? Is he pulling them up or down?” asked Cally.

I laughed. “That is the question, and we don’t have any good ideas yet. It’s a guy fashion, and one they don’t understand. White boys pretending to be hood.”

“Hood?”

“Urban, poor neighborhood, black usually,” answered Tamara. “The ‘fashion’ started in the 1990s and was brought to the streets when imprisoned black men were released. But the term ‘sagging’ comes from the ‘60s American prison system. They would take away belts and shoelaces to prevent suicides but the clothes didn’t fit the inmates. So they sagged. These white boys have no idea what it means. It’s disgraceful, and I’m glad it’s on the way out.”

"My, you're a fountain of information," said Kalisha.

"I asked my dad, and he told me. He hates seeing white boys mimic something they don't understand."

"I can see that," agreed Kalisha.

"And they look stupid!" I cried.

"Oh so stupid," said Tamara, laughing. We all joined in.

The guy had stood on his chair and picked up a pitcher and was about to tip it up and chug it down. He got partially there, then his chair wobbled and he went ass over head, crashing through the table and landing on the floor in a puddle of beer.

The five of us howled with laughter. "I knew that was going to happen!" I said through my tears and hiccups.

The rest of the guys at the same table turned and were watching us. One was glowering, but he was too drunk to get the face right. Security pushed their way through the crowd, got them all up, and escorted them out of the pub.

"Oh, look at that one," I said, nodding to the girl leaning over the bar counter with her pants riding low. Her tramp stamp was exposed between her thong and her top.

"Oh no! Is that trend coming back?" asked Lisa.

"Trend?" asked Cally.

"In the early 2000s, getting a tattoo on your lower back a la Britney Spears was considered provocative," I explained. "So was wearing a thong and leaving it exposed; it was considered an open invitation. It was a misogynistic point of view, but it was what was thought."

"What's a thong?" asked Cally. "Who is Britney Spears?"

"Where have you been hiding? Mars?" asked Tamara.

"Anyway, yes, it's coming back," I said. "Now it's seen as an empowerment choice for women."

“I don’t,” said Kalisha. “To me it just looks like your underwear is showing. I prefer to not have my underwear showing.”

“You prefer to not wear underwear,” said Tamara.

“Boom!” said Lisa.

“That’s not entirely true. I wear underwires,” said Kalisha. “I need to frame these babies properly.” She pushed her breasts together to plump them up.

A table full of cute guys was watching our table when she did that, and one started to walk towards us.

“Oh, now look at what you've done,” said Lisa. “You’ve attracted the peg and ball club.”

I glanced up and saw the young man walking toward us.

“Good evening, ladies. Are you all having fun tonight?” he asked. It sounded like he had a drawl of some kind, so probably a tourist.

“Just fine thank you, sir,” said Tamara. “We prefer the company of women.”

D’Oh! You didn’t say that. It piqued their curiosity and challenged them to “convert” you.

“You don’t say?” he said smoothly. “May I join you, because I too prefer the company of women.” And before we could say no, he was sliding in beside Cally and ordering a drink for himself.

“Hi,” he said to Cally. “I saw you from across the way. You are gorgeous.”

Blushing, Cally looked at me and then turned back to him and said, “Thank you.”

“Do you want to go and party?”

“No thanks,” I said firmly.

"I was asking your friend here," he said. "What's your name, pretty lady?"

I banged her knee under the table hard, hoping she would understand not to say anything. Instead she gave him her Irish name.

"Cailleach Dhé."

"Excuse me?" he asked.

"That's my name, Cailleach Dhé," she said, grinning at him.

I couldn't help myself, I burst out laughing. He scowled at me.

"I'm sorry, I didn't get that clearly."

"Ní ormsa atá an locht go bhfuil tú dúr agus neamhíogair. Gread leat," said Cally. Her face said it all.

"I think you had better leave, please," I said.

He got up and muttered "Bitch" under his breath and left with his drink.

"Well, done, Cally!" cried Tamara. "What did you say to him?"

"I told him it wasn't my fault he was stupid and insensitive and to go away."

"Bravo!"

"Hey this is a great song, let's go dance," said Kalisha. So we all got up and went to the dance floor and made a circle and danced. Three or four songs later, I realized we had left our drinks unattended. I returned to our booth to find those guys sitting there looking smug.

The rest of the girls were behind me when I told them all to leave.

Instead, one of them said, "Come and sit with us, girls. There's lots of room here." He was patting his lap to show us where we could sit..

"Get out of our table, now!" I said again, loudly this time. "If you don't, I'll call security."

"Why don't you be nice and just talk to us?" he asked. He was looking at Cally's ass when he spoke.

"We'll give you one shot. If you disrespect us one more time, you will suffer consequences," said Cally.

The guys slid out and let the girls slide in so that it went girl, boy, girl, boy, and so on. The last two guys got chairs and sat outside of the booth.

The booth was not large enough for this many, so we were pretty tight. Full contact between us. The guys put their arms around the back of the booth to provide a little more room. Conversation started out stilted, but eventually we learned they were in Montreal as a group and here for a sports event. They were from Des Moines, Iowa. When they started ordering more pitchers of beer we all loosened up a little. We were laughing together and drinking; it was becoming fun. When they ordered a whole tray of shots, each of us got two. We started a drinking game. Every time we heard someone say OMG, we would have to drink.

That got out of hand quickly. Another tray of shots, more pitchers of beer, and we were all having way too much fun. It's when I felt the hand slide up my leg that I knew I had stopped paying attention. I put my hand on top of the guy's—I didn't remember his name, looked at him, and shook my head, no.

Then I looked around the rest of the table, and saw that three of the girls were kissing boys. Tamara, Lisa, and Kalisha, each had a guy they were necking with. Tamara's guy had his hand between her legs, and Kalisha's guy was already feeling her boobs. Lisa was almost sitting on her guy's lap.

I glanced at Cally and she looked stricken. The guy beside her was sucking on her neck, giving her a hickey. But the thing that blew my temper was his hand had traveled up between her legs and was rubbing her crotch.

I pulled his hand out and said, "Enough of that, stop." He looked at me smugly and said, "The lady didn't say no, so shut up, bitch."

The guy who had tried to handle me reached over and dropped something in my drink. It fizzed a second and then cleared.

Cally found her voice and said, "Stop, I don't want you to do that."

"Come on, sugar, let's have some fun. I gave you a party drink."

I glanced at her drink and couldn't tell if he had spiked it too. Cally found her strength and pushed the guy off her. He backed up into the table, knocking over some of the empty glasses.

Incensed, those two guys left our table, leaving the other three groping my friends.

"Can you do something to know if your drink has been altered?" I asked Cally quietly.

I watched her say something in Gaelic and snap her fingers. All of the girl's drinks on our table turned bright green. I looked around the bar and saw that many others were too.

"Our drinks have been spiked! Security!" I yelled. "Security! Help!" Three big guys wearing tees with SECURITY across their chest, rushed to our table.

"What's wrong here?"

"These guys and their friends have spiked our drinks!" I exclaimed. Glancing at my friends, I saw two were in real trouble. "Now, two of my friends are falling unconscious."

"Okay, fellas, time to leave," said Security #1 as he pulled the table away from the bench. Security #2 and #3 started pulling the guys off my friends. Cally and I got out of the way. Tamara slumped in her seat when she had no one holding her up. Lisa sat there dazed, and Kalisha was acting weird, falling over and holding her head as if it was about to explode. One of the guys fought against Security #1, but the last two guys gave up and went quietly.

"Tamara, Kalisha, have you had any of your drinks?" I asked.

They both nodded yes. Kalisha was starting to fall over. Lisa was also looking sleepy.

"Cally, can you do anything?" I whispered to her.

"Perhaps." She murmured more in Gaelic under her breath, and the glowing green glasses became normal. Our three friends perked up a bit, but were still woozy. However, in the rest of the bar, where there had been green glasses, there were now guys dropping like flies.

"Absolutely wonderful! Good thinking! Let's go. Now!" I cried. I pulled out my phone and was dialing my father by the time we cleared the table. The five of us made our way around the bodies on the floor and escaped outside into the cold fresh air. That went a long way to waking up Kalisha and Lisa too. Rick said he had stayed downtown so he would be close. He was such a good father. I needed to tell him that.

Sure enough, Rick's car rolled up just seconds after we got to the sidewalk.

"Girls, do you want a lift home too?" he asked the other three once Cally and I were seated inside.

"No, Mr. Benal. It's okay, we'll Uber home."

"Are you sure?"

"We're good. We're all going to one place. We'll be safe."

"Good night, then," said Rick, closing the car window. He turned in his seat and looked at us in the back. "Are you girls okay?" he asked me.

"Yes, thanks to Cally's magic."

"Cally's magic?"

"Yes, she made the spiked drinks glow, and then the people who spiked the drinks got the symptoms."

"Oh boy," he said. "Let's get you home." Rick turned to face forward and start driving, but a knock on the window stopped him. He rolled the window down.

"Yes, Officer?"

"Excuse me, sir," said the police officer. "May I have a moment to ask you a question?"

"Oh, sure," said Rick. "What's it about?"

"About the incident that happened in the bar tonight. Were you at the bar this evening?"

"No, I'm just picking up my daughter and her friend."

"Were they at the bar tonight?"

"This one here? Yes," said Rick. "I believe they were there with three other friends too."

"May I ask them some questions about a strange thing that happened?" asked the officer.

"They are a little drunk and tired. Is it necessary? Can you ask them tomorrow?"

"I suppose, yes," said the officer. "I'll take your contact information, then, please."

Rick gave him his business card and his home number before closing the window again. Then he started the car and pulled away from the curb. I looked back at the bar and saw a couple of police cars there, along with some ambulances. I wondered what happened but I fell asleep and didn't wake up until the car stopped in front of our house.

"Girls, wake up, we're home," came Rick's voice from the front seat.

I opened my eyes and he was looking at me earnestly.

“Is there something I need to know about what happened there tonight?”

“I don’t think so,” I said. “But why were the police and ambulances there?”

“I don’t know, so I’m going in to watch the news. You girls get to bed.”

“Rick … Dad … you’re a good father. Thank you for being there for us.”

“Any time,” he said, getting a little choked up.

20— PI Progress

PI Adams

I started digging around in New Orleans, because the Canadian police were already investigating in Canada. When I called their office and introduced myself, I told them I had been hired by the family to locate the deceased. They were not helpful. They said, "You've found him."

"Thanks. Can you tell me anything about his death?" I asked.

"No, ma'am, we cannot. Even if you were an immediate family member, we could not tell you anything about the case while we are investigating."

"What about sharing information?" I asked.

"What information would you have that may be relevant?" asked the officer.

"I have his background, who he worked with, what he did, and what his kinks were. They are sort of special."

"Can you come to the station and make a statement?"

"No, I'm in New Orleans. This is where he's from." *Oops, I shouldn't have given them that. Damn!*

"New Orleans, huh? Thanks. Please leave your contact information with our communications officer and we'll be in touch." The line clicked several times before a new voice came on.

"Comm Officer Brady, how can I help you?"

"Uh, hello. I'm investigating Derek Staung here in New Orleans, and I'd like to be in the loop with your investigation please. The detective told me to leave my contact info with you."

"Oh, okay, go ahead, then."

"I'm Marcy Adams. I'm a private investigator, license number 246985663 in New Orleans, Louisiana. My phone number is 941-555-6889. That's a cell so you can text or call."

"Very good, Ms. Adams, I'll add that to their file. Good day." And the line went dead.

"And I thought Canadians were polite people!" I said out loud to the phone. Well, it seemed I needed to travel to Canada. First, I would check with the police here to see if they could do anything to get the case information shared.

"NOLA PD, this is Officer Pentacast."

"Hello, Officer, is Captain Adams available?" It always helped to have an inside man.

"Hello, Marcy. Yes, your dad is here. Let me check to see if he's free. One moment."

I sat on the phone humming a few bars of the jingle from *Jeopardy!* Pentacast came back on the phone: "Go ahead, Marcy."

"Dad?"

"Yeah, hun, what's up?"

"I'm working a case and it leads me to a DB in Canada. Is there anything you can do to request they share information on the case with us?"

"A DB you say? Hmm, I'll have to check on that. Unless the body has some connection in crime to this city, I don't think we can compel them to share. But let me dig and let you know, okay?"

"Thanks, Dad."

"Marcy, who's the DB?"

"A man named Derek Staung. His daughter has hired me to find him, and find out what happened to him."

"Staung, Staung, that name is familiar. Just a moment."

I could hear my father typing on his keyboard, clearly looking something up.

"Oh yeah, that dude is creepy. He has a sheet. He runs a 'club' for youth down in Ward 9, and there have been suspicious activities associated with that club reported by various neighbors for years. We've never had enough on him to convict him. So perhaps we can reference one of the open cases. I see there is a missing youth connected to the club. Give me a few hours and I'll call you, okay, Marcy?"

"Thanks, Dad."

I liked traveling and I didn't get the opportunity often, but this time I decided I'd make a point of it. Montreal was like a sister city for New Orleans, right? French culture, great food, yessir, I was not missing this opportunity! I looked into flights to Montreal.

However, before I could book a flight, I needed more information, and to bring my client up to date on my findings.

21— Finding Steve Bushing

Andrews

When I left Justin, I drove to my office. I immediately went to the washroom and cleaned my hands and mouth, because, well, you know. You don't stay that way; proper etiquette dictates you clean up after sex. I wanted to make a note of the guy who visited the condo and do a facial rec search on the photo that Justin sent me.

He had given me his name as Jackson Perry. I didn't have him in my notes as an associate of Bushing, so I wanted to do a deep dive on him. First, logging into the Canadian police criminal database, I was able to get a known address for Perry, in Ahuntsic. That was the detail that the media had received too. I thought when I heard it they were referring to Bushing, but they weren't, they were referring to this guy Perry. So what did Jackson Perry have to do with anything?

More reading on the Canadian police database disclosed that Perry was a known associate of a right-wing group that had headquarters in Lacolle, Quebec. Their group was anti-immigration, in particular Americans gaining access to Canada near the Lacolle border. That would be a perfect group of people to hate Justin and Rick coming to Canada from the US to open a new restaurant. Huh!

Okay, now, what is the connection to Bushing? Could it be they hired Bushing for his explosives expertise? My phone rang, which was strange for a weekend evening.

"Andrews speaking, how can I help you?"

"It's me, Perry."

"Hello, Mr. Perry. Are you going to tell me what you know?"

"Not over the phone I ain't. Can you meet me?"

"Sure, there is a coffee shop on the ground floor of this building. It should be open. I'll meet you there in fifteen minutes. If you're late, don't bother coming, I won't be waiting."

"In fifteen."

I spent another ten minutes reading more on the file about Perry to see if there were any significant details. He seemed to be a blowhard, hatemonger, and all-around nasty fellow. He had a chip on his shoulder the size of Manhattan, and wielded it at anyone he thought was preventing him from living his "best life." It must be so sad to be that small.

I packed up my briefcase, brought a recording device, and left my office after double-checking everything was locked tight. The elevator ride down was two minutes, so I arrived with three minutes to spare. I selected a table in the back, ordered a coffee and donut, and waited.

On time, Jackson Perry entered the shop, looked around once, and made his way toward me. That was at least a good sign that he meant what he said.

"Mr. Perry," I said, by way of greeting as he slid into the booth opposite me.

"I have some information for you."

"Why wouldn't you give it to the police?"

"I don't trust po-po."

"Okay, why would you trust me?"

"Cause you're ex-military, like me."

I hadn't read that in his file, so either he was lying, fantasizing, or the Canadian police didn't know that. The third option was unlikely.

"Where did you serve?"

"US. I was part of Desert Storm. I flew helicopters."

"You're an American citizen?"

"No, I'm Canadian, but I wanted to fight in Desert Storm."

Of course you did. "So what did you want to tell me, Mr. Perry?"

"I know where Bushing is."

"And who is Bushing?"

"Steve Bushing, he's the one who designed the bomb that went off on New Year's Eve."

"Who was he working with?"

"Ah, I can't tell you that."

"Why was the bomb made?"

"I can't tell you that."

"Who was the bomb made for?"

"I can't tell you that either. I can tell you where he is."

"But knowing where he is, is irrelevant if I don't have the other information."

"He's the one responsible for the bomb," said Perry, getting exasperated.

"How do you know that? Why? For who? For what reason?" I fired at him. "You see, it's not a complete picture, and therefore it's not of interest."

I got up to leave, throwing a twenty on the table. I was halfway to the door when he called after me.

"Alright, I'll answer some of those questions too."

I walked back to the booth. "Which ones?"

"He wasn't hired by us, he was working independently. But he needed a place to work in secret, so we helped him out."

"Who's 'we?'"

"My club." Meaning the right-wing gang out of Lacolle.

"So you gave him a place to work. Does your club often make room on their premises for strangers?"

"No, that's the thing. We've never done that before. He had some ranking over our leader."

"Do you know what that was?"

"No, but it came from the States."

"Do you have a specific state?"

"New Orleans."

"How do you know?"

"I picked up my leader's phone to give it to him and it rang in my hands," said Jackson. "Looking at who the incoming call was from, it was a New Orleans area code. I looked it up later."

"Did you recognize the number?"

"Yeah, um, it belonged to the boss."

"You do realize this doesn't make any sense, and it makes you look like a suspect instead, don't you?"

"How's that? It wasn't me that made a bomb for them!"

"Them?"

"The gang."

"Steve made a bomb for the gang?"

"Yeah, as payment for use of the space without asking questions."

"Okay. So do you know why they wanted the bomb?"

"No, I think the instructions came from the New Orleans number."

"Was it designed for the restaurant?"

"I believe so."

"Why would someone in New Orleans order a restaurant in Montreal bombed?"

"I don't know!" He was now whining.

I doubted I would get much more from him that was coherent. Still, I had one more detail—the order for the bomb came from NOLA, and was executed by Bushing of NOLA, here in Montreal, using the gang out of Lacolle. Clearly, the gang was being used as a patsy so the crime would hang on their heads. The evidence of that was that Bushing had already left the city.

So Bushing, NOLA, and an unknown were involved in this bombing. *Now I have to find out why.*

"Mr. Perry, thank you for your information. I'll put it to good use," I said, turning my attention back to the squirming little rat in front of me. "Good day." I got up and left. I heard him speak up to try to stop me once, but I ignored him and kept going. Back on the sidewalk in the fresh air, I detected a nasty smell in my nostrils and realized how much the man had stunk. Inhaling deeply, my lungs were grateful for the fresh sweet-smelling air.

So now I needed to look more into the connection between Bushing and the Lacolle gang. They had a boss in common that was in New Orleans. Going back to my office, I pored over the reports from the agencies about the leaders of the Lacolle gang. There were no obvious connections. All were born in Canada within a stone's throw of Lacolle. None had made recent trips to the New Orleans area. The only connection was the phone call Jackson referred to.

I obtained the phone records for the gang's leaders and went over the numbers that were coming from out of the country. Only one number was listed in New Orleans so I dialed it.

"Brotherhood of the Blade and Snake," answered someone.

"Hello. I'm sorry, I think I may have dialed the wrong number. Did I call 504-555-9245?"

"Yes, that is this number. Who did you want to speak to?"

I decided to do something risky. "I was looking for Derek."

"Derek is no longer here. Is there anyone else you want to speak to?"

"Ah, no. Thanks anyways. Have a good day." Hanging up, I felt a little thrill juice me. I had a definite connection between the Lacolle gang and Staung's organization. They had changed the name of it slightly, but it was still them, and the person who answered wasn't unfamiliar with Derek's name. I could now go to the police with this information.

"Detective Meunier's office, may I help you?" said the voice on the other end of the phone.

"Hello, this is Robert Andrews, I work for Mark Chisholm. He asked me to look into the bombing of L'Escalade for his friends, the owners Justin Madera and Rick Benal."

"Wow, that was a mouthful. How can I help you, Mr. Andrews?"

"Is the detective there? I have some information for him."

"Just a moment please."

I sat there and sang the *Jeopardy!* song in my head for a few minutes until I heard a click on the line.

"This is Detective Meunier."

"Detective, Robert Andrews. I am a private security officer for—"

"Yes, Mark Chisholm. I got the rundown from my officer. What can I do for you?"

"I had a conversation with a person by the name of Jackson Perry today. He claims to know where the bomb came from, who built it, and a possible reason. I have also discovered a connection to an international terrorist organization in New Orleans."

"Oh?" asked Meunier. "Can you come to the station and put that in writing? And do you have proof to back this up?"

"Of course, and yes. I recorded the conversation I had with Perry, and also the telephone calls I've made. That, along with the documents I've collected, should provide some good evidence for you."

"Thank you. Ask for me when you get here, and we can debrief."

"On my way."

Three hours later, they had sweated every detail I had accumulated out of me. At one point, I suspected they suspected me, but it was clear that they had no reason so. Still, to be under their scrutiny made my skin crawl.

Detective Meunier was a thorough man. He left no stone unturned. We agreed that the connection to Derek Staung was a little thin, but the fact that Staung was left dead here, and that one of his organizations was in the Montreal area building bombs, seemed to be a connection. Meunier was in a position to reach out to NOLA authorities and gain further evidence. At least now we had a possible motive for the bombing, and the leaders of the Lacolle gang were being brought in for questioning.

I just had a niggling thought that the body they found and identified as Staung wasn't Staung at all but a plant. I couldn't prove it here though.

My next stop was to update Rick and Justin.

22— Another Lead

Andrews

Grisham came back with a sheet on Steve Bushing. It was an interesting sheet too. As recently as last year he was picked up on suspicion of being involved in a political right-wing group who had planned various terrorist attacks. That was dismissed and he was let go. But his rap sheet told me that he had the skills and experience to build a bomb like the one at L'Escalade.

Bushing was ex-military. He was a munitions expert who specialized in shaped charges and quiet entries. He was deployed in the Middle East in several missions to "remove" terrorists and bring them into custody. After his second deployment, he was discharged with a wound that left him non-deployable. It was not specified on the sheet, so I suspected it was a missing limb or something. He was living in Hamilton, Ontario—known as a rough town, a former steel town. There were some pretty seedy areas there.

His current whereabouts were unknown, although it was believed he might have gone down to the US. The rest of his sheet showed lots of B&Es, time in and out of jail for that, and one assault. His parents were not in the picture since the late 1990s, "unknown" was listed as to what happened to them. He was born in Hamilton, and was currently thirty-five. No next of kin listed, no girlfriend or boyfriend, and no associations.

"Hmmm, you're an enigma, aren't you?" I asked for the file in front of me. "Well, we'll just have to peek under the covers and dig a little deeper." Grisham had managed to get his photos from the service and included them in the file. So the first thing I did was put that on the police wire. I also decided to put it out to the American authorities in three cities: Houston, Atlanta, and New Orleans. I had a feeling there was a connection somewhere.

That is going to take some hours to produce any fruit, if anything, so what shall I look at next?

My call to the fire chief gave me little in the way of new information, but they had successfully collected the pieces of the detonation device on the bomb. It was a simple device, designed for maximum damage spread over the largest range possible. The bomb had been set up to blow in a fan shape outward from the location. That was something I could link to Bushing. The fire department also detected that the bomb used a high explosive packed into a container with a hollow pipe through the middle to create a cavity. It was all contained in a thin metal box with a detonator on the outside. This was a signature, I was sure of it.

The fire chief also believed this sort of bomb had been used before. He promised to get me the data on that and send it over.

The police had spoken to everyone that had been at the restaurant that night, both sittings, and had come up empty except for the two cooks. Those leads we were already following up on.

I was reading through the material the fire chief sent over when my condo line called me.

"Andrews speaking."

"Andrews, it's Justin."

"How are you doing?"

"I'm much better than I have a right to be, that's for sure. Tell me, do you have any leads?"

"Yes, we do. We're following them down. If we're lucky, we may get something really concrete in a week or so."

"Oh, that is good news. Listen, it's been haunting me. Is there any chance our place in Atlanta is at risk?"

"That's a good question. I thought of that myself, and I'm looking for connections that turn that way too. I haven't found anything yet though. I was going to send one of my guys down to thoroughly go through that restaurant."

"I will pay you extra for that knowledge and protection," said Justin.

"No need. I'm compensated Well, by Mark."

"But I want to. Think of it as a nest egg for the future."

"If you insist."

"I do," he said. "By the way, thank you for the experience you shared with me. I didn't thank you before, and that was just rude."

"No need. Did it help?"

"Yes, very much so. It helped me consider my options. What was it like becoming immortal?"

"Well, the bite was a little painful at first, then the euphoric properties of the venom hit my blood and I was flying. I passed out for a day or two while my body was being changed. When I woke up, I felt stronger, faster. I could hear better, I could see better. Sex was certainly better—and that wasn't something I expected."

"I now know what you mean about the sex."

"The procedure is much simpler now. We can use an injection. But, if you ask me, the bite was more fun. Even mock-fighting Mark was interesting. I tested my own strength against him. By the way, no competition. That guy is beyond strong."

"So Mark was the one to bite you?"

"Yes, because we didn't know at that time we could just inject the venom. Aggression also produces venom and it's used between men."

"Hmmm, aggression or love."

"This species is very sexual. The immortals I have met are all very fluid in their sexuality. They often orgy, and it's not only couples, but three and every combination you would like."

"I would do Mark too, he's a cutie."

"Immortals also generate magical power through sexual energy. It's how we brought those witches through a portal from another dimension."

"Freaky. I sense a story there."

"Perhaps, but useful. Their magical power is used for healing and creation."

"Well, I'm a testament to the healing part, that's for sure!"

"I gotta run, but I will keep you informed about my progress," I said.

"Thanks, and Godspeed!"

23— Fallout

Lora

I was sitting waiting for Rick to get home from picking up the girls from their night out. I turned on the television to keep me company. An overnight news broadcast had an item that was about the bar the girls had gone to tonight, so I turned up the volume to listen.

> *"...several people became sick and fell unconscious to the floor suddenly and there doesn't appear to be a reason. Eyewitnesses said the only thing they noticed was their drink glowed green for a second right before the person they were talking to fell over. We'll have more on this developing story later. This is Trish Noray for IBC news."*

"Glowing green?" I said out loud. "Why does that sound suspiciously like magic?" I heard the garage door open and then close, and a few minutes later Rick came in with the girls. He was about to send them up to bed, but I intercepted them.

"Minni, wait, come here girls please," I said. "Cally, did you use magic at the bar?"

"Yes, Minni asked me to see if our drinks were changed," said Cally.

"I asked her because I saw a boy drop something into Cally's glass," said Minni.

"When it showed that there was something in it, Minni said the drinks had been spiked with a drug, and we needed to leave."

"And what happened then?" I asked.

"Well, I noticed my friends were so wasted they were going to pass out," said Minni. "And then I noticed it wasn't just our drinks, but there were lots of others that way in the bar. I called security."

"And then what happened?"

"Security helped remove the boys and get us out of the bar," said Cally.

"But I asked Cally if she could reverse the effects of the drug on my friends."

"And then?"

"Then the boys fell down unconscious."

"Hmmm. So the boys who had dosed the drinks became the ones dosed?" I asked.

"It would appear so," said Minni.

"I didn't mean to do any harm!" cried Cally. "I just wanted the girls to be okay!"

"I understand. Your intention was good, but we just can't use magic in public, Cally. Next time, girls, if you suspect a drink has been dosed, dump the drink on the floor, okay?"

"Okay, Mrs. Benal."

"Call me Lora."

"Off to bed, girls," said Rick.

"So what happened?" I asked him.

"Well, as to what happened inside, I don't know. However, the girls were really drunk when I arrived. I didn't want the police to see that. Two police cars arrived at the bar just after me, and then two ambulances. They seemed to have taken two males into the ambos, and the police were asking patrons what happened. They tried to ask me questions too, then the girls and I used their drunkenness as a reason not to."

"Okay. The TV said they spoke to a witness who remembers the drinks glowing green right before people started falling over."

"Hmm, that matches what the girls told me. If I understand correctly, Cally transferred the drug's effects back on the person who spiked the drink."

"Clever spell. So what reason are we going to come up with for the glowing green?"

"That's a good one. No idea, but we better think of something, because I expect the police to call tomorrow to ask the girls some questions."

"Damn," I said.

———

The following morning came and the news didn't add anything to the story other than that four men had fallen ill and been taken to the hospital. The symptoms were described as lowered inhibitions, loss of balance, feeling sleepy, visual problems, confusion, nausea, and vomiting. Two of the men were unconscious. The reporter suggested that the men had been roofied, which would be the first case of women using the drugs on men. I laughed when I heard that.

"Well, girls aren't going to roofie a guy, because then he'd be as useless as a wet noodle," I said to the television. "That's a stupid conclusion. But if you had been roofied, you would know that, so you're one of the lucky girls who has never been subjected to that."

I had agreed to let my eighteen-year-old daughter take Cally out with her friends last night. I thought it would be a good experience for both of them. I did NOT anticipate that Cally would need to use magic in public and create a panic in a bar.

Oh my!

Now I had to deal with the fallout. I was not looking forward to this. It wasn't like the girls did anything wrong, but they could not display paranormal skills in public. We couldn't afford the exposure.

Still, I can't fault her for thinking on her feet. She just needs to think differently next time.

Cally came downstairs first.

"Good morning, Lora," she said, looking chagrined.

"Good morning, Cally. How are you feeling today?"

"I've got a serious headache and I feel really sick to my stomach," she said.

"This is called being hungover," I said. "That happens when you have too much alcohol the night before. Your body is severely dehydrated, and it's affecting your brain. The first thing you should do after a night out like that is to drink two large glasses of water before you go to bed. Come with me, I'll fix you up."

We walked into the kitchen and I gave her a large glass of water to drink, then gave her some Motrin to swallow with another glass of water.

"Now go and lie down for twenty minutes until the medicine works."

"Thank you, Lora."

Minni came down a few minutes late. She was not as badly hungover, as she had remembered to drink water before bed. She still looked really rough though.

"Ah, Minni, so you had a lot to drink last night, eh?"

"Yes, Mom. More than I realized or intended. It was the guys who joined us. They kept ordering pitchers and shots and we all kept drinking. I watched one guy spike my drink, and suspected the others had done the same. I asked Cally if she could do something."

"Can you tell me again what happened?"

"I can tell you what I remember," said Minni. "These guys, they were tourists, wanted to sit with us. Tamara at first told them to leave, but that seemed to have incentivized them. When we got up to go dance, they sat at our table waiting for us. One of them charmed Tamara, and she let him stay. Then Lisa invited them all to join us, I think. Anyway, they all ended up at our table. Some of the girls were flirting way too much for normal. So maybe they had already spiked our drinks. I remember one of the guys had his hand up Tamara's dress. Or was that Kalisha? I'm not sure. I do remember Cally being upset because one of them was trying to give her a hickey. And the guy's hand was between her legs and he was rubbing her. I pulled his hand out and yelled at him to stop.

"Cally found her voice then and told him to stop, but he said no and told her that he had given her a party drink so they could have some fun. That's when I realized that the drinks had been spiked. I asked Cally to do anything. She did and all of our drinks glowed green.

"Then I yelled for security. Three big dudes came and removed the boys. It was then I looked around the bar and saw other drinks in front of girls were green too. Cally had a solution for that too, and then we left quickly."

I glanced over at Cally, who was lying on the sofa. I said to Minni: "Let's get you some Motrin and water and then talk to Cally."

"Cally, are you asleep?" I asked.

"No, but the headache is disappearing, thank you."

"Cally, are you fully immortal?"

"What do you mean?"

"Have you had sex with a man? Do you have fangs yet?"

"Ah, no and no."

"Okay, that may explain why the drug didn't affect you as much, but that you still got drunk. My God, you must have had a lot!"

"My last count was that we were on our tenth pitcher of beer for the group, and I personally had ten shots and five glasses of beer. The boys kept ordering more and more."

"Wow. Okay, this is what is going to happen today. The police will be calling to ask you girls questions. Since you discovered the drugs in the drinks, they're going to want to know how. You cannot tell them magic. Understand? Minni, you simply tell them you saw one of the boys spike a drink."

"What about we're developing a tool that you can put in your drink that will indicate when someone spiked your drink by turning green—and we gave out samples?"

"I like it, except we don't have any samples to give the police if they ask for them."

The doorbell rang. "Hold that thought," I said, as I went to answer it. Opening the door, there were two officers there, a man and a woman.

"Come in, Officers. Can I get you a coffee?" I asked.

"Please," said one.

"No thanks," said the other.

"Is there somewhere we can sit?" asked the woman.

"Of course, the girls are in the living room. Why don't you join them?" I asked. "How do you want your coffee?"

"Black is fine."

I followed the officers into the living room with the coffee and sat down beside my girls.

The man asked, “Can I get you girls’ names please?” They answered him. “Cally, are you a member of the family?”

“Sort of. My sister and I have been sort of adopted by Lora and Rick. They are fostering us.”

“Your sister, is that Minni?” she asked.

“No, my sister is Alison. She’s just fifteen.”

“Alright. Cally, in your own words, can you tell us what happened last night?” asked the lady cop.

Cally told her basically the same story Minni had told me, just from her perspective, up to the point of the drinks glowing green.

“Did you see the drinks glow green last night?”

“I did,” said Minni. “I was trying to get that creep off Cally when I noticed the sticks had turned green. We have been working on a prototype stir stick that would turn green in the presence of date rape drugs. We gave samples out at the bar.”

“Did you tell anyone what you were giving them?” asked the cop.

“No, I just put it in their drinks. I thought it would be better if it were a blind test,” said Minni.

“Do you have any more of those stir sticks?”

“Ah no, we only had about a dozen. They’re kind of one-use-only things. We’re working on that part.”

“You’re a clever girl,” said the cop. “I hope you finish that project. It will help a lot of girls your age.”

“Thank you.”

“Okay, Mrs. Benal, I think we’ve got everything we need. If I have any more questions, can I find the girls here?”

“Yes, they both live here,” I answered.

“Have a good day, folks,” said the male cop, as they turned and left the house.

———

"You know, we should actually try to make those," said Minni, once the cops' car had left the driveway.

"What?" asked Cally.

"The stir sticks. Imagine if we could actually come up with a solution that could be sold in bars and drugstores."

"It would be a worthwhile endeavor, that's for sure," I told them. "Why don't you look into that. You could pick chemistry as one of your courses in university and patent the idea."

"Hmm, Cally, are you game?"

"To go to university? Now, in this time? How would I qualify?"

"We could prepare you for the GED exam. That's an exam that allows a foreign student to show they have the equivalent knowledge of our school system to gain them entrance to our universities."

"I would love that. What is chemistry?"

"You would have called it alchemy in your time," I said. "Do you think you could do it with magic though?"

"Maybe, I would need to experiment. Is there a room where I could do that?"

"Yes, I'll take you back to the ship. There are lots of rooms you can use there. What materials would you need?"

"Let me think about that and get back to you."

"Good," I said. "Girls, I have to go out right now. Minni, why don't you and Cally look into the GED exam?"

"Okay, Mom."

24— Young Ladies

Lora

Forever, it'd been Minni and I with the two boys. Now we had two more girls living with us, one older than Minni and one younger. Even though they were not wise to our world, they still had a maturity Minni didn't have yet. Having them here was good for her.

The three girls hit it off immediately. It was like they were suddenly one entity. Minni would be their best introduction to all things twenty-first century better than I could be. Especially better than the boys.

The first night, all three slept in Minni's room. The boys complained that the girls were getting a sleepover party, but I explained to them that they were doing "girl things." So they accepted that and went and did their own thing. I'd have to see if there was a young or teen boy we could foster as well.

Minni came to me one day asking me questions about female anatomy and menses, and all that stuff.

"You know all that," I told her. "I've taught you that several years ago. Why are you asking now?"

"Because they have weird ideas and I wanted to make sure I was right."

"You mean Cally and Alison? Hmmm, sounds like a mom talk is needed."

"Yeah, I think it would be better if it came from you. Cally has started her flow and she didn't want to use the tampons I gave her."

"Ah, I get it." I went upstairs with Minni to find Cally sort of hiding in the bathroom.

"Hey there. Are you okay? Is there a problem?" I asked, knocking on the door gently.

"Nothing, I have just started my bleeding, and I have nowhere to isolate myself."

"You don't have to do that anymore. Today, women go on with their normal life while we are bleeding. It's called menstruation. It happens to every healthy human female," I explained. My daughter looked at me funny, and I shook my head.

"But the blood will cause sickness and will get all over my clothes."

"That may be what people believed hundreds of years ago, but it's not true. It doesn't spread sickness. And we have products to prevent messes from happening."

"Really?" asked Cally. "How does that work?"

"We use pads and then dispose of them when they are done."

"You throw away your blood in the trash? But that can be used against you in ritual!" cried Cally.

"You're going to have to trust me on this one, there are no witches that will use your blood against you in magical rituals in this century."

"No?"

"No," I said with certainty. "Now, let me help you. Let me in please."

I heard her scramble to the door, and the lock clicked open. The door opened a crack and she looked out.

"It's okay, Cally, let me in." The door opened wide enough for me to slip in.

"First, let's take off your skirt and underwear. Don't worry about the blood, we will wash that out and they'll be as good as new. Just leave them in the tub for now."

Cally stood up and removed her lower clothing and looked ashamedly at her body as the blood ran down her legs.

"Look at me, Cally," I said. "Look me right in the eye. This is normal, and it is nothing to be ashamed of. You'll see, once you are using the right product, this won't happen again." I helped her wash up with a hot cloth and got her all clean. Minni went and got her some new underwear and some pads.

"I used to know what to do and I would just do it without anyone knowing."

"No one will notice in this century either. It's just a new process for you. Let's start with sanitary napkins."

"What's that?"

"It's a pad that absorbs the blood. It has a sticky side that you use to hold it in place in your underwear. Here, I'll show you. Once you're comfortable with those, I'll show you another device that we use called a tampon," I said, showing her one. "They work like a cork in a wine bottle. You insert the tube and push the cork into place."

"Where?" she asked quizzically. "Where do I insert this?" she looked at the device with a little horror.

"Into your vagina," I said. "Do you know what your vagina is?"

She looked at me like I'd grown horns. "I put this inside my baby channel?"

"Yes. Hmm, okay. It appears we need to start at the beginning."

"Mom, let's give her that whole lesson thing later. She needs to be able to leave the bathroom."

"You're right. Cally, use the pad now for simplicity," I said. "We'll leave the rest later. For now, here's a fresh pair of underwear. You'll want to check the pad every hour to see if it needs changing."

"Get dressed and come out when you are finished," said Minni, as we left the bathroom. "Mom, I think they both need those lessons."

"Yes, I believe so. Let's aim for a couple of days from now, to give her time to adapt to the pad."

When Cally came out of the bathroom, Minni explained how to dispose of the pad when it was finished. We'll empty it every day. After her first week, she was quite comfortable with the process and knew what to do. I told her to let me know before she ran out of pads so we could have more in the house. With three girls in the house menstruating, we'd need lots of supplies.

A couple of weeks later, I got all the girls in the living room and sat them down.

"Girls, I need to teach you more about your bodies, and what we do in the twenty-first century."

"What do we need to know?" asked Alison.

"Oh, about pads and things," said Cally.

"That's right. Alison, you have started your cycle too, right?"

"Yes, a year ago."

"You will each have your preferred products to use. Don't run out. Make sure you have enough sanitary products before your period. Now, there are two kinds. One is what we showed Cally. They're called pads. There are different kinds of pads, different thicknesses for different flows."

"Different flows?"

"Some women have very heavy flows, they lose a lot of blood, others barely anything. Some women go for a whole week, others for a day. We're all very different. Your flow will change from day to day too, perhaps heavy at first, and then taper off on the last day."

"Oh," said Alison.

"Minni can show you the different products online, and you can purchase them online as you need them."

The two witches remained silent at that point, and I waited while understanding and ideas flitted across their faces. Cally was the first to grasp the idea that she didn't have to go out to shop for sanitary products.

"The other form is called a tampon. It works the same as a cork does in a bottle of wine. It's made from an absorbent material that stops the flow before leaving your body."

"Where does that go?" asked Alison.

"Inside your baby channel," said Cally.

"How?"

I tried to explain how to do this. I used a wine bottle with a tiny bit of wine left to demonstrate. It was something I had to learn on my own as my mother never taught me. So many feminine things we have to learn on our own in a vacuum without knowledge or the benefit of a friend.

My first time was terrifying. Suddenly I was bleeding out of a hole in my body I was barely aware of. I was at school of course, and it was gym class. We had swimming. Yup, I had swimming class on the day of my first period. Oh God, that was horrible. I tried to explain to my teacher, a woman, who I thought would be sympathetic. Nope, not sympathetic at all. In a loud voice she told me to get my ass to the change room, put in a goddamned tampon, and get my ass back to class. I felt so humiliated. I vowed right then if I ever had a daughter, I would teach her how to use them before she needed them, so she would not go through what I did.

Minni has known how to use all kinds of sanitary products since she was ten. Now I had two girls who had already started, but due to the time they came from had no clue about modern knowledge, or convenience. Their sex-ed was nonexistent, and they had no clue how their bodies worked. I had to fix this. Sooner rather than later.

Once she had practiced on the bottle a few times, we switched to putting the tampon inside herself. Cally was in the washroom and we were standing outside giving her encouragement. After she successfully inserted a tampon this way, she tried again without coaching.

"This certainly feels strange," Cally said, when she was finished and came out of the bathroom.

"You definitely need some training about your body. Remember, you don't leave them in longer than a day. It's important to remove used ones as soon as you are done."

"How often do I change?"

"Again, that depends on how much you bleed. So you'll have to learn that about yourself, by watching your underwear for spotting. I will give you some panty liners to use. They temporarily stick inside your underwear to protect it from blood stains. When you see blood spots on the liner, change the tampon."

Now it was Alison's turn. I congratulated the girls for their work and bravery. It was a big deal for them—well, for any girl to go through this. Suddenly your body bleeds for no apparent reason, and even if you were "taught" about it in school or by your mom, it still takes you by surprise.

"The second part of this talk we'll do now."

"Girls, Minni has had this talk, but there's nothing wrong in hearing it again, and you two have not."

"Ah, Mom..."

"What talk?"

"The talk about sex."

Cally and Alison both went white, then bright red.

"Girls, you're in the twenty-first century. Sex is part of life, and it will be part of your life too if you want it to be. So you need to understand your bodies and what they do for you. All the boys are out of the house. I got Rick to take them to the movies. And Anita is on her day off. So it's just us. There is no embarrassment, and no shame."

"We know how babies are made," Cally said. "That was common knowledge from watching the farm animals."

"Well, sex for humans is not just about making babies. It's also an expression of love, tenderness, play, and it can be ownership too, if I'm honest with myself.

"When humans have sex it's more complex than with animals. At least from what I know, animals don't necessarily derive pleasure from mating. We do. There are all kinds of places on our bodies that are designed to give us pleasure. Humans are very tactile. We love to touch. We learn through touch, and we experience pleasure through touch. For example, when your feet hurt you rub them. It feels good. Someone else can rub your feet and it also feels good. Sometimes it feels better than good.

"These places on our bodies that give us pleasure are called erogenous zones. When stimulated during sex, they release chemicals in our brains that give us extreme pleasure. Most of these places you can reach with your fingers, or someone else can reach with their fingers."

"Where are these places?"

"Your breasts are one area, especially the nipples. The place between your legs is another. Inside the folds of skin is a little bump—that is a very big one. Just inside the opening of your vagina is another. There are a few hidden ones that you need to find for yourselves."

"How?"

"Tonight, you're going to lie in bed naked, and I want you to touch your own bodies. Use different kinds of touching, find out what your body responds to, what it likes. Try for those three places first. Then we can discuss it if you want."

"This will be strange."

"Yes, but you will enjoy exploring your own bodies."

I left the girls watching a rom-com in the theater and I went to watch TV. A movie about fourteen coming-of-age stories was not my thing. I liked something much more naughty. All this sex talk had me randy for my man. I hoped the boys got home soon. *Because I swear I'm going to rip Rick's clothes off and ride him like a steer.*

25— Chemistry is Fun

Minni

Cally and I were sitting in the family room reading when she asked me if I meant what I said, and would look into creating a device that would detect drugs in drinks. I thought about it for a minute.

"Sure, why not. Let's go do some research."

The two of us went to my room and opened up a browser. I entered in *what chemical is used to detect drugs,* and pulled up a list of things explaining how drug tests are done, and how to use spot tests for urine and blood. That was obviously not what we were looking for. So I tried another search: *products that detect drugs in drinks.* That got us a list of things that had been invented already.

I ran down the list: Coasters, cups, nail polish, a wristband, and a smart device.

"What would you do with a coaster?" asked Cally.

"I dunno, spill your drink on it?"

"Wouldn't that look obvious?"

"I would think so. So too with nail polish. What would you do with that? Stick your finger in your drink? Yeah, our idea is better. Stir sticks are commonly used in drinks anyway."

"How are we going to figure out how though?"

"Maybe my chemistry teacher can help us," I said. "Why don't we ask him after class today."

"I'll meet you there at 3:00."

———

I was standing at the front door of our school when Cally walked up waving at me. Picking up my backpack, I fell in step with her as we went through the doors.

"Mr. Warlex is waiting for us," I said. "I did give him a primer first to see if he would help. He got excited about the idea, and told us to come to the lab and he'd help us figure out what would work."

———

"Mr. Warlex, this is my stepsister, Cally," I said. "We're the ones who came up with the idea when we were out at a club a while back."

"Hello, Cally, nice to meet you. Come on, girls, let's see what we can do," he said. "We'll need to figure out which drugs to test for first."

"The three biggest problems are ecstasy, Special-K, and roofies," I said.

"The actual names of those drugs are GHB—gamma hydroxybutyric acid—ketamine, and Rohypnol. There are already established tests for those drugs, so maybe all you need to do is adapt those reagents to the delivery method of your choice."

"Oh, maybe that's easier than starting from the beginning."

"It will be," he said. "Now what were you thinking of as a delivery method?"

"A stir stick," we said together, and laughed. "'Cause they are usually around drinks, and people carry their own now to reduce plastic waste."

"The reagent we need is called the Mandelin reagent. I believe I have some books here that will help us recreate the compound." Mr. Warlex went to the bookshelves behind his desk and searched until he found the book he was looking for.

"Here it is. This should be fairly simple, we have all the necessary chemicals in the lab. Okay, girls, we'll need the following materials." He went on to give us a large list of tools, beakers, and chemicals that we ran around the lab and collected. He set up a station and got Bunsen burners working, and set up the desk to "cook" the compound we needed.

We watched him very carefully as he worked through all the steps listed in the book. It was more like a cooking recipe than anything else. I made sure I took a photo of the recipe while he wasn't looking. When he was finished, he had a crystalized powder that sort of looked like sugar.

"Now what do we do with it?" I asked.

"We need to apply that to sticks somehow," said Cally. "What material will the stick be? Metal, wood, or plastic?"

"Metal may be reactive," said Mr. Warlex. "What about glass? After all, we created the compound in glass beakers."

"Wood would work too. There are already stir sticks made of wood," I said. "Glass is too breakable to put in your purse to carry around."

"What if we package it in an unbreakable tube?" asked Cally.

"Oh, that's a good idea. Kind of like a case for a thermometer or a pen."

"Exactly," said Cally.

"How do we get the test on the stick?" I asked. "Wait, is this compound toxic? I mean, would it make someone sick if it gets into the drink?"

"No, not likely. We won't need very much for a test," said Mr. Warlex.

"What about dipping one end of the stick in the compound?"

"That would only work once though, and we'd like it to be reusable."

"I don't think you can do that," said Mr. Warlex. "Reagents don't tend to stick around, they are part of the test, and once the test is complete, the reagent is gone. You're looking at a disposable, I'm afraid."

"Hmmm, then we don't want plastic or glass. Wood is the best? Would that work?" I asked.

"Let's try. We'd need to get our hands on some drug to test," said Mr. Warlex. "In the meantime, let's see if we can bond this to different surfaces without destroying it."

They worked for another hour or two, trying to come up with a usable delivery, and the only thing that seemed feasible were plastic sticks.

"Ladies, let's call it quits for now. I'll try to get my hands on some of the drugs so we can do tests. Let's reconvene this tomorrow after classes?"

"Okay, Mr. Warlex. See you tomorrow."

We got home around dinner and excitedly told Mom and Rick about the idea and the progress we made.

"Oh, honey, you should have spoken to Gwen about this first. You need to patent ideas like this or else someone will steal them," said Rick.

"Rick, I doubt our chemistry teacher would do that. He's our teacher."

"Well, I'm going to call Gwen anyway."

———

Gwen arrived after dinner and had coffee with my parents. Rick called Cally and I downstairs to explain to Gwen what we had done so far.

I sent her the recipe from the textbook, and told her about the compound. Cally explained to her our thinking about the kind of delivery we needed, and that we still had to test delivery methods still. We told her that our teacher was going to get drugs to test against.

Gwen quickly took notes and asked us what we wanted to call the product.

"Smart Stix, we want to call them Smart Stix." [See Endnote]

———

We returned upstairs after Gwen thoroughly questioned us about our idea.

"What do you think that was about?" asked Cally.

"Probably so Gwen can put a patent together for us," I answered. "We'll need one before we try selling it, or someone will steal our idea."

A week later, Mr. Warlex let me know he had secured small samples of all the drugs so we could start testing our idea.

This was exciting. We bought a package of both plastic and wood stir sticks to use.

"You know, the wood ones are really obvious, I'm going to split them in half," I said. I split three sticks so we had enough to run three samples.

Then we liquified the test compound and dipped the sticks in the test liquid and hung them up to dry with clips. Mr. Warlex made up three different drinks and put a tiny amount of drug in each. We had three different tests.

First, we tried the wood sticks. Cally dipped one into the first cocktail. It took a second but the beverage turned blue. A positive result. Then I dipped the same stick in the next drink, and it didn't do anything.

"So that's a single test. A customer would need a package of them for a night if they wanted to test every drink."

"What if we dried the sticks before using them?" asked Cally. So we brushed the compound on the outside and kiln dried them thoroughly before putting them in the drink. Same result.

"We need to find a way to prevent the compound from coming off the stick."

We struggled with this for a few days until we had a breakthrough. Suffice it to say, the beverage did not turn blue, the stick did, in the presence of one of those three drugs.

With that success, we quickly prepared the rest of our sticks and another package and took them to the popular university hangout the following Saturday night. Mr. Warlex came with us to help convince the pub owner to give our product a try. Once convinced, he agreed to put a stir stick in every drink ordered by a girl, even the beers. We sat back and watched. Cally and I kept track of who got a stick and what they ordered. Mr. Warlex kept track of how many turned blue.

At the end of the night, we had several positives for drugs. Each time we saw the stir stick turn, we quietly removed the drink and told the girl.

We didn't get out of the pub until two in the morning, but we were all jazzed by our success.

"Mr. Warlex, we couldn't have done this without you! Thank you!" I cried, and hugged him. Cally shook his hand. Mr. Warlex handed me over the data he had accumulated. I bundled that with mine and then we separated for the night.

The next morning, we told my family about our success. They called Gwen to make sure the patent was sent.

"Yes, I sent it the following day," said Gwen. "It is registered as a patent pending, and the finalized results, schema, and chemical analysis has to be delivered to the patent office within thirty days of that filing."

Cally and I got busy coming up with a social media strategy. The owner of the pub we tested our sticks in wanted to place an order immediately. That left us manufacturing them ourselves at home. Rick set us up a lab in the basement and outfitted it with all the equipment and chemicals we needed.

"Hey, this isn't that much different from molecular gastronomy," said Rick. "There are chefs that exclusively use chemistry to select foods to put together. So this lab is perfect."

The whole family got involved in the making of our stir sticks. We had our first order.

Once we had our first order finished, Cally and I worked with Gwen to finalize the patent. Now we needed marketing, packaging, manufacturing—*oh my*. We were going to need help!

We posted all kinds of photos on social media showing our stir stick working. The pub ended up getting swamped with customers because girls felt safer there. Soon orders were piling in from other bars.

I had to consult with my family on how to manufacture these sticks quickly, because we were doing it at home. Perhaps Gwen had some ideas.

"Gwen speaking."

"Gwen, it's Minni, Lora's daughter. How are you?"

“I’m doing well Minni. What can I do for you?”

“I understand you filed patents for us on our stir stick invention, so thanks for that.”

“You’re welcome. It’s important to not bring a product to market without one. As a matter of fact, I received a message from the patent office yesterday. I was going to call you.”

“Oh? What about?”

“Someone tried to file a patent of their own for the exact same product. A Mr. P. J. Warlex of St. Eustache, Quebec, filed a patent application for Strawz, a personal drug-testing device. The contents of the patent application matched one—yours—already applied for and approved.”

“Huh! That’s my chemistry teacher. Why would he do that?”

“Probably because he saw a winning product and decided to steal it from you and get rich off of it. If we hadn’t filed before him, he could have sued you to cease production.”

“Oh no! What a creep! Gee, I didn’t see that coming.”

That’s why you always hire a lawyer!” said Gwen. “Now, what can I do for you?”

“We’ve run into a problem: we cannot manufacture them fast enough. We have too many orders to fill. Do you have any suggestions?”

“Hmmm, let me look into this. Perhaps we can find a company that we can outsource to. But it will need an air-tight contract. Let me work on this, okay?”

“Thanks, Gwen!”

26— Learning Magic

Lora

I was sitting reading a book on magic, when Minni and Cally came and found me.

"Mom," started Minni, "we'd like to learn magic—well, I would, and Cally is volunteering to teach me."

"That's a good idea," I said. "In fact, we should all work together. I'm sure there is something for everyone to learn."

"Do you mean to bring in the others too?" asked Cally.

"Yes, I think so. It's high time we start to get the measure of the talent in the coven."

"How about we go down to see everyone?" Minni suggested, jumping up and down in excitement while Cally smiled knowingly.

———

We reached the spaceship where the witches were living about two hours later. I sent one of the young ones to collect them all to the platform so that we could have a meeting.

As soon as everyone was present, I launched my idea.

"Hi everyone, you must remember me? I wanted to speak to you about something. As my daughter and Cally were practicing magic, I watched them combine their balls of light into one. That gave me the idea of us combining our magic to work cooperatively. This would let us create defensive maneuvers."

I heard murmurs all around and saw some heads nodding in agreement and that gave me the courage to continue.

"Now I realized I'm not the most experienced magic user here, but I would like to start a weekly project where we get all the witches together to practice and share magical knowledge," I said. "In particular, working toward some cooperative defensive magic."

More nodding and agreement.

"I don't think that is a good idea," said a voice I recognized in the back.

"Why not, Amarlyis?"

"Magic is not intended to be wielded cooperatively," she answered.

"I disagree. There is much we can do together as a group. We proved it when we brought all of you back, remember? Perhaps one day our security will depend on a cooperative magical solution. Or perhaps we'll need to work together to defend against an enemy."

"Fine, in those situations, I agree with you."

"I know I'm not the strongest magic practitioner here, but will you let me lead you in this exercise?"

There were nods all around.

"Great and thanks. We will work on defensive magic that can be done in a group. Can I have everyone pair off? We'll start with two, and add from there."

Once everyone was paired off, Cally stood beside Minni, and I smiled. I walked into the center of the crowd. "Now, everyone, focus on creating a ball of energy between the two of you. Whoever forms it first takes the lead. The other person will then focus on that ball and the two of you will make it larger. Understand?"

A chorus of yeses.

The witches fell silent as they all tried to make a ball of energy. I walked over to Amarlyis, who did not have a partner and said, "Work with me."

Together, we stood facing each other. I focused on my ball and it popped into existence quickly. Amarlyis was surprised. "That's a good trick."

"Now, help me make it bigger," I said.

We both poured our focus into the ball, drawing our hands apart until it was the size of a beach ball. It was spinning around; its skin looked like the aurora borealis as colors spun and waved across the surface. There was a hush around us and I felt the magical energy drop. I looked up for a moment to see most of the witches were watching us.

Amarlyis noticed too. She glanced at me and I nodded. Together, we stepped farther away and widened the ball until it looked like a small portal. I felt it was stretching too thin with the power that just two of us had. And I was right. A moment later the bubble burst and the energy dissipated.

"Wow, that was spectacular!" someone said.

"How many of you got a ball?" I asked.

Four hands went up.

"Good. Were you able to make it larger?" I asked.

Three said yes, but not as big as mine.

"That's to be expected. It takes practice. Let's try again everyone! Make a ball, and try to get it as large as a beach ball.

Keep trying when you fail. Do it again. Switch people if it's not working for the two of you."

For a few hours, I drilled the witches until everyone could make a ball and expand that ball into a large bubble. The color of the auroras was different with each pair, so the whole place looked like a rainbow.

When everyone was exhausted, I stopped the exercise and we all sat down in a circle.

"What did everyone learn today?"

"We can work together," said a witch.

"Combining our magic makes it more fun," said another.

"We are more powerful together," said another.

"All these things are correct. We're going to do this again next week, same day, same time. In the meantime, I want each and every one of you to practice. Practice making your energy bubbles, and making them as large as you can on your own."

We all got up, and went our separate ways.

The following week, I saw a big improvement in not only casting the bubble, but in the confidence of all the witches. They now threw their bubbles into existence easily and were able to make them the size of beach balls on their own. So this week, I got them to work in threes. I worked with Minni and Cally.

Our little group was able to expand our bubble large enough to cover Minni from head to toe. She could stand inside it. All the other trios were getting nearly the same size. So, halfway through this week's session, I told them to make foursomes and to make their bubbles large enough to encase the whole group.

That was fun. As the bubbles got larger, they started bumping into each other and sizzling. Once the bubble was large enough, the group would jump inside. A game started then of running up and knocking the next bubble over. The bubbles bounced off each other. With everyone inside their group bubble, the platform indeed looked like a bumper car game with ricocheting bubbles bouncing around.

This suggested to me that the bubbles could indeed act as defensive tools.

"Okay, everyone, that was wonderful, silly, lots of fun, and instructional. Next week, let's see if these bubbles can be defensive. We will divide the group in two. One group will form a single bubble and the other group will attack. Practice, practice, practice!"

They split up and walked back to their rooms in groups, discussing the next week's project.

Amarlyis approached me and asked, "Why are you doing this?"

"Because I have this feeling that we need to know how to do this. I don't know why."

"Alright, after learning how to create these bubbles, let's also look at how to create magical attacks."

"I agree. Can you bring some next week? I don't know any myself."

"Yes, I'll devise three simple ones we can all practice."

27— Turning Justin

Justin

Mark's physician made a special trip and declared me healed. Apparently he looked after the immortal family. He wasn't very happy with examining me, and that was mutual, but he made sure that all my injuries had indeed healed completely.

The doctor grumbled about giving a human immortal blood, and that the youth are going to be their downfall. I felt for him, because this was a very real risk they were all running in bringing me into their circle. But I had promised I wouldn't peep a word of this to anyone. After all, I would become the subject of their little experiments too.

Oh God, I can see it now. "GAY IMMORTAL IN CITY" How can this be??? The headlines would be all over everything. Nope, not going there. *Ever*.

I still needed to figure out how to deal with Greggory though. My propensity for wanting new lovers all the time didn't bode Well, for long-term relationships. Without the desire for that, I couldn't tell anyone. Basically, I could tell only one person. That's it, one. That would be my one and only. My true love. I hadn't felt that yet. Lust, yes, bordering on love, yes. But true love? Na-ah. Not the kind that Rick had anyway. I saw how he fell for Lora. It was instantaneous. He was head over heels within minutes, and I laughed at him for it.

He told me that it wasn't "love" but a connection so deep, so complete, that he couldn't deny it. When he was away from her he couldn't think of anything else, yet when he was close, just touching her brought him calm, oneness, and a feeling of rightness.

I didn't have that with Greggory. So it would be fun, until it ended, but it would end—probably sooner than later. I wanted that connection Rick talked about. I wanted that sex that Andrews showed me. If he wasn't mated, I would pursue that man.

My next goal was to become immortal. Later that afternoon, I called Abeo and asked him if he could be here in an hour or so. I was excited—nervous but excited. What will it feel like? The venom bite I received from Andrews blew my mind, I mean really! It was like nothing I'd ever experienced before. Would this be just as intoxicating?

"Justin, make sure you're comfortable," said Abeo an hour later, "because when I give you this injection, you won't be moving for a while." He had me get into bed again and lie on my back. "This will pinch, but the euphoria will take over quickly."

I felt the large needle go in for sure, *ouch!* But as he said, it was only momentary. The drug in the venom took over quickly, making me as loopy as the bite did. *What a feeling!*

Then everything went black.

Two days later, I surfaced to find Rick sitting beside me and Lora on the other side. Rick was holding my hand.

"How long have I been out?" I asked.

“Two days,” answered Rick. “That is about average. But now Abeo has to give you a second dose.”

“Really? It’s not one and done?” I asked.

“No, it normally requires multiple doses. You have had one via my blood, so another should just about do it.”

I didn’t tell him that Andrews had bitten me. It felt conspiratorial. Abeo was there again a minute later with another large needle that, this time, seemed larger somehow.

“Is that needle bigger?” I asked.

“Yes, the dose is larger too,” answered Abeo.

Again, the needle hurt for a minute, but it was replaced with a floating feeling that took me away, and then blackness.

This time when I woke up, it was dark and no one was there. I glanced at the clock on my desk and it said 3:15 a.m. *Well, that’s a good reason for no one to be here, I thought.*

I tried to get out of bed but my legs didn’t want to work. A moment of panic started, but I managed to get myself calm again. I was probably just immobilized, that’s all. I tried my fingers, a smaller target, and sure enough they moved, then my hands, then my arms. I shook them vigorously to get the pins and needles out.

Lifting myself up, I had a bit of a headrush, but steadied myself before looking around some more. A bottle of water was beside my bed, and I took a long drink from that. My throat and mouth had been very dry. I took hold of one of my knees and manipulated it until it could move on its own. Pins and needles danced up my legs as if they were doing a cancan. Eventually, the feeling disappeared and I put my feet down on the floor and tried standing.

Wobbly at first, I lurched for the back of a chair to steady myself. I got myself straightened out and took another step, then another, and soon I was standing at the window and looking down on the skyline of Montreal.

I examined myself closely. Other than the stiffness of being immobile for who knows how long, I felt pretty much the same as before I started this process. I didn't feel stronger, my eyes couldn't see more, I couldn't hear more. So far no net benefits. Maybe they would come in later. I was famished though, so after putting on a robe, I made my way down the stairs to the kitchen to find food. I didn't care much what food it was—heck, a peanut butter and jelly sandwich sounded delicious right now. And that was exactly what I ended up making.

I was sitting on the sofa watching the sunrise, eating another PB+J, when I heard footsteps upstairs. The other guys must be waking up. *Oh goody!* Seamus appeared first.

"Good morning, Justin, how are you feeling?" he asked.

"Not bad. Normal, I guess," I said. "I didn't make coffee yet, sorry."

"Oh, no worries! I'll get on that right away," he said. "Do you want something to eat?"

"No thanks. I have been eating PB&Js. I had forgotten how satisfying they were."

"I discovered that myself when I moved in here. In my day, we didn't have food like that," said Seamus. The doorbell rang.

"Oh, that's early! Who could it be?" I asked.

"I'll go look." He peeped through the hole. "Oh, it's Abeo." He opened the door.

"Justin, good morning," said Abeo. "I've come to see how you're doing. When did you wake up?"

"I woke up at 3:15," I answered.

"Good. Let's see if you're making progress."

"How will we do that?" I asked.

"I will make a small incision in your hand."

"Ouch!"

"It won't hurt—well, not much anyway," he said, teasing me. He walked over to me and took a hand. Pulling out a penknife, he poked a small hole in the heel of my hand. It bled for about one second, and then closed up.

"Wow! As a person who has cut themselves frequently in the kitchen, I know just how much that should have bled. That's amazing!"

"Good progress. You've passed the initial phase. For the next six or so months, you will experience changes in your body. Your senses will become sharper and more sensitive. Your mouth will get sore, because you'll grow new teeth—your fangs. Your tailored clothes may not fit Well, anymore, because humans usually grow taller and become bulkier when they change. Other than that, you're now an immortal. So, welcome."

———

One day not long after, Duffy, Seamus, and I had a discussion about bachelorhood. We decided that the arrangement of renting this condo together worked well. So we asked Andrews if we could continue. He was delighted to let us stay.

"We all have enough privacy," said Seamus.

"Yes, I agree with that," said Duffy. "I'm not as likely to be bringing anyone home anyway."

"And why not?" I asked. "You're a ruggedly handsome man. I'm sure we can find a lady or gent right for you, depending on what you're interested in."

"Uh, ladies, thanks," said Duffy. "I'm not over my ex yet. I still miss her."

"Ah, I understand. You need to get laid for fun," I said.

"No, that's not what I meant!"

"Come on, Duffy, you know you need to. You just can't deny yourself," said Seamus. "I'm catching up on a very long dry spell myself."

"Seamus, it's fine for you. You met Anita and made an instant connection. There ain't a woman who would want me."

"Are you sure?" I asked. "I say we have a little soirée here and invite some of the peripheral people in the immortal group and see if sparks happen."

"Interesting idea, Justin," said Seamus. "I know there is a woman staying with Margaret and Abeo who is single and immortal. Plus, there are all those witches that were rescued."

"Leave it to me, boys," I said. "I'm a great party planner."

28— Creepy Morgues

Andrews

Looking over my handwritten notes, the picture had more pieces, but it was far from clear.

- Derek Staung's body was found outside of Montreal. Or at least that was the ID on the *—note to self, prove or disprove that*—could be a red herring.
- The cook led me to Steve Bushing.
- Inquiries about Steve brought Jackson Perry out of the woodwork.
- Jackson told me Steve was an independent contractor taking orders from someone in New Orleans.
- Bushing was working out of a warehouse owned by the Lacolle gang, who were an extreme right-wing group hellbent on removing and blocking any immigrants from the country.
- Bushing made a bomb for them in payment.
- The phone number in New Orleans was answered by the Brotherhood of the Blade and Snake.

- There is a connection between the brotherhood and the Lacolle gang.
- The person answering the phone was familiar with the Staung name.
- Was there a connection between the Fraternal Order and the Lacolle gang?

I'd given all my information to the Montreal detective, and updated Rick and Justin on my progress. My next move would be to go down to New Orleans and poke around there. But first, I wanted to see if I could get into the morgue to see that body.

Arriving at the Montreal morgue, which was downtown in a sub-basement of an old building, I took the elevator down three levels, and when the doors opened I had the sense of being in a horror movie. The halls were genuinely creepy and dark, with flickering lights casting a greenish pall over the walls. Or were the walls green? I couldn't tell. *The gurneys lining the hallway are a nice touch,* I thought. *Stephen King would be proud of the set dressing.*

The door I needed was, of course, at the end of the long hallway. Making my way toward it, my head started to throb from the strain on my eyes because of those damned flickering lights. *How typical. Incapacitate the human! Ha! I'm not human!* Pushing the doors open, I walked into a brightly lit, exceptionally clean, white and stainless morgue.

"Wow, that's refreshing!" I said out loud. "Hello? Anyone here?"

"Who goes there?" came a voice from an office off to the left.

"My name is Robert Andrews, I'm investigating the bombing of L'Escalade. I believe you have a body here that may be connected."

"Hullo, I'm Dr. Mort," said the coroner. "Yes, it's the French word for dead—I've heard every pun in existence, so don't start."

"Wouldn't dream of it," I said, smiling. This guy was fast.

"So who are you looking to peep at?" asked Dr. Mort.

"Derek Staung. He was brought in about a week ago I think?"

"Oh yeah, the decomp body. It's over here, follow me."

Dr. Mort pulled out a shiny stainless-steel drawer with a black body bag on the bottom. When he unzipped the bag, the most awful stench oozed out.

Gagging, I planted my hand over my nose and started breathing with my mouth.

"Yup, the smell gets you every time!" chimed the coroner. "It's why we carry around Vicks." He handed me the small dark blue glass jar with mentholatum gel inside. I gratefully applied some to my nose.

"So what were you hoping to see or not see?" asked the doctor.

"Well, I need to confirm the body is actually Staung. If it is, then my lead evaporates. But if it isn't, then my next step is to find him."

"The only evidence of who this is right now is the driver's license he had on him."

"Just a driver's license?"

"Yes, and that is weird."

"No wallet, money, or credit cards?"

"Nope, nada. Just the driver's license inside the pocket of his jeans."

"May I see the license please?"

"Sure, his personal effects are over there in a bag marked with the drawer number."

"Number 273, okay. Thanks." I went over to the shelf and found the appropriate bag. There was nothing in it but the license, and it was a Quebec license. That was proof it wasn't Staung.

"Doctor," I called out.

"Yep?"

"Derek Staung is from New Orleans, Louisiana. He wouldn't have had a Quebec driver's license. It would have been from NOLA."

"So you're saying this ID doesn't go with him?"

"Well, it does, but it's fake. So very likely the body is not his. Do you have dental?"

"I have taken imprints, but there have been no matches in Quebec or Canada. But now that you tell me he's possibly from New Orleans, let's try that database right now."

"Excellent. May I watch?"

"Yes, of course. Come with me."

It took about thirty minutes before the database spit out some information. However, it was definitive: the dental impressions were not from the body. The dental pictures from Derek were very different.

"So the body is not Staung. Good for you, I take it," said the doctor.

"Yes, good for me. My investigation has a new place to go. Thank you, Doctor."

"Watch out for the zombies on the way out."

Laughing, I pushed back through the doors into the creepy hallway. *Zombies, I wouldn't be a bit surprised!*

29— A Meet and Greet

Justin

It didn't take me long to speak to everyone in "the circle" that would be interested in coming to our soirée. I started with Rick and Lora, of course.

"I think that is a wonderful idea, Justin," said Lora. "We'll bring Anita, Cally, and Minni too. Since both girls are adults now, and will be immortal, they should meet everyone."

"Good idea," I said. "This is going to be a good crowd!" *Gosh, it feels good to be doing something again!* My next call was Margaret.

"Margaret speaking."

"Margaret, it's Justin—Rick's business partner?"

"Yes, hi, Justin. How are you feeling?"

"I'm all healed up, thank you, and now I'm planning a party. Think of it as a welcome back to life soirée. I understand there are a few members of your household who may be interested?"

"Yes, I'm sure that Mary and her daughter would be. Both are adults and immortal, and new to this world, so making friends would be very important to them. Don't forget to call Abeo. He may have friends to invite too. I just have to find a babysitter for the kids."

"Oh my, I forgot, you have five babies, don't you?"

"Uh huh, but there are a couple of fifteen-year-olds that can help. Leave that to me."

"I'll let you know what the date will be."

"This is exciting!" exclaimed Margaret.

My next call was to Abeo. He was currently out of the country, so I had no idea where he was, but his cell phone connected quite easily.

"Hello, Justin!"

"Hi, Abeo, how did you know it was me?"

"Your contact is on my phone as the person to call when I need catering."

"Oh, lovely! Thank you!" I said. "I'm calling because I'm doing my favorite thing: planning a party. Margaret told me to call you to see if you had any friends to invite."

"I take it that it's a party for immortals?"

"Yes, and near immortals."

"I have a few people I can include. They would enjoy a party for a change. So thank you. When will it be?"

"Yet to be determined. I will send out a text announcement for the date."

"Good, I will make sure I'm available."

Next to call would be Gwen. Again, she was delighted to hear of a social event for "the circle" of friends. She told me that she knew of a couple of singles who might be interested too.

Last to call was Mark and Falon.

Mark was more concerned about the security of it all. Was it smart to put so many of our kind in one spot with a loud party? I didn't have an answer for him, but I put it in the back of my mind. Perhaps our witches could be of help in disguising the party, or soundproofing it. I would ask Seamus when I finished inviting everyone.

The people-mill was working on its own. Word would spread of an immortal party. I had no idea how many would show up, so I'd better plan for a hundred, just in case. Catering was next. Since my own restaurant was out of commission, I needed an alternative. This might be a good opportunity to test out Carlos. After all, he wanted to start his own business.

I called Lora's house again and asked for Carlos.

"This is Carlos. Who's calling?"

"Hi, Carlos, my name is Justin. I'm a chef. I'm having a party soon and need someone to cater it for me. Anita told me you want to start your own company, so I wanted to give you a chance."

"Si, señor, I do want to start a business with Anita. I would welcome an opportunity to show you what I can do. May I cook lunch for you?"

"Oh, that would be fun. Yes. How about tomorrow?" I asked.

"Si, that would be ideal. Do you have any requests?"

"No, let me see what you want to show me."

"*Gracias*."

Carlos arrived about 10:30 the next day to start his prep for lunch. I invited Seamus and Duffy too, and let Carlos know there would be three of us.

"That is good, señor, the more the better."

"Oh stop calling me señor, *por favor*. Justin is just fine."

"Si señ—ah, Justin."

Carlos got busy in the kitchen, chopping, puréeing, baking, and lots of other stuff. It smelled wonderful and I was getting very hungry. It had been ages since I'd had a nice meal. Seamus and Duffy arrived in good time and we all watched him work. Duffy went and set the table for us, making four places. I didn't know if Carlos would eat with us, but I welcomed it.

When the food had been plated, Carlos brought it out and set it down. It was colorful, with lots of textures, spicy and savory, and beautifully presented. I applauded.

"Bravo, Carlos! This looks amazing. I may hire you for my kitchen when I rebuild my restaurant."

"Really? That would be an honor, señ—Justin. Thank you."

"Now, tell me what we are eating," I said.

Carlos gave us descriptions of each of the dishes he prepared. They were culturally Colombian, his favorites. Everything was perfectly cooked.

"Carlos, can you cook other styles of cuisine? French? Italian? Asian?" I asked.

"Si, Justin, I can cook many, but not as expert in some. I would like to practice before I cook for a restaurant. But it would be my pleasure."

"Carlos, I want you to cater the party please. Make enough for one hundred people, and I'll leave the menu up to you. We'll match the food to beverages when I get the mixologist."

30— Witches Assemble

Minni

Being part of learning magic with the witches was amazing. Suddenly it felt like I had a special purpose in life.

Cally, Alison, and I would practice in the back yard together. My brothers weren't really interested, but that was okay. They each had their own thing. Trent was into sports, and Pascal was into being non-binary. So us three girls were left quite alone to do what we wanted with no interference from younger siblings.

Of course, Cally and Alison were way beyond me already. They were patient with me and helped me learn. The exercise we were working on together was to form bubbles of energy. It was difficult to stay focused on one thing. My mind kept wandering to questions I had.

"Minni, focus!" scolded Cally. "You'll never learn if you let your attention drift."

She was right, I was thinking of other things. *Focus, Minni!* I was supposed to be creating my own bubble or ball of light. So far I had made a spark—just a spark—while both Alison and Cally had balls about the size of baseballs balanced in their hands.

"I don't get it. What am I doing wrong?" I asked.

"You're not doing anything wrong. There isn't a right or wrong way, just your way," said Cally. "What I do is try to picture in my head what I'm trying to create. I look at it from all sides, forming it as completely as I can. Then I stare at it and try to feel its presence. Eventually, it becomes real."

"So start with seeing the ball in your head…"

That was difficult. I opened one eye and looked at theirs. They were translucent like a glass sculpture. So I pictured a glass ball. I thought of nothing else but that glass ball floating in a black space with nothing around it. A clear glass ball imperfect but round, swirling around and around like a planet. I turned it over and rotated it the other direction. I looked through it, and noticed how the imperfections distorted the view of the other side of the glass ball. I raised it up high and dropped it down low—but not too low. I spun it around me and eventually stopped it in front of me. I saw my hand come into view under the ball and it continued to spin and my hand did not touch it.

I opened my eyes and there was a spinning clear ball of energy hovering an inch above my hand.

"Wow!" I managed to say before it went poof and disappeared.

"Very good, Minni!" applauded Cally. "That was a significant improvement. I liked when you spun it around your body. That was cool."

"That actually happened?" I asked.

"Of course it did. Is that what you pictured in your head?" Alison asked.

"Yes, but I thought that was me just getting a full picture."

"Nope, you had your own ball and you made it do things. So, excellent work today!"

"Thank you, Cally. Coming from you, that's high praise," I said. "But why is mine clear and yours and Alison's green?"

"Did you picture it as clear?"

"Yes, but I was likening it to a glass ball."

"Well, what you picture is what you get. Still, there should be a color to your magic. Perhaps that will develop later with experience."

"Now that we all have balls, can we combine them? I asked.

"Let's find out," said Cally. "Alison, bring yours right up against mine and let's see if we can push them together."

The two girls worked together on this step. It was clearly a difficult thing to do, because beads of sweat broke out on their foreheads as they concentrated on their efforts. I watched in awe as they slowly smushed the two globes together. Finally, they popped into one bubble that was twice their separate sizes. Cally took control of that larger one while Alison slumped to a chair, breathing heavily.

"Phew, that was tough," she said. "It felt like I was trying to push a ball through a wall!"

"Yes, I agree. That was difficult," said Cally. "But we did it. Can you remember what you thought about Alison?"

"Yes, I was thinking about pushing my ball inside yours. I got a lot of resistance though as they kind of flattened against each other."

"Shall I try?" I asked.

"Let's give it a go," said Cally. "Remember to keep your focus very narrow, only on one thing."

I formed a new ball, more quickly this time, and moved it up against Cally's. With the difference in size, it looked like a planet circling the sun. Cally's sphere had wavy aurora-like lines moving all over its surface and mine didn't.

I started to tell the ball to push up against the larger sphere. It did, but then it stopped. It was like my ball had hit a wall. I commanded it to move forward, and it tried but didn't go anywhere. I pictured my ball pushing halfway into the other one, and kept that visual in my head as clearly as I could as I tried to add movement to it.

Slowly, my ball pushed against the sphere. I could feel the resistance as it crackled and snapped like lightning. Eventually, I could feel my ball push through the sphere's "skin" and then things got easier. It didn't take nearly as much effort to push my ball completely inside as it did to get through initially.

As soon as I felt my ball was completely inside, I opened my eyes and looked. There it was, my clear ball floating inside the green sphere, intact. Now all I had to do was let it go. I released my spell and my ball disappeared, but the energy that it contained stayed inside the sphere, making it grow again to the size of a beach ball.

"Yippee!" I cried, jumping up and down with the joy of accomplishment. "I did it!"

"Very good, Minni," said Cally. "You've got natural talent. We'll make you a powerful witch yet!"

"Let's show Lora!" said Alison. "She'll be impressed we did this."

"Yes, she will," said Cally.

"I think this is wonderful!" said Lora, when we found her later. "Good work, girls. I'm very proud of you. Let's show this to the coven as well. Perhaps you can demonstrate it? This may be another way to combine our power for defensive measures. I was on my way down there this evening. Do you want to come along?"

"Yes," all three of us said.

We made our way down to the ark ship platform. The witches had set up a bell to call everyone to the platform easily, and Alison rang it when we arrived. The witches soon started coming in ones and twos.

"Ladies and gentlemen, I have a new exercise for us to practice. My daughter, Cally, and Alison came up with it. Girls, will you demonstrate please?"

Pressure! I had never done magic in front of others before, much less accomplished witches. I gulped and faced Cally.

"It's alright, Minni. Just do the exact same thing you did back at the house," said Cally. "Narrow your focus to us three and block out everything else."

We started. Each of us created balls of energy. When all three were visible, the witches clapped and cheered our accomplishment. Next, Alison merged hers with Cally's. She said it wasn't as difficult the second time, because she understood what was happening.

The crowd cheered again as Cally's sphere grew. Next it was my turn. I too found it easier this time. It didn't seem like it took as much effort—*So practice does help. Huh!* When my ball was inside Cally's, the group applauded again. When I dissolved my ball and Cally's grew again, they cheered.

"That is quite something," said one of the witches. "Imagine if we could all do that!"

"Well, that's the purpose of today's practice," said Lora. "Everybody, form groups of three and replicate what the girls have just shown you. When we have one sphere per group, let's try combining more and see what happens."

As the witches worked on achieving the first sphere, we three girls did the same thing again. Each time we did the exercise, it became easier, until we could basically make our spheres inside one another, cutting out a step entirely. It was much easier than trying to enlarge someone else's sphere. After we had done the exercise again a few times, I suggested we try to create more balls inside.

Cally went first. She created a blue ball inside the sphere and released its energy. Then Alison made a red one, and I made another as well. Now the sphere was nearly as big as Cally.

"Let's keep going!" she said, as she made another ball in quick succession, followed by Alison and I. Soon we just kept making balls inside the original sphere until it towered over Cally, and was wide enough for the three of us to stand inside. But we were all breathing heavily, because it was hard work.

"Can we all stand inside the sphere?" asked Alison.

"Let me try first," said Cally, as she drew the huge sphere over her head and then brought it down to the ground. She was standing inside the sphere and had a big grin on her face. "Alison, you're next."

Alison stepped toward the sphere and tested a finger against it. It snapped a little, but didn't hurt and she felt no resistance. So she punched her hand through the bubble's skin. Following her hand, she pushed her arm, head, and then shoulders inside too. Finally, her feet followed and she was standing beside her sister.

"Okay, Minni, your turn!"

I repeated what Alison did. Once we were all inside, we clasped hands in a triangle and worked together to maintain the sphere, which was draining Cally.

Outside, Mom had been watching. She gasped when she saw us making multiple balls inside the larger sphere, but when we actually walked inside? She smiled and got everyone else to watch.

"Cally, release your energy please," said Lora. As Cally let go of the sphere, its collapse caused an energy wave to push out from the center like a seismic wave. Everyone felt the power until it dissipated.

"Wow, that was an impressive use of power, girls," said Amarlyis, who had joined the group in the middle of the exercise.

"Thank you, Amarlyis," said Cally.

"Folks, I believe we have our next goal to achieve," said Mom. "Let's replicate what the girls have done, on a larger scale. I want to get everyone inside a bubble of energy."

"Why?" asked Amarlyis.

"Because this could be a good defensive strategy," said Mom. "Once we can get people inside, we can test if the bubble can protect them."

"Good idea," said one of the witches.

"Okay, let's get to work. We have a lot to achieve tonight."

Everyone dove into this exercise, working with increasingly larger groups of people until everyone was inside one bubble. Amarlyis and Lora stayed outside to create the offensive magic to throw against the bubble.

By the time morning came around, we had devised and mastered an energy bubble that would hold together against most magical spells. But the witches were exhausted; many of them had dropped to their knees after the last trial. So we all agreed to stop and get rest before continuing in a few days.

"This is exciting," said my mother. "We're developing our own defenses. And somehow I think we're going to need them."

"It is exciting," agreed the girls, but they were too tired to make much conversation.

31— The Plot Thickens

PI Adams

My father did get back to me with more information on Derek Staung. It was too bad I hadn't asked him about this person before I took on this "missing person" case. Turns out, this dude was bad. Real bad. Apparently, his daughter didn't know that. I needed to speak to her again, and challenge this aspect of his life.

Derek Staung's daughter, Analise, lived modestly. She was a simple school teacher in a grade school. Knocking on the front door of her modest house, I didn't relish the conversation we were about to have, but it couldn't be helped.

"Oh, hello, Ms. Adams," she drawled. "Do come in. Would you like some sweet tea?"

"Thank you, please."

"Have a seat in the sittin' room. I'll bring us some cool glasses." Analise disappeared for a few minutes and returned with a silver tray carrying glasses and a pitcher of sweet tea and ice. After pouring me a glass, she sat opposite me and settled in.

"Now what can I do for you today?" she asked.

“Well, I’ve come to give you an update on my progress.”

“Truly grateful.”

“I think I may have located your father. But it’s in Canada—Montreal to be specific—and it’s a body.”

Analise gasped and her eyes went wide with surprise. A second later, water was collecting in her lashes, threatening to release a torrent of tears down her face.

“Now, the ID is not for sure yet, and I mean to find out definitively if it is your dad. In the meantime, though, I've uncovered some information about your father’s activities that I need to address.”

“Go ahead,” she said bravely. “I’ll tell you what I know.”

“Did you know that your father once was a member of a group called the Fraternal Order of Monks?”

“No.”

“Did you know that your father founded a separate group called the Brotherhood of the Blade and Snake here in New Orleans?”

“No.”

“Have you ever heard of either of those two groups?”

“A long time ago, my father used to rant and rage about a group he was associated with that he said never had the balls to take the fight to the enemy. Could he have been speaking about them?”

“It’s possible,” I agreed. “Did he ever say anything specific about them?”

“Well, most of his ravings were that, ravings. He believed in vampires and werewolves! My mother divorced him because she couldn’t take the nonsense anymore. He so truly believed that stuff that he went hunting them. He even roped some friends into going with him.”

“So he was off his rocker a long time ago?”

"I was just a girl of twelve when they split up. So yes."

"I'm sorry you had to live that way. Is there anything else you can tell me about that part of his life?"

"He used to hang around the Ninth Ward a lot because there were some voodoo priests and such living there. I never went down there. It was a scary place to go."

Especially for a lily-white woman! I thought. "Thank you, Analise. If I find anything else, I'll let you know."

"Okay, then," she said, standing up. I nodded to her as I opened the front doo,r and let myself out.

———

*Well, that was almost useless,*I thought as I got back into my car. I needed to touch base with that detective in Montreal again to see if they had anything new.

Pulling up his number on my phone, I used my car's integrated speaker to call while I was driving.

"Meunier."

"Detective Meunier, this is PI Adams from New Orleans again. How are you today?"

"I'm fine. What can I do for you, Ms. Adams?"

"I'm just following up on that DB you had to find out if you have confirmed the identity as Derek Staung."

"One moment," he said. "Oui, that file has been updated. The body is not Derek Staung. Dental records confirm this. Is there anything else?"

"No, *merci*," I answered. "That's all, thank you."

Click.

"My, there is an abundance of rude in that police station!" I said out loud. "That means Derek is not dead in Montreal. But was he in Montreal? And if so, why?"

Back at my office I dove into research. I looked up flights from NOLA to Montreal stretching back before he disappeared. I found a couple of instances where he was there for a week or two at a time. The last time was just before his disappearance—so that was progress.

I also looked up city records on the Brotherhood and the Order going back about two decades. About three years ago, there used to be a chapter of the Fraternal Order here in New Orleans. Huh. With some more digging, I found a manifesto for the group announcing their dedication to remove all things supernatural and dangerous from New Orleans. They went on a binge of raiding magic shops, and voodoo shops. New Orleans has been a hub for the supernatural long before the Anne Rice books came out. People voluntarily walked around with tattoos and piercings to make themselves look like vampires. There were social groups who pretended to be vampires and hid in buildings where they blackened out the windows.

People were strange. *But this Fraternal Order takes the cake.* Apparently, the group was incorporated and had to file minutes of shareholder meetings with the city. One such document indicated that the group was on to a Mark Chisholm of Houston some years ago. They believed he was a vampire for real, hiding in plain sight. They claimed he appeared out of nowhere without any history.

If they were sworn to eradicate vampires, and they thought this Chisholm guy was one, perhaps they were after him…?

Next were flights between New Orleans and Houston. *Lots of those!* Staung was spending lots of time in Houston three years ago. Lots of time. So where did Chisholm go? Did Staung follow?

More searching gave me a bounty of information. Chisholm was in Montreal numerous times, and Staung was there at the same time. So Staung was following him around. There was a big splash in the news about a gala for a big charity event that Chisholm and his new wife were hosting. It was going to be a big thing with the media. *Hmmm ... if I wanted to take down a vamp,*

I'd want credit, and what better way to do that than doing it in public!

More digging through news archives pulled up a small news story about an assassination attempt on Mark Chisholm and his wife at the gala. *Bingo!* Dates? About a year before the body was found.

"Okay, Adams, what have you got?" I asked myself.

- Staung was associated with the Fraternal Order and ran a chapter here for more than twenty years.
- He had a hate for all things supernatural.
- New Orleans is a hotbed for vampires.
- Staung had identified Mark Chisholm as a vampire and was following him everywhere.
- There was an assassination attempt on Chisholm's life a year ago.
- Staung renamed the order the Brotherhood and recruited kids who wanted to vamp hunt.

I have to go find that warehouse. That was my next move.

The address was easy, because the "club" was registered with the city, and the address was on file. However, you couldn't describe the level of creep there. Sure, there were new homes built in the ward. A number of celebrities had jumped on the bandwagon and helped out. But even those projects had gone awry. There were still many lots left vacant and the original buildings torn down. There were lots of land where there was nothing but high fences preventing people from going there. There were lots of unused warehouse buildings too, and that was where the club lived.

But they were trying to revive the ward. The trouble was, the people moving back were "gentrifying" the area with fancy solar powered homes on stilts. The people who used to live there wouldn't, and couldn't, afford those. *Does anyone want to move back into a death trap?*

Evil thrives in vacant places and dark corners. Those empty buildings had desperate people lying around with needles in their arms, or people trying to make a living on their backs. If you were to take a trip on Google Earth, it would look sunny and happy. But behind that shine was a hidden world. In some places, every third house was missing. Stone walls outlining property remained, but the houses were gone. Those that could not be repaired still had their single storey homes. The new constructions were all elevated and two storeys. There were still so many abandoned homes. The people who used to live there lost everything. The ONLY people who were living down there now were those who bought up the land for nothing and built fancy new houses way up on stilts. It was disgusting.

It didn't take me that long to find the "clubhouse." It was a rundown warehouse along the water that was missing most of the outer wall on one side. Where the wall was gone, so was the roof. There were two internal sections to the building, one of which was unusable because of debris still piled up inside. The other two were nominally workable. The third one was the most intact, and that was where I found their meeting hall.

The building had no power and only one window by the door, so it was as hot as stink inside. The walls were lined with boards held up by broken pieces of furniture to make tables of sorts. The tables were covered with candlewax because of the fifty or so thick candles that lit the space. No lights. On the walls, over top of the mold, mildew, and dirt, were sheets with sayings painted on them like "Fight the Good Fight" or "Vamps = Death." At one end was an altar. At least that's what I interpreted the platform to be: an altar with a table that had two large candles on it, and was covered with a whitish cloth. It was too dirty to call white.

About thirty people were inside, sitting on the floor facing the altar. A young man in his twenties was on the platform and was speaking with great enthusiasm; his hands and arms flying around like a helicopter. I couldn't make out what he was saying, but the audience made humming sounds in response to some of the things he said. If I didn't know better, I'd say they were all jacked up on something and he was brainwashing them. Every one of the people sitting was male. No females at all. That was telling. They could all be incels.

I couldn't do more right now. I needed to set up surveillance on this place. Looking around, I spotted a building across the way that might suffice.

32— Brainwashing is a Thing

Andrews

My trip down to New Orleans was fairly uneventful. It was your typical business trip: cramped seating, no food or drink, and long lines for security and customs. After checking into my hotel, I picked up a map of New Orleans and took it back to my room with food to study it carefully. I needed to understand the layout of the city, where people congregated, where the tourist areas were to avoid them, and where the underbelly was. Every city had an underbelly. It was just a matter of finding it.

I poked around talking to workers, like the doormen about the city. Racism was still a big thing, and the hatred seemed even more palpable. One of them told me the air was "thick" with it. An apt description. In a city where the wealthy whites still ruled, and corruption seemed to be embedded in the culture, racial problems persisted.

Another doorman explained how drugs were killing the youth of the city. Young men and women were being seduced by the plethora of drugs available now; their futures were being stolen from them. The fentanyl problem was everywhere, but in poor neighborhoods it was worse.

Using the data my team provided, I was able to use city records to find addresses for many of the players in the Brotherhood. I would need to speak to some of them to find out who was running the show right now. Perhaps I would have to go undercover.

Except I discovered the members were all white.

A report was sent to me from Grisham that let me know he had a breakthrough. He found evidence that the Fraternal Order had removed Derek to Switzerland when they intervened on the night of the gala. He said he was eighty-nine percent sure based on airline data, filed flight plans, and chatter he'd picked up recently. He believed the Swiss group left another body to be found in Montreal with "evidence" to point to Derek to discredit him. The Order had distanced itself from his New Orleans group.

Using some of Duffy's surveillance, Grisham pieced together that the Order held Staung for about six months before letting him go. They returned him to New Orleans, but since then he'd disappeared. Duffy said they had a room at the compound that was used for programming initiates. Maybe they tried to reprogram Staung?

So now my goal was to find Staung alive in New Orleans. My first steps would be to check known associates, addresses, and family. Then I'd look through shelters and rooming houses, and finally the homeless population of New Orleans. That was a large population too.

I'd get started tomorrow.

33— Immortal Mixer

Justin

With all the plans finished, I was busy putting the finishing touches on the decor. My guests were going to start arriving soon, and I wanted everything to be perfect. Yeah, I was OCD and proud of it. It was a pain in the ass for everyone around me, but I didn't care.

I wanted an elegant affair, so I chose gold and white as the colors. I had fairy lights dancing in branches that were strategically placed all over the main floor in white planters. The branches had been spray painted in white, and I had gold-colored leaves wired to the branches in clusters. The effect was quite enchanting. I used clear glass tables along the walls as buffet tables, with clusters of white and gold pillar candles inside large vases. The base of the vases were clear, with opaque pebbles inside to add weight. I had those vases placed on just about every horizontal surface I could find. They spread a warm light and softened the dreary gray industrial look of Andrews' ultra-modern home.

Not that I didn't like Andrews' decor, it just wasn't me. I had to admit I was a bit of a fairy when I wanted to be. I love magic, and what's more appealing than magical-feeling decor?

Carlos and Anita had prepared all the food offsite, but they were using the kitchen as a staging area. There was nothing I could do about the fact that the kitchen was being used. It was an open plan, no walls, so everyone would see. My idea was to create a glittering curtain of beads suspended from the ceiling. It didn't hide the kitchen, but it broke up the visual. The curtain stretched the length of the island counter and came down to about eye height so that it wouldn't interfere with food prep.

The food smelled awesome! My tummy was grumbling from hunger just smelling all those wonderful spices.

Carlos and Anita were plating all the food onto gold and white dishes that would look amazing on the clear tables. They had arranged the food into groups. Three kinds of salad and several different vegetables were arranged on one table. On another table, there were delightful finger sandwiches and canapes. Yet another table had at least three kinds of meat appetizers like wings, meatballs, shrimp, and my favorite "pigs-in-blankets". The last table had different entrees like grilled salmon, prime rib, and a yummy looking leg of lamb. In this way, the guests had to travel around if they wanted a complete meal.

I had arranged with Carlos that once the food was served, he didn't have to stay. We would clean up the day after. He thought my plan was odd, but went along with it, saying that having the night off would be nice. He would go to a movie with a friend he had made.

I had moved all the sofas and chairs into conversation settings in the center of the space, rather than as they were around the perimeter. Cozy intimate groups were better for mixers when you wanted people to connect.

Andrews' condo had a wet bar already, so I didn't have to do anything about that. The only thing I wanted to do was design a special cocktail for the evening. Glancing at the clock, I was down to an hour and a half before people started arriving. Seamus and Duffy were out picking up extra alcohol and mixers for the bar.

I ran upstairs to change. I had a white tuxedo that I paired with a white shirt, gold tie, gold cufflinks, and a gold belt. I had a white rose tipped with gold as a boutonniere. A final check in the mirror and I felt I looked smashing. I just needed to find my white patent leather shoes. As I came down the stairs, Seamus and Duffy were coming in with their parcels.

"Justin, you look like a groom. Is there something we should know about this party?" asked Seamus.

"Really? No, I'm not getting married," I answered. "I just wanted to be like my decor, elegant and magical."

"Well, that you are, my friend. That you are," said Seamus. "We'll stock the bar, then I'll go get dressed. But I'm not wearing fancy clothes, Justin."

"That's quite alright. Wear what you're comfortable in. I must admit, I've always loved getting dressed up."

The guests started arriving right on time. *Figures!* That's why I wanted to be ready. No one remembers the "fashionably late" rule. There is always someone who arrives early or on time. I don't like getting caught without pants.

Well, unless I've planned it that way of course.

The witches were the first guests to arrive, which made sense. They basically used a portal to get here. I greeted them at the door. I wasn't going to remember any of their names, but it was nice to have new blood. Amarlyis had done a respectable job dressing them all. The ladies were wearing cocktail dresses and the men were all in suits. It was a split of five ladies and three men. Since they were here first, I showed them the food, and the bar, and told them to help themselves.

Carlos was just finishing up, and I heard him say goodbye to Anita.

"Justin, I'm leaving now. What time do you want me back to clean up tomorrow?" he asked.

"Not before 10:00, my friend."

"Okay. Have a good party," he said as he closed the door behind him.

The next people to arrive were Lora and Rick's family. They didn't bring the two boys, but they brought their daughter Minni and Cally. The girls were both adults now. They were all dressed elegantly, and Lora was wearing my favorite color on her—emerald-green. Her baby bump was adorable, and that dress hugged all those curves the right way. Rick was in a classic tux with an emerald-green shirt; the girls were in chic little black cocktail dresses. Anita, who was already here, was crushing it in a black and red lace number with a decidedly Spanish twist. She looked hot, and I wondered who that was for. I didn't have to wonder long, as Seamus made a beeline straight to her. They gazed at each other with such heat, I thought they would spontaneously combust right there.

I walked up to them with a glass of water ready to douse the two of them.

"Do I need to use this or do you want to get a room?" I asked under my breath.

Seamus broke his gaze on Anita, glanced at me, then my hand, and laughed. He took Anita's elbow and led her into the party to introduce her to the others.

I will keep my eye on those two!

Margaret and Abeo were next to arrive. She wore a smashing off-the-shoulder red number that hugged her curves lusciously. He was dressed in a suit, black on black. *Impeccable.* He always dressed well. They also brought along their two boarders, a woman named Mary and her adult daughter Siobhan. Both were immortal, but her daughter wasn't "finished." With their arrival, all thirteen witches were now here.

I think I am going to introduce Duffy to Mary. I think they may hit it off. At that moment, Duffy came downstairs. Duffy looked out of place, poor guy. He wasn't much of a social butterfly. *I'll change that!* I walked over to Duffy and grabbed him by the arm.

“Duffy, I want to introduce you to someone,” I said. “Now relax, you look great and it’s time to meet people, ladies in particular.” He sputtered beside me, but followed. When I reached Mary’s position, I took her elbow and turned her around to face us.

“Mary, I would like to introduce you to a wonderful friend of mine, Duffy.”

Duffy, this is Mary, and her daughte,r Siobhan.”

“Pleased to make your acquaintance,” said Duffy, bowing slightly. Siobhan blushed slightly as Mary looked straight at him.

“Duffy, pleased to greet you. What’s that short for?” asked Mary.

“Ah, well, you see, it's me nickname. My proper name is Johnson McDuff. But everyone calls me Duffy.”

“You’re Irish,” said Mary. It was a statement, not a question. And it smacked of approval.

“Yes, guilty. Normally, me accent doesn’t come out this much. I’ve lived in Florida for years now.”

“Oh? You live in Florida?”

“Well, sometimes. I have two places now,” said Duffy.

“Well, I don’t mind you telling me all about them and your business,” said Mary, as she slipped her arm through his and guided him away to chat. That left Siobhan and I standing there together.

“Well, that was easier than I thought it would be,” I said.

“Wha’ you say? Introducing ma t’a man?” asked Siobhan.

“Getting Duffy to speak to a woman!”

Laughing like a tiny bell, she said, “Ma is no wallflower. Ne’r ‘as been, and Duffy’s a nice-looking man. E’en ifn’ he wasna in’eres’ed, she’d‘ve made a go for ‘im.”

That made me laugh out loud. “Good luck, Duffy!” I crowed. “I don’t think you’ll be needing introductions either.”

“No t’ank you. I’ll do just fine meself, t’anks.” She gently placed a hand on my upper arm and smiled as she walked away to say hello to the other witches. It occurred to me that she already knew most of them, and that she hadn’t seen them since being placed with Margaret.

Falon and Mark walked in the door as I was saying so long to Siobhan. I had to say, both Falon and Lora looked radiantly pregnant. Their bodies just seemed to agree with the hormones! Falon was a bit more conservative, in that her black cocktail dress didn’t hug her body quite so much. But the sleeveless sweetheart neckline certainly framed her ample bust nicely. Mark, of course, was hovering. But he was very protective of his mate. Mark looked like the Greek god Adonis in his perfectly cut double-breasted tuxedo. *Damn, I wish he was bi! Surely an immortal has the time to consider all options?*

It was amazing to have so many fashionable friends! Was I expecting any more? *Oh, how silly of me, Gwen and Andrews still aren’t here. They should be here shortly.* I decided I should mingle, then I heard the door again.

As it turned out, Andrews let himself and Gwen in, seeing as he had a key. Gwen was stylishly dressed in another black cocktail dress that was tailored to fit her to a tee. Andrews was more casual in a perfectly fit turtleneck cotton sweater under a well-fitting suit. His combo of black on charcoal was elegant even though casual. I loved that man’s look!

Sometime later, Abeo answered the door and let in some of his associates. He brought them over to me to introduce them.

“Justin, I’d like to introduce you to two of my oldest friends,” said Abeo. “May I present Tuata, my once captain and now business partner, and Lucas, a pilot and also a business partner.”

"Tuata, Lucas, welcome to my humble party. Thank you for coming. Please, help yourself to food and drink. Mingle. All the people here are part of our circle of immortal beings."

"Really?" commented Tuata. "That's different. I don't recall ever having a party with our kind before."

"That's a shame!" I said. "I love parties. We need to know each other, and socialize together."

"I agree," said Lucas. "We feel so isolated normally, it's nice to be able to speak freely and not worry about keeping secrets."

"Do. Go! Be! Have fun!" I chanted. I watched as Abeo introduced his friends to Margaret and then made the rounds to everyone else before showing them the food and drink. I stood for a moment and took in all the people here. A good showing, diverse in color, all supernatural, and plentiful enough to make some fun with. I hoped we had some new couples after this. I for one was on the lookout.

Lucas returned to my side while I was musing on the composition of my get-together.

"Ahem," he said quietly.

"Lucas, right? What can I do for you?" I asked.

"I was hoping to corner you for some conversation," he said shyly.

I took a second look at the man. He was nicely built, polished even, with wild gray eyes that spoke volumes and volumes. I hadn't looked him in the eye yet. Once there, I felt almost trapped. I couldn't look away. Those depths needed to be plumbed. I swallowed and smiled.

"Of course, I'd be delighted to," I replied. "I didn't notice at first, you're my kind."

"Gay?" he asked. "Yes. I sensed this from you too, so…"

"You were hoping to make a connection? I hear you. It's been a long time."

"I think I have you beat on that one. I'm not even going to tell you how long it's been for me," he chuckled. He looked me in the eye again, and that pull was stronger this time. "I don't want to be presumptuous, but I really want to kiss you."

I stepped closer and realized we were the same height. I took his face in my fingers and went to place a chaste kiss on his lips. As soon as I touched him, he held me tightly and the kiss became sensual. No tongue, but long and soft but demanding. A promise of more, and a request for more as well.

He broke the kiss and I leaned back a little dizzy. All the blood rushed from my head to somewhere else.

"Wow, that was nice," I said. "Do you often kiss perfect strangers like that?"

"Never before. But somehow you don't feel like a stranger."

"No, you don't either," I realized at that moment. I'd forgotten about my guests entirely. I was in a little bubble and I didn't want to leave. Tearing my eyes away from his, I glanced around the room. No, you don't either," I realized at that moment. I'd forgotten about my guests entirely. I was in a little bubble and I didn't want to leave. Tearing my eyes away from his, I glanced around the room. Nearly everyone was engaged with someone or something. Except Abeo. He was watching us from the edge of his vision. Perhaps he had hoped his friend and I would click. I turned back to Lucas and took his hand.

"Come on, let's go mingle together. Maybe we can turn some heads!"

He laughed and accompanied me into the party.

People were eating, drinking. The noise level was not loud, the music was fun, some people were even dancing. Everyone was having a good time. It wasn't a bold good time, but people were making connections. That was good. Lucas hadn't left my side all night long. He cornered me in a back room for a short necking session, in which we both got so hot we had our ties off. But I put a stop to that. I wanted to get to know him, I didn't want a typical hookup. I didn't want sex.

What? That's just stupid. Of course I want sex! I just want more than sex. That's it.

Lora was being a dear and keeping things light and fun. She'd even proposed a game of some sort, but I didn't hear any takers yet. I did overhear her describing the habits of the group of immortals they met on the Caribbean island—how they went about their life completely naked because they never knew when the urge to fuck would come over them.

People laughed. It wasn't so much a nervous laugh. Rather it was a laugh of a group that wanted to try but didn't know each other Well, enough. Lora would change that pretty quick. I had to run upstairs and get my camera from my room. I wanted to start documenting the success of this party.

I spent a few seconds making sure I was still photo-ready before grabbing the camera and exiting the room. However, I ran into Lucas as he had followed me inside.

"What a fortuitous place to run into each other," he said to me. His gray eyes were drowning me in sex and lust.

"Um, I just came up here to grab a camera," I said. *Why was I like a schoolgirl, all nervous?*

"I want to kiss you again. I need to kiss you again, Justin. Don't make me beg."

I put down my camera and he was in my arms in a flash. He had me backed up against my bed in two steps, and pushed me over until I toppled. He was lying next to me before I could blink, he moved so fast. He physically stopped me from moving by placing his leg across mine and his hips on top of me. I could feel everything I wanted to feel, including his knee gently stroking my cock that was so fucking hard right now it was painful.

He held my head gently between his hands, but that was the only thing gentle about it. His lips were crushing mine in an erotic kiss designed to melt steel, and it very nearly was. I was quickly becoming a puddle of hormones, incapable of doing anything other than fucking this glorious man.

"Oh God, fuck me," I said between kisses.

"My pleasure," said Lucas. He rolled off of me and quickly removed his clothing. Fuck, he was perfect. He stood there a moment just so I could admire him. Everything was perfect, from the low hanging balls to the very long cock that was arcing toward me. He had a twelve pack, I was sure, because there were more muscles than I'd ever seen before. And his chest was cupped by beautiful pecs that were perfectly shaped for my hand to hold. The shining perfection was topped by nearly hairless, flawless skin that glowed a lustrous caramel color. Shit, he was so good I could eat every inch of him.

I was still clothed. Damn! I sat up and started taking off my jacket. He sat next to me and helped. His cock was standing up looking at me. I could not help myself, I went down on him right then. Taking his cock in my mouth, I ran my tongue across the tip and listened to him shiver and moan. He jerked in my hand as I sucked on him slowly and took his balls and squeezed them gently. His cock loved the attention, but he pulled me off and kissed me again, taking his time to explore my mouth thoroughly, while his fingers undid my shirt and pulled it off my body.

He pushed me down on the bed again and started kissing my chest, nipples, and the crease between my breasts, leaving little bites on the flesh that sent zings across my body. I was flying so high, I could barely contain my excitement. When Lucas got to my pants, I thought I would ejaculate right there and then. But he took my cock from my pants, as flooded as it was and ready to go off, and he took it into his mouth. It felt so hot that when he started sucking on me, I could help it, I let go.

He swallowed all of it and continued. Not content with one orgasm, he was building another, and it would not take long. He paused long enough to pull off my pants, and straddled me, gazing down at me.

"Geez, you're beautiful, Justin. Your body is a symphony, and your soul is the light. Let me gaze at you a moment before I take you completely and make you mine."

“Take me? Do you want to grab a condom?” I asked.

“No need, we don’t transmit disease. But if you have some lube…”

“Of course.” I reached over to my bedside table, but couldn’t reach. “It’s in there,” I said, pointing.

He leaned over and pulled out the drawer and the lube. He started slathering it all over his cock, then grabbed my ass and gave me a good lube job too. I lay back wondering what his next move was, when he lay down beside me. Reaching around, he started to play with my ass, first one finger, then two. I flipped over on my stomach and did a downward dog position to give him full access. Kneeling behind me, he gently pushed himself inside up to his head.

“Ah fuck! Oh God, that is good. So tight,” I screamed. “Give me more!”

He pushed in more, and I was singing his name. “More!”

Little by little, I felt him take more of me, push farther into me, until I felt his balls bang against my legs. He was fully inside. Oh God, that was amazing! *Fuck, fuck, fuck, fuck!*

“Justin, how do I feel inside?” he asked.

“Fucking amazing, Lucas. Are you completely in?”

“Yes, you’ve taken all of me,” he said, sounding surprised.

“Baby, fuck me, make me scream.”

“My pleasure,” he said in my ear. He wrapped one arm around my waist, held my hips with the other, and started to pump. The long slow withdrawal was excruciatingly exciting. As he withdrew, the anticipation of his thrust had me nearly peaking. When the thrust came, it again was slow and persistent. Lucas was a master, playing my body like an instrument. He climaxed on his fourth thrust. He tried to hold back on going fast because he wanted a slow burn, but that last thrust, he couldn’t wait and he pushed hard and fast. It nearly wasted me too, but not quite. My cock was ready to go. Giving me a minute while he got his breath, I changed positions with him, lubed up, and returned the favor.

"Ah no, not slow, Justin, fuck me hard," he said.

"Are you sure, hun?"

"Mmm, yes."

I bent down first and rimmed him, using my tongue to excite him. Then a little finger action to goose up the excitement. When I placed my lubed cock at his gate, the man pushed backwards on me to impale me halfway in one shot. He screamed out as I gasped in surprise.

"Fuck! Ah, ah, ah, oh that hurt a bit," he said.

"Are you alright?" I asked, as I started to pull out.

"I think so. No! Don't pull out. Please. Stay there, let me get used to your size. You're a big boy, and I love that."

"Okay, let me add some lube and go slower."

"Uh huh. Push again, all the way."

"If you say so."

With that, we both thrust together, and my cock slid home fully inside him. I'd never been fully inside a man before. It was quite the sensation. My cock was firmly held like a tight hand; I could feel him all around me. My tip was up against something, and that might be what hurt him. But he was groaning in pleasure as he moved around on my impalement. Eventually, he rose to his knees so that we were skin to skin, my front against his back while I pumped both of us into a lather. He was holding me with an arm to get leverage to push against me harder, while I wrapped my arms around his chest. My other hand was fisting his cock into a beautiful erection again.

My goal was that we both climax together.

The sweating, moaning, and low screams we were both emitting as our bodies took over our minds must have sounded loud. How did no one hear us? We fucked each other into oblivion and it was so good. Our climax was stupendous, exponentially higher than anything I had ever felt. We both collapsed on the bed together, glistening with sweat and feeling oh so satisfied.

"Oh my God, that was the best fucking sex I have ever had in my life!" I said.

"That was for me too," said Lucas. "I'm never going to want to fuck anyone else again, you know that?

"Lucas, hun, I don't ever want anyone else but you," I echoed. "But I have to get back to the party I am hosting."

"I know. I'll be waiting here for you, okay?"

I looked at him. He was serious, he wanted to stay in my bed. "Stay as long as you want, love. If there is more lovemaking later, nothing could make me happier."

I rolled off the bed, got dressed, splashed some water on my face, and tried not to have a JFL—but I couldn't help it. When the fucking is that good, nothing hides your feelings. Walking back downstairs, my legs were like jelly. I had to hold on to the banister so I didn't give myself away too much. I swear I could still feel him inside me.

With my camera in hand, because that was the reason I went upstairs, I rejoined my party, happy to see that it was still going strong, even after my hour-long vanishing act. A few people had left but it was only some of the witches from what I could tell. The rest, who were coupled up, were all sitting in a large circle in the middle of the living room.

I wonder what game Lora got them to play.

Approaching, I overheard Mary say to Duffy, "Would you like to go to dinner with me next week?" I didn't wait for the answer, but Duffy better have said yes!

Moving along the floor around the circle, taking photos, I overheard Seamus and Anita too. They were basically ignoring everyone else in the room and had eyes only for each other. It was adorable seeing the scruffy ginger man sweep the pretty senorita Anita off her feet. They were an unlikely looking couple, but their chemistry was off the chart.

Lora had some magical device floating in the air and spinning around. When it stopped, it pointed to two people on the opposite sides of the circle. They had to get up, and one would pantomime a word for the other. It generated lots of laughs and camaraderie. It was like a game of spin the bottle, without the teenaged necking.

I continued working my way around, taking photos of everyone, the food tables as empty as they were, and the decorations. I was happy with the way my party turned out. It was a success. Lucas came down the stairs a few minutes later and we made space in the circle to sit with everyone. Because we were late, Lora made us get up and do a turn immediately. The word I drew from the hat was kiss. Well, that was easy. I reached over to Lucas and kissed him deeply to a chorus of oohs and ahhs from everyone.

Life was getting much better.

34— New Orleans, LA

Andrews

My wakeup call came too early. I was still tired from the trip yesterday. However, I had too much to get done. A shower helped, and walking to a local restaurant and having a traditional breakfast of grits, eggs, and ham was a good way to get the brain going.

My journey to locate Staung started at the city registry. There were no records of Staung after the date of the gala. Even after he was supposedly released, if he returned to New Orleans, he didn't take up a tax-paying residence. So he was in the wind. That meant I had to visit halfway houses, rooming houses, and shelters.

With a list in my hand, I started pounding the pavement. Place after place the answer was no, they didn't know the man in the photo. A couple of times I got a yes, they had seen him, but no, didn't know where he was now. He was a ghost.

My last stop was a well-known alley for the homeless. I walked past these poor sods huddled in tents. There must have been more than a hundred people. At least they didn't have to contend with weather like we got in Montreal. Still, they got hurricanes here, and these folks weren't likely to be evacuated. Face after face, none was Staung. No one recognized his photo either. It occurred to me that Falon's charity could do some real good here. I would have to tell her.

I took a cab back to the hotel because I was too tired to walk. A message was waiting for me at the front desk when I returned. It was from Grisham. So I called him back.

"Andrews, we've got some very interesting data," said Grisham in a rush.

"Good morning to you too," I said.

"We've been monitoring that phone number," he continued. "It has had several calls to Bushing but also to a Swiss number we traced to the Order. When we looked into that number, we learned it has been in contact with Bushing's number for years. We looked up dates corresponding to the calls. We discovered there was a suspicious event, like a bombing, shooting, drowning, or something similar to a prominent local person with a sketchy background, in each case. Not only that, Bushing was booked on flights before and after those events each time."

"So what does all that mean?" I asked.

"I think it means Bushing was working for the Order, not for the group in New Orleans."

"What would he have been doing?"

"We think it was wet work."

"So does that mean they hired Bushing to take out the immortals in Montreal again?"

"Don't know, boss. But I'll keep digging."

Clearly, I needed to find out who was running the Brotherhood now. It was time to check out the address for their clubhouse.

Arriving in the Ninth Ward, I was struck first by the shiny new houses that were being built over the destruction of Katrina. But everywhere I looked I saw reminders of the devastation. The warehouses along the river, which once had booming businesses, were now vacant, broken, and falling apart. It was in one of these buildings the Brotherhood had claimed to have their meetings. Casing the place, I discovered their part of the building had no windows, but it still had four walls and a roof. So that was a bonus for them. The ground was littered with debris, and the entire property had been fenced off by the city with barbed wire to prevent people from exploring.

That was what must have attracted the Brotherhood to this location: That people were prevented from entering. I found a section of the fence between two buildings that had been cut, leaving a gap large enough to walk through.

There was a single door on one wall, and a small window beside it. It didn't look like a great place to sneak a peek, so I carefully walked around the building looking for another spyhole. Around the back, I found a loose piece of siding near ground level I could pry up. Working with my pocketknife, I was able to wiggle out the nails and pull back a section of siding large enough for me to crawl through.

That got me into the very back of the building. Several stacks of chairs were in the corner that could afford me cover. I was looking toward the door. There was a stage in front of me with a raised dais on it. An old door turned into a table was covered with a filthy cloth, and that was held in place by two large candlesticks. That must be an altar of some kind. But this wasn't a religion, so what was with the altar? Was the new leader turning it into a cult?

There were some excellent places for me to place surveillance equipment. I needed a couple of cameras and some directional mics. Since the building was empty at the moment, I went back to my car and grabbed my kit bag. I always traveled with basic equipment in the event I needed to do something in a hurry. My kit included tools, miniaturized directional mics, and wireless button cameras. It was just enough to cover the altar and the door.

It took me nearly an hour to install and test the cameras and mics, but I was satisfied they would not be detected. Next, I needed to find a place to sit and monitor them. There was a building across the street that was also abandoned, and would be close enough to get the signals. I decided to set up there.

Anticipating that their meetings would take place at night rather than during the day, I returned to my hotel to get supplies like food and water, chairs, blankets, and pillows. There was no point being uncomfortable on a stakeout.

I returned just before sundown and parked on the far side of the abandoned building across the street. It was an old two-storey house with all the windows boarded up. Boards were nailed across the door, but the door was unlocked. It was easy to gain entrance.

Going up to the second floor, I saw the filth accumulated in the building from Katrina. The walls were covered in mold up to the ceiling, and the wallpaper was peeling. Much of the drywall was gone and it was just studs. Upstairs was nearly as bad, but the higher elevation meant not as much mold. I chose a room closest to the warehouse, and it turned out to be the cleanest room in the whole house.

I took off a door and set it up as a table. I put two laptops on the table and hooked up the extra battery supply. It would kick in if they ran low on power. One would show me the feeds from the two cameras, while the other let me communicate with my team in Montreal. But I had a good eight hours before that. I unfolded my camping chair and made myself comfortable.

I didn't have to wait too long before people started showing up.

I hadn't noticed this during my initial foray into the building, but they were lighting the space with candles. Lots and lots of them. Candles lined the walls and there were large candelabras on the stage. It looked like a play set in the eighteenth century. I half-expected people to walk in slow procession wearing monk's robes. Surely they weren't playing that kind of cult game!

I had good views of the people coming in the door, and was able to snap clear photos of each face. This was good intel that we could hold on to—all the members of the cult could be identified.

When most of the chairs were filled, which was surprising, someone came out from behind a small wall at the back of the stage. It must have been used as a change room. The guy was wearing a robe with a hood, so I wasn't able to get a photo yet.

He approached the altar, said some nonsensical words in a chant, then threw back his sleeves and pulled out a knife. Making a cut horizontally on each arm, he held up his arms to the ceiling and yelled more nonsense. The "congregation" was mesmerized. In response to his words, they all threw up their arms to the ceiling with fists. This looked too much like a … Nazi meeting.

After a moment of silence, the person leading this fantasy threw off his robe and I finally had a face to take a photo of. I didn't recognize him at all, so when the data came back almost immediately as Douglass Staung, son of Derek, I was surprised. He looked too old to be Staung's son. Perhaps that was the drugs—they had a way of aging a person prematurely.The data came back almost immediately as Douglass Staung, son of Derek.

"Gotcha!" I said quietly. The data sheet kept scrolling past on the screen. He was a decorated vet, served two tours, and during his last tour had been a drone pilot, apparently a very good one. He had a half-sister named Analise who was a school teacher in New Orleans. They were estranged. Since being back on US soil, he'd had a lot of run-ins with the law, mostly small misdemeanors, but one was an arrest for murder—it was thrown out due to lack of evidence.

Douglass had been standing silently for about three minutes, just staring out at the followers seated in front of him. They were staring forward like zombies, utterly captivated by his every word.

"Brothers, I have sad news," opened Douglass. "Our initiative to remove the filth in Montreal has failed."

The entire audience gasped in sync.

"Not only that, my spies believe they are multiplying."

"This can't be allowed!" cried one of the voices.

"No, it cannot," said Douglass. "We must fight back. We must eviscerate them. We must rid the world of vampires!"

"You really are insane," I said to myself quietly. "Daddy taught you well, but perhaps you drank too much Kool-Aid."

"My father, praise his soul, would not stop. He would not rest. He would pursue them to the ends of the Earth. And so shall we!" yelled Douglass.

"How, Master?" asked a voice from the audience.

"I will handle this task this time. Clearly, I cannot trust anyone else to succeed. So I shall use the tools we have at our disposal."

"What tools are those, you idiot?" I asked the screen quietly.

"We shall rain fire down on them when they least suspect it! We shall be God's wrath! We shall burn them in hellfire!" he yelled.

"Yeah!" cheered the whole audience.

I had heard enough. I now had proof he was behind the bombing, and that he was going to do something else. I didn't know what, but I knew the significance of the term "hellfire." It referred to incendiary devices used by the military. And they were deployed by drone, something Douglass could do himself. Did he have those weapons? I needed to figure that out next.

35— Homeless

PI Adams

I had a few hours before I needed to be back at the warehouse to spy on them, so I decided to focus on trying to find Derek Staung.

The first place I went to, I discovered someone had been there already, asking about him. After visiting three other places and hearing the same thing, I knew someone else was working either the same case, or a related case. If it was a related case, perhaps they could share information.

My last stop was to a little-known sheltered spot where a number of homeless people could get out of the rain. It was a condemned rooming house. Closed since Katrina, the inside was littered with debris from the floods, and a lot of the lumber was rotted out. But when you're homeless you'll take just about any port in a storm.

My instinct proved good. There were at least five people sheltering inside. Without water or power, there was no heat or sewer. The smell was incredible. Lit only by burning oil rags or candles, the dim light showed no colors, but then you might not want to see in color in that setting.

I eventually found an old man, debilitated beyond thinking, lying on a pile of filth, drooling. There was a younger person with him, who seemed to be trying to care for him. I couldn't tell if it was a woman or a man.

I shone my flashlight on the face of the old man, and compared it to my photo. It was a match. This was Derek Staung. Who was the younger person?

"Hello there, my name is Adams."

"Go away! This is our place, you can't have it."

"I don't want your space. I just want to find a person, and I think I may have."

"Who are you looking for?"

"Derek Staung. Is that him?"

"Yes, this is my father."

"Your father?" I was surprised. "What is your name?"

"Douglass," he answered, elongating the S on the end like a hissing snake.

"Douglass, do you know you have a sister who has been looking for her father?"

"I don't have a sister. She's only half my blood. She and my father stopped speaking before I was shipped out."

"How old are you, Douglass?"

"I'm twenty-nine."

That was sad. He didn't look twenty-nine, he looked seventy-nine, but then his father didn't look the fifty-nine years he was either.

"Is this where you're living?"

"It's close to our clubhouse, and free, so yes."

"Free is important to you?" I asked. Poverty, poor nutrition, and lack of shelter would do this to anyone.

“Go away, there’s nothing here,” he said, waving his arm at me.

I had my quarry. My job was basically done now. All I needed to do was let my client know.

Except I was too curious to see what was happening at Staung’s “clubhouse.” I decided to return tonight and spy a little. I walked out of the rooming house as quickly as I could, holding my breath. I was sure there were dead bodies in there too. The stench was making me gag.

Clear of the building, I walked down the street. Under the dim, flickering streetlight, I pulled out my phone and called my client.

“Analise, it’s Marcy Adams speaking, how are you?”

“I’m fine, Ms. Adams. Have you found my father yet?”

“In fact, yes, ma’am, I’ve just located him,” I answered. “He’s alive, barely, and living in an abandoned rooming house down in the Lower Ninth. He’s with your step-brother. His name is Douglass, and he appears to be caring for your father, more or less.”

“Hmm,” said Analise. “Well, I thank you for your service, Ms. Adams. That concludes our business.”

“Is there anything you want me to follow up on?” I asked.

“No, that won’t be necessary. The fact that he’s still alive means that his will won’t be executed yet.”

“Of course, you were waiting to see if he was deceased,” I said. “It probably won’t be long. From the looks of him, he’s either starving or overdosing.”

“I will send people to the address you provide me, and we’ll handle it from here. I thank you. I know now who I can contact for future endeavors. Good day, Ms. Adams.” She hung up abruptly. I planned to send her my final invoice tomorrow morning, but this conversation left a cold feeling between my shoulder blades, and a bad taste in my mouth. I decided to send the invoice now. The sooner I got paid, the sooner I would not have any further contact with this family.

Back at the clubhouse, I'd just finished placing my directional mic as the sun was setting, and I was looking for a spot where I could sit and listen. Perhaps a room with a view, so that I could take photos of people going in and out of the building. That house across the street looked promising, so I made my way there. The front door was boarded up, so I crept around the side to the back door. It was unlocked but there were boards across it. Still, there was enough space for me to fit under, so I squeezed through and got inside.

The place reeked of decay and rot. It was pitch black; the only light was from the weak streetlight across the street. Not even as much as moonlight. It was utterly silent too, except for the tiny scratching sounds, indicating there were rats living in the walls and floorboards. I didn't mind rats as long as they kept to their own business.

I started walking toward where I suspected the staircase was and the floorboards creaked with each step.

"Stop right there!" came a masculine voice out of the dark.

"Eek! Who are you?" I asked, jumping out of my skin. I swallowed, took a deep breath, and calmed my heart rate down.

"Never mind who I am, who are you?"

"My name is PI Adams. I'm working on a case and I don't care why you're here. You can go on with whatever activities you were doing and ignore me. I'm just listening to the building across the street."

"PI, huh? Hmmm, listening across the street," said the voice. "Are you working on a case involving Derek Staung, by any chance?"

"Yes! Yes I am. Are you?" I asked. "Oh, you must be the person I was following asking about him."

"Yes. My name is Andrews, Robert Andrews. I'm not a PI, but I own a security company. I'm investigating a bombing that happened in Montreal. I have reason to believe Derek Staung's group is involved."

I flipped on my flashlight and shone it in the direction of the voice. Sure enough, a well-dressed man wearing headsets was standing in front of me. "Hi," I said lamely. "Perhaps we can work together?"

"I think that may be a good idea," said Andrews. "Let's compare notes, shall we?"

That was a great idea, because he had photos of all the members in the group. He also knew that they were responsible for the bombing, and I connected them with the gala. I told him I'd found Derek and that he was homeless and living in an abandoned rooming house. I also told him he was a vegetable and his son was caring for him, sort of.

"So what is this group? Do you know?" I asked.

"Yes, I do," he answered. "It's a group of people who believe in vampires, and they believe they are hunters."

"You're kidding!"

"No, sadly, I'm not."

Andrews then pulled up some footage he had shot the previous night. I watched Douglass come into the room and walk around theatrically before standing and delivering a speech that would make most people in their right minds laugh nervously.

"Wow. Isn't that something," I said. "I just don't know what."

"I think I need to infiltrate the group," said Andrews.

"I don't know about that," I said. "They're all white, you're black. In this town, that doesn't wash well. I suspect they're all incels as well."

"Incels?"

"Involuntarily celibate," I answered. "Young white men who can't get dates with women that lead to sex. So they blame all women."

"Now you're kidding."

"No, it's a thing."

"What are you looking for?" he asked me.

"I was hired by Staung's daughter to find him about a year ago. It's taken me all this time. Once I did, I discovered he has a son as well. They mentioned their clubhouse and I was curious about what sort of club it was. My research uncovered lots of unsavory things about Staung. I know his organization was involved in drugs and weapons, as Well, as a number of other illegal activities."

"Huh."

"Have you connected them to the bombing?"

"I think I have. Staung, or rather his son as I have found out, was the one that put the hit out. He planned for, hired, and executed a bombing meant to murder a number of people back in Montreal."

"That rant he did last night proves that, doesn't it," I said.

"It would seem so. Now I need to find out if he is planning anything else. I need to provide enough proof that the NOLA police and the FBI will act on it."

"There is another meeting tonight. Perhaps we'll get lucky," I said. It took a moment before I realized what that sounded like, and blushed red hot. Good thing it was dark. I heard him chuckle quietly.

"Perhaps we will. But I'll let you know I'm a married man, Ms. Adams."

"I am sorry, I didn't mean…"

“I know what you meant! I’m just giving you a hard time.” My turn to laugh.

“A hard time? I do declare!, Mr. Andrews, surely, you don’t believe I’m a girl of such low morals!” I said in my best Southern accent.

“Not at all, Ms. Adams, I wouldn’t dream of it,” he said, with a John Wayne accent. “Let’s keep watch here to see if we can learn more about his next action.”

“Agreed. Then we can both work on having this group arrested and shut down permanently.”

36— Surveillance

Andrews

PI Marcy Adams and I watched the Brotherhood's clubhouse for a week. Not much happened during the day, but the evenings were busy with meetings and practice sessions. Sharply at 7:30 p.m., the riffraff that was the membership started filing into the warehouse.

The same faces showed up, so we were able to get multiple images of each, confirming their identities. Most of them turned out to be runaways. Many had rap sheets filled with misdemeanors, and a few more had long sheets with robbery and assaults included.

Douglass, on the other hand, had a very long sheet. He was convicted for robbery, assault, sexual assault, grand theft, and conspiracy to commit murder. He had been in and out of juvie since he was eleven, and had spent three years in the pen recently. Douglass was bad news, not just batshit crazy.

Every night he ranted about the injustice of society against "his kind" and how they could not get any advantages because others stole all of them or were given them all by the government. He ranted about women, government, police, big business, you name it, and everyone else was to blame for his lot in life.

The breakthrough in our surveillance came six days into our operation, when he finally mentioned the Brotherhood and what its main focus was.

"Brothers, I don't need to tell you how many are against us, we all live the life. But there is a villain above all that controls humanity, that manipulates humanity into slavery to serve them. They alone hold wealth beyond measure because they have existed for so long. In one long continuous existence, they have accumulated power unparalleled to any billionaire today. They have stolen OUR wealth, OUR money, OUR jobs, OUR lives."

Douglass held the audience in his hand now. They were all rapt with attention.

"That is the supernatural, the long-lived, the undead," he said in a quiet tone. "Vampires, my brothers. They exist, they walk among us, they hold us in thrall, and they feed on our people."

The audience gasped in one breath. Then we heard all kinds of murmurs and chatting.

"Brothers, heed me, we need to destroy these monsters!"

The murmuring got louder.

"Can you prove they exist?" yelled one voice from the thrall.

"Yes, I can. I can not only prove they exist, but I know where they live and I know their plans. They inhabit every city."

My own ears perked up with that statement. I glanced at Marcy and she nodded to me.

"I heard that too," she said. "He claims to know their plans. But who is he talking about?"

"I'm afraid it may be my friends," I said, turning back to the meeting.

Douglass now started an elaborate story, telling the listeners how his father had tracked down a nest of vampires in Canada that were currently growing their numbers. They were living in plain sight and walking among the humans undetected.

"How can this be? I thought they couldn't go out in the daytime!" cried one of the voices.

"That is nonsense. Forget what you know of vampires from the movies," said Douglass. "They can go anywhere they want, anytime they want. They are faster and stronger than us. And they drink blood, but they can also eat human food."

"How do we kill them?" asked another voice.

"You have to remove their heads," said Douglass.

There were a lot of "ewws!" from the audience.

Douglass shushed the audience. He told them that a plan had been put into play to execute the leader and his minions a few years ago, but it had been thwarted. So he had developed another plan, this time to take the vampires out with a bomb.

I glanced at Marcy and she gave me the thumbs-up. I had them. I had the evidence now.

Douglass continued to tell them the details of his plan and how they had hired local specialists to carry it out. I got it all on tape, both video and audio recordings. The only thing I needed now was to find out if he planned to do anything more. But the meeting was breaking up. There were lots of little conversations.

"Do you think he's going to try again?" asked Marcy.

"Yes. It's just a matter of when," I said. "I need to keep listening. I don't want to get the authorities on them until I learn what his next plan is."

"Understood," she replied. "I guess we're back here again tomorrow."

"I guess so. I'll hang around a little longer to make sure they all leave."

"Okay," said Marcy as she got up and left. "See you tomorrow. Don't get caught."

I pulled out a sandwich I had packed and poured myself some coffee from my thermos while listening to the audio. Douglass was still there, milling around doing who knows what. The camera didn't show anything, because it wasn't focused on where he was. *I would need to fix that once everyone left. He may be doing something I need to see,* I thought to myself.

"Sir, can I have a minute?" said a new voice. I perked up my attention.

"Yes, son. What can I do for you?" asked Douglass.

"I want to be a member of your group, sir. I want to hunt vampires," said the obviously young man.

"Son, I would be honored to have you join my organization, once you've reached adulthood. You're what, fourteen?"

"No, sir, I'm seventeen. I'm old enough to fight for America," he sneered. "Why isn't that old enough for you?"

"America takes them younger than they should. I don't."

"What's the difference between seventeen and eighteen?" he asked. "Really?"

"You have to have finished high school to join me, son."

"Alright, then I can come back?"

"Yes, son."

I heard the young man leave. I got a look at him as he left the door, and he was certainly younger than seventeen. At least Douglass stopped at that. I heard him pick up his task and he walked back into view of the camera. He was on the podium setting up something. My exposure to Lora and magic told me it was a pentagram of some kind, as he was drawing an elaborate symbol on the floor of the stage, pouring sand or something to create a continuous line, first a five-pointed star and then a circle outside of it. Then he stood large pillar candles in each point of the star and drew designs between each point near the circle. He drew another circle in the middle of the star between the lines that crossed. He sat inside the inner circle cross-legged on the floor. Positioning his body in a meditation pose, he started chanting.

He was ramrod straight, sitting there for an hour or two, chanting quietly. Nothing happened. Then the candles suddenly blew out. There was another source of light, so the cameras could continue observing.

"Master, you have come!" cried out Douglass.

A whirlwind started up outside the largest circle and moved around the stage as if guided by remote control. When it stopped in front of Douglass, a wispy black form floated there, transparent and wavy in nonexistent wind. Two red orbs glowed near where the "head" would have been. This was clearly some sort of demon or ghost perhaps.

"Yes, Master!" answered Douglass without a question being asked.

"Master, how?" continued the one-sided conversation.

"I can do that, Master," he said after a minute of silence.

"It will be done!" cried Douglass after another minute of silence. Then the apparition was gone and the candles started burning again. I checked my video, and it was still recording. *Good, no one will believe me when I tell them about this! I thought.*

Douglass stood, leaving everything where it was, blew out the candles and left the building, locking up the front door. I spent the next thirty minutes rewinding and checking my surveillance video and audio, making sure it was good, making copies, and sending them off to several people. I wanted Lora's take on what that was, as Well, as Mark. I sent it to Grisham for research and to keep it on file.

I sent an email to Mark to tell him I had definitive proof that Douglass had ordered the bombing, not the Swiss. I also told him that I had the pictures and names of all the members in the group here in New Orleans.

I needed to spend another couple of nights here, to find out what the future plans were. But for now, I packed up my gear and bugged out of the old house and made my way back to my hotel.

After returning to my room, I made some quick calls home to update Justin, as Well, as to speak to Gwen to see how she was doing.

We spoke Well, into the night, some of it dirty enough to leave me Well, frustrated to not have her body there. But a cold shower helped. Food and sleep was what I needed.

37— The Final Plot

Andrews

It was around midafternoon the next day when I heard back from Grisham on the files I had sent him. He had conferred with Lora and Mark, and they didn't have a clue who or what Douglass had spoken to the night before. They were going to keep digging though.

Back in my spot, I set up the equipment again and got ready to wait for the meeting. Seven thirty arrived and I heard Marcy downstairs. She wasn't coming in stealthily this time. When she stepped on the top stair and it squeaked, I announced my own presence.

"Hi, Marcy."

"Hi, Andrews. I brought sustenance for the evening."

"Oh?"

"Yup, fried chicken from Willie Mae's Scotch House. The very best in N'Orleans."

"Oh wow, thank you. And cornbread too. That's my favorite."

"Well, you can't eat N'Orleans without cornbread, or sweet tea."

We sat in companionable silence, noshing on the great food and listening for the meeting to start.

"Hey, what's with the candles on the stage?" asked Marcy, when she looked at the laptop screen.

"Last night, after everyone left, Douglass did some kind of ritual and brought some kind of entity into the building."

"Entity?"

"Don't know what I was looking at, but I caught the whole thing on video."

"Can I look at it?" she asked.

"Sure. I'll send it to you. What's your email?" I pulled up the video on my laptop and sent it to her phone.

"Oh! My! Really? Wow!" she gasped, a few minutes later. "Um, I think I know what this is."

"Yeah?"

"Maybe. Can I show this to anyone?"

"Yes. If you can get some answers, that would be helpful," I said. "Look, people are coming in again."

We watched as the same people came in and took seats. There weren't as many tonight as the previous times I had been here. Roughly half of them were missing. They were all sitting in the front two rows as well. That didn't usually happen.

When Douglass came in, they all got to their feet and did an elaborate bow that reminded me of a Nigerian greeting. But instead of putting one hand on the floor and one behind the back, both hands were down in front, not touching the floor. They waited until Douglass touched their head before standing up and sitting again.

That little ritual was all about control. His control over them.

"Huh," murmured Marcy.

"Brothers, we have been given the word to go ahead with our next mission," said Douglass quietly.

The small crowd murmured quietly.

"Our master has told me what to do, and how to do it. We will try one last time to take out the vampires in Montreal, to burn them from their very nest. We will rain hellfire down on them."

"So they're going to use Hellfires?" I asked out loud.

"Do you know what this is?" asked Marcy.

"Yes, I know the term. It refers to an incendiary drone strike, air-to-air or air-to-ground missiles, military issue. They are hard to get."

"Do they look like this?" asked Marcy, holding out her phone with a photo displayed.

"Yes, that's a Hellfire missile. Where was this taken?" I asked.

"I was poking around the neighborhood a week ago and came across crates in an adjacent building from their meeting hall. I pried open one or two and found these. I snapped photos to show the authorities as soon as I knew what they were and who owned them. I also found five of these…" She flipped through photos until a drone displayed. "Will they carry those missiles?"

"That's a military issue drone and yes, it's designed to do stealth attacks with those missiles," I answered. "Can you please send me those photos and anything else you found?"

"Sending now."

"Let's find out what he has in store, shall we?"

"…at the appropriate time, we will let them fly and they will take out the entire compound. We just have to wait for the best opportunity when they gather together. Now, I need volunteers, four of you, to come with me on this mission." Everyone's hand flew up like a class of grade-schoolers eager to please the teacher. “Who has military training?” asked Douglass.

Most put their hands down, but six were still up.

“Okay, you six will start training with me tomorrow. We will meet here at noon. The best four will accompany me on the mission.”

“When will the mission happen?”

“I expect mid-summer.”

“That does it, Andrews,” said Marcy. “Now you have the means, we know who, and roughly when. Can we call in the cops now?”

“Yes, it’s time.”

We packed up all the equipment. I was going to sacrifice the mic and camera by leaving them in place. Who knows, they might come in handy in the future. Marcy and I arranged to meet at the main NOLA police headquarters the next morning at 9:00 a.m. She told me her father was the police captain there. We would make our report to him. Then it was back home for me to prepare.

But tonight, before I left New Orleans, I’d visit Bourbon Street. See what all the fuss was about.

38— Bourbon Street

Andrews

On my last night in New Orleans, I decided to go out and experience the French Quarter. I had heard so much about it, it would be a shame if I didn't spend a bit of time there.

Bourbon Street turned out to be a party—the whole street was the party. Booze everywhere, drunk people everywhere, and it was packed with tourists gyrating to the music spilling out from the clubs onto the street.

Between the women taking off their clothes, the free-flowing booze, and the beads being thrown around liberally, it was an easy place to find sex. While it's NOT a tradition, in spite of what you hear, women do NOT have to bare their bodies in exchange for gifts, but it seems tourists buy into this claptrap. But, of course, the tourists are there to have license to behave in a way they would not otherwise behave.

The disturbing part was the number of women quite alright with subjugating themselves like that. It was not surprising to see the number of men willing to take advantage of these poor drunk women, and that was a sad, black mark on my former species' behavior.

I had found a bar not too far from my hotel in the French Quarter where I could get some food as Well, as alcohol. I took a booth with a table for myself. It didn't take long before women were trying to sit down opposite me, propositioning me for any number of favors from squeezing their nipples, to outright fucking them on the table. It wasn't difficult to put them off. I told them I was gay. That made the occasional woman try harder to "convert" me, but most women it chased away. My bluff was blown when a group of women with a single man showed up and my gay line prompted him to make advances too.

Once I finished my meal, I walked back to the hotel. To my surprise, or not, I was tackled once or twice by women throwing themselves at me. One woman started humping me as she grabbed my pants. I had to pick her up and pull her off my body, placing her down on the ground and away from me. She was so far gone, she turned around and humped the next guy. Sigh.

As I made my way through the crowd, a pair of hands slid under my shirt and up my stomach to my nipples and started tweaking them. I had to grab those hands to stop them. Pulling the arms out from under my shirt, I turned around to see a woman standing behind me dressed in a Brazilian samba costume with layers of beads and feathers around her neck enough to cover her breasts, and wearing a bikini bottom appropriate for a Mardi Gras parade. It was a French-cut thong, strung with feathers, beads, and fringe worthy of the best Vegas dancers. She started shaking her body and pivoting so that I could see her lovely ass as she shimmied and shook what "her momma gave her" for all she was worth.

The woman had changed my grip so that she was holding my hands instead of me holding her hands. She took my hands, and pressed them against her well-endowed breasts. Then she leaned against me full-body, still shaking her ass, and pushed against my growing erection. Sometimes you just have no control over your body's reaction. As she continued her dance against me, she moved her hands down to her pussy, pulling my hand along, and as she pressed my fingers into her pussy her squirming intensified. The other hand left mine on her breast and reached around her and pulled my head toward hers. She turned her head and laid a deep kiss on my lips as she pushed my fingers into her vagina. Her tongue mimicked the action.

My breath hitching with the excitement that was building in my body, she took that as consent to leave my hand in her panties and reached into my pants. Her hot soft hand found my stiff cock in short order. As she wrapped her lithe fingers around my member, it stiffened more and danced. Somehow, she got my zipper open and had me out of my constricting clothing. She made her intent clear as her body rotated until she had her front pressed up against mine as hard as could be. She never broke the kiss. One hand was wrapped around my neck and the other was on my cock. She wrapped a leg around my hips as she thrust my cock between her legs.

It missed entering her, barely. She whimpered a little at her error, and tried again. She'd forgotten my hand was in the way. She removed my hand and my cock slid home inside her. Her gasp of delight was contagious, and the pleasure took me too. But this had gone too far, I had to stop.

"I can't do this," I said.

"Why ever not? You're hot. I'm hot. We're here, and you're oh so ready," she murmured into my ear. Her hips started moving again. I had to physically separate us, and held her by the shoulders at arm's length.

"Stop!" I said. "I'm married, I'm a father, and I don't want to do this."

"Liar! You do want to do this."

"I may have once upon a time, but now I'm loyal to my mate. Please, find someone else to play with." I turned away from her, tucked myself back together, and pushed my way through the crowd to return to my hotel room.

39— The Amazon

The woman stood there pouting. She was hot and bothered, and had felt the connection that she had with that man was genuine; she sensed they were the same. She needed sex, now. She turned about face and was about to walk into the crowd in search of another male when before her was this vision.

Tall, blond, fair, chiseled cheekbones, eyes like deep pools of water, and a body that was delicious to look at. She stepped close to him and wrapped her arms around his neck.

"Take me," she breathed into my ear. "Fuck me hard."

"Here?" he asked, as he briefly glanced around at the crowd around them. No one was paying attention to anyone in particular—most were engaged in similar behavior. In fact, there were so many bodies crammed in together in the street, they were supporting each other as they danced, shimmied, and fucked. There was a whole lot of copulating going on. The lewd behavior seemed normal for the crowd as no one was stopping it. He looked at the Amazon, deep into her eyes.

"Where, then?" she asked, licking her lips.

"Where are you staying?" he asked.

"I am in the hotel on the corner."

"Let's go. Lead on," he said. She grabbed his hand and walked toward the sidewalk. It only took them a few minutes to get to her room, and once the door was closed she was on him like fly paper.

This was definitely a no-name sex session. No words were exchanged, only grunts and moans. She repeated her performance from the street, leading him to the bed. The beads around his neck nearly strangled him, so he removed those in order to pay proper homage to her wonderful breasts. Her beaded thong didn't last, breaking under the strain his hand put it under. Another of his hands was between her legs, penetrating her with prejudice, working the Amazon up to a lather. Her moans of delight were enjoyable to listen to. When she started panting and begging him to fuck her, he slid out of his pants and took her. She wrapped a leg around his hips so she could lift herself up and give him wonderful access. As he pushed deeply inside her, she screamed with ecstasy and held on tightly.

"Oh God, that is perfect," she murmured, as he thrust again and again, going deeper each time.

Her climax was delicious, as her body flooded with endorphins and the scent of her bloomed on his nose. He held off his own orgasm, wanting to make her come again. She reached up with both arms and pulled him down on her chest. He felt her lips kiss his neck, then a gentle lick, before a slight sting. The drug hit his blood, surprising him totally as he rode a wave causing him to climax, but not come.

He sucked in his breath to cover his climax, and suddenly realized what or who lay underneath him. She didn't know what he was though.

"Do you like it rough?" he asked her, in a rough voice due to the arousal he was feeling.

"Yes, I do," she said coyly.

He pulled out of her, which made her cry out, flipped her on her stomach, and then took her from behind, driving into her with all his length, causing her to cry out over and over again. He was pushing the limit, but if she was what he thought she was, this would only heighten her orgasm. As he grew harder, he started tipping her, and the sensation caused him to moan loudly, and she gasped first in pain, then in delight as he filled her completely. Their orgasm was epic. They both came, their bodies shuddered, synchronized, releasing endorphins.

She glanced around her shoulder to look at him, and saw his visage was that of his true self, glowing eyes and fangs. She smiled and bit him on the bicep. He leaned down and bit her shoulder, giving her his venom as she had given him hers.

He woke up and looked at the clock on the side of the bed. It was flashing 6:43. Disoriented, he shook his head, rubbed his eyes, and looked again. The room wasn't right. This wasn't his room. He rolled over and discovered the Amazon sleeping contentedly next to him. Oh yeah, he had truly amazing sex last night with her. He still didn't know her name, but she was like him.

He was watching her sleep, when she opened an eye and looked at him.

"Morning," she said with a sultry voice. "I knew you would be a good fuck."

"Really? How?"

"I could smell you. I could sense who you were, what you were. Like me," she said.

"I don't have that skill yet," he said.

"No? How strange. I thought all our people could."

"How many of our people are in New Orleans?"

"A few. Not many. We used to have a bigger community, but it was getting difficult to hide. So we split up."

"Hide?"

"Vampires, we have to hide, because there is a group here that tries to kill us."

He choked on her last statement. "Vampires?" he asked incredulously.

"Yes, you're one too—you bite and have venom. The stories have it wrong, we don't drink blood at all, but we do bite."

"You think you're a vampire?"

"What else would you call us? I was turned many years ago by a very old vampire. He's gone from the city now, but he taught me what we were."

"How long have you been like this?"

"About seventy-three years. I was turned during the early twentieth century."

"What's your name?" he asked.

"I don't give out my name, hun," she replied. "What's yours?"

"Mine? It's Torion. How about I just call you Amazon."

"I like that. Let's go with Amazon."

"Amazon, you're not a vampire. You are not human, and you're like me, but we're not vampires."

"What are we, then?"

"I don't know, yet. Something else, I just don't know what yet. But I intend on finding out."

"Well, if you don't mind, I'll continue with what I think until proven otherwise."

"Suit yourself. I've gotta go. It's been nice."

"Yeah, maybe we'll knock boots again."

"Knock boots?"

"Have sex."

"I'll think about it. If I change my mind, I'll come get you. Or I'll see you on Bourbon Street again."

40— Police Update

Andrews

Meanwhile, grateful I escaped the woman in Bourbon Street last night, I decided to meet PI Adams at the police station. Walking into the station, an officer asked me if she could help.

"My name is Robert Andrews. I'm an investigator from Montreal. I'm here to see PI Adams." The officer smiled and went back to her desk. PI Adams walked in a few minutes later.

"PI Adams, nice to see you again," I said.

"Oh, stop with the PI this and PI that. Call me Marcy. We can go right on back to the captain's office," she said walking through the door.

She knocked on the captain's door, and we heard "Enter!" from inside.

"Dad—uh, Captain, this is Robert Andrews, an investigator from Montreal. He and I have unknowingly been working on the same case, and we have some information for you."

"Good morning, Andrews," said the captain. "Please, have a seat and tell me what it is I can do for you."

I ran the captain through my case, giving him enough detail to merit a look, and all the details we had uncovered here in New Orleans.

"Okay, son, what am I supposed to do with this information?" he asked.

I bristled under the word "son," but ignored it as an affectation of the South. "I was hoping that you would arrest them."

"It doesn't work like that, son," he said. "I can't go arresting white folk without proof of wrongdoing."

Would you arrest black folk without proof? I thought. The blatant racism in his statements was hard to take. But I couldn't antagonize this man.

"I just laid out for you the connection between this club in New Orleans, a hitman specializing in explosives in Montreal, and a bombing of a restaurant in Montreal. Does that not merit an investigation at least?"

"Now, boy, that isn't anything done here," said the captain. "He has to do something here."

"Please, stop calling me boy. I'm not your boy, nor your son."

He looked at me and the anger was visible. Luckily, his daughter distracted him.

"Dad, uh, Captain, this club, the bombing, and all is connected to Derek Staung. We located him here in New Orleans."

"I see," he said. He was quiet for a few minutes while I silently seethed at the racism— unintentional or not—of his statements and actions.

"Moreover, Captain, we have proof that he is planning on another action," she continued. "We don't know when exactly, but we have enough to know how and where."

"What sort of proof?"

"Surveillance footage, both audio and video," I said.

"You bugged them?" asked the captain.

"I planted a surveillance camera inside their meeting room, and a microphone near the stage of the meeting room, yes. Then I have electronically recorded whatever was said inside the meeting hall over the past three nights."

"What did you hear?"

"We both heard that they were the ones behind an attack in Montreal about two years ago. They were also the ones that ordered the hit by bomb this past New Year's Eve, and that they are going to try a third time to kill a group of people in Montreal. The son, Douglass Staung, has a deep revenge-lust for this."

"May I please have a copy of that surveillance footage?" asked the captain.

"Yes." I pulled out a flash drive and handed it over to him. "I made a copy for you."

"Thank you," he said, taking the thumb drive from me. He slipped it into a USB port and opened the video file. The captain sat there watching the video for a few minutes, shaking his head at the language and antics of Douglass as he hopped around the stage. The ritual he performed alone alarmed the captain, and he turned it off at that point.

"Do you know what he was speaking to in that ritual?" I asked.

"No, sir, I do not. But I have my people looking into it."

"You'll likely not find it anywhere but here in N'Orleans," said Adams.

"What is it? Do you know?"

"I'm afraid I do," said the captain. "That there is a demon." The captain pointed to the image frozen on the screen. All we saw on the video was a grayish black smudge of smoke.

"He is speaking to a demon," continued the captain. "There is a lot of demonic worship in this city. It's done for the tourists, and pretends to be voodoo, but it's just claptrap."

"Demons?" I asked. "You're telling me they're real?"

"As far as Voodoo is considered, absolutely," said the captain.

"So what do we do, Dad?" asked Adams.

"What can you do, Captain?" I asked.

"Not much. I will send some officers to look for the weapons you mentioned. We can arrest them for as long as we can prove they are the ones who own them. We will watch the group now. If they look like they are building up to another attack, we can stop them then. But now … there's nothing we can do. Foreign crimes are foreign crimes. Now if the Montreal police want to do something, we can assist."

I left the police station feeling as though I'd been slimed. The lack of interest in this group was astounding. At home, they'd be all over a group like this. I was glad the daughter was not like her father.

My flight back home was uneventful. I landed in Dorval and Gwen met me there. She immediately picked up on something.

"What's wrong?" she asked.

"A few things," I said. "Let's talk when we get home."

Gwen brought me up to date on what was happening here with everyone. As I turned into the driveway, she looked sidelong at me. Her expression was pensive. I put my suitcase upstairs, looked in on my son, and came downstairs to see Gwen paying the babysitter and saying goodbye. I poured us each a drink and sat in the living room.

Taking her glass, Gwen sat beside me.

"Okay, give it up, what happened?" she asked.

"I almost had sex with a strange woman."

Silence.

I didn't look at her face. I must admit I didn't have the courage.

"Almost? Why?"

"It was a Bourbon Street thing. I was a little drunk."

"But you didn't."

"No, I stopped her."

"What's her name?"

"I have no idea. What's interesting is that she is one of us."

Silence.

"How do you know?"

"I could sense something different about her. She didn't smell like a human."

"Perhaps you should bring her to Montreal. Maybe we can mate her to one of our people."

"I thought of it, but I don't have a way of contacting her."

"That's good because you're mine."

"And you're mine. I love you."

41— Case Closed

Justin

I got a call from Andrews. He'd figured out the case. He knew who bombed the restaurant, and more importantly, why. He told me that he had one more thing to do in New Orleans and that was to speak to the police there to make arrests. Then he would be back in Montreal to have the Surêté du Québec arrest the responsible people in Montreal.

It's done. I felt a huge weight lift from my shoulders. The weird thing was it wasn't about me or the restaurant. It had been another plot by the same people who had tried to assassinate Mark and Falon at their gala nearly four years ago. The son of the man they eliminated was taking revenge. It was a good thing we hadn't had all the immortals in the restaurant that night.

Then I remembered the mixer I had recently and my blood ran cold. *Good thing he didn't find out about that event, or there would have been dead immortals.*

Andrews assured me that there wouldn't be another attempt on my restaurant.

I called Rick and suggested we get together to talk about the future of the restaurant. He agreed.

We met downtown at a café that served amazing beignets.

"Hey, Justin, how are you feeling?" asked Rick.

"Great, thanks. Much better since hearing from Andrews about the case."

"Fill me in," said Rick. So I repeated what Andrews had told me.

"I think we can start to look forward again. Since the Atlanta restaurant is basically managing itself now, we don't need to be there anymore. You haven't been down there in ages, and neither have I. The chef and I speak every week, but he's doing wonderfully. So I propose we cut him into the profits there. That will make him even more autonomous, and will leave us to develop this property."

"Hmm, do you want to do that again here?" asked Rick.

"Yes. Just because we were bombed doesn't mean I am not committed to building in this amazing city. Besides, we own that property. We have to do something with it."

"True. So what do you want to do?"

"I'd like to rebuild the property like it was, with two floors of apartments, a main floor dining, and a second-floor dining."

"Do we have the funds?"

"Some. Here's the good thing: the city of Montreal, because it's a heritage building, will provide some of the monies we will need. The insurance will pay for about sixty percent of the replacement value, and that leaves perhaps thirty percent for us to come up with."

"Put that into dollars for me."

"Well, I have to get some quotes. But if you're not interested, I won't bother."

"No, I'm interested. I'm just putting some of my funds into a new project with Mark. It's a long-term project. But, you know, I'll bet Abeo would be interested in investing in the restaurant. What about Lucas?"

"Lucas?"

"Yes, the new guy in your life?"

"He has money?"

"Well, he's as old as Abeo, and he's part of their bank. He should be as well-heeled as Abeo is."

"Hmmm, I'll speak to both of them. Okay, so I will gather the quotes, make a financial plan, and then we'll touch base again."

"Sounds good."

Lucas didn't live in Montreal, so we didn't see each other frequently. However, since the mixer, we had spent a couple of weekends together. I didn't know him Well, yet, but what I did know I didn't want to do without. When I called him and asked if he'd be interested in investing in our new restaurant, he jumped at the chance.

"How much do you need?" he asked.

"I don't know yet, I still have to get quotes. But I wanted to see who or where the funds would be coming from before I did that."

"Well, count me in. I'm good for seven figures if you need it," said Lucas.

"Seven figures? Wow, thanks, hun."

"Justin, I'm interested in more than weekends with you and temporary trysts."

"I just need to go slowly."

"Why?"

"Because I'm not great at relationships. I'm good at sex. But relationships elude me," I said honestly.

"Slow it is. It's not like we'll run out of time," he joked.

When I spoke to Abeo later, he too was interested in investing, to the tune of seven figures. I don't think I would need that much from either of them, but it was nice to know it was there. My next call was to the city of Montreal, to establish the scope of the project, to get the name of a builder that would do the restoration, and to get a quote.

Once the building was figured out, I could go shopping again. I think I'd simply reconstruct the exact same style, decor, and furniture. After all, I didn't really get a chance to wear that look out, did I?

42— Back in Build Mode

Justin

I'm building again! Yeah!

First things first, I consulted with the city about the restoration of the building, and the highly skilled artisans who would make a new building look like a two hundred-and fifty-year-old one. Frankly, I'd believe it when I saw it.

I was lucky that Montreal already had a lot of experience with restoring their heritage buildings. They even had websites for DIYers who wanted to try their hand.

At least I was smart and took lots of photos of the building before and after we finished our renovation the first time, so I had detailed photos on the cornices, windows, doorways, and stonework that would make it simple to replace. Well, simple, no, but at least they'd have something to guide them.

It started with the structure. Nothing was salvageable. We packed up the two upper floor apartments and put them into storage. I had been paying for a hotel for those two families already. That would continue until they could return.

The next step was to salvage any stonework we could for the facade. Then we demolished the rest. That was easy, if not cheap. Bringing down an old building without damaging the ones next to it was an art form. The demolition company's work was flawless.

On the day they brought it down, it was announced on the news. A huge crowd gathered to watch the show. They had draped the lower two floors that were damaged by the bomb with heavy tarps beforehand. Then, at precisely 11:00, a whistle blew to tell everyone to clear out. They started a countdown from ten, and boom! The dynamite blew on every corner and every floor, causing the rest of the structure to pancake on itself inside the confines of the building. A humongous cloud of dust exploded out from the base, covering everything in its path, and when it cleared a few minutes later, there was no building. In fact, all the rubble was down in the basement with a small hill in the center. It had been mostly masonry, so it came apart easily.

Now the task was to clear the site to the foundation and start new. The new building would be modern construction with steel guts. Then we would use masonry for the street sides of the building, but modern cladding on the other two walls. The new building would not be attached to the one next to it this time, keeping it a free structure. That was the fire code now. That would have an impact on the inside square footage, so I had to adjust our blueprints accordingly. That was an expense I hadn't anticipated. *C'est la vie!*

Once all that was started, the foreman was in charge and my hands were freed up. I could go shopping for the interior. I started with the same furniture cabinet maker I used the first time, Soufrière et Fils in Trois-Rivières.

"Pierre Chenotte, how nice to see you again!" I cried when he came out of his office to greet me.

"Justin Madera, it is a pleasure. Do you need more furniture for your restaurant? Are you expanding?" he asked me in perfect English.

"You speak English!" I said, smiling.

"Yes I do. At first I wait to see if a customer is going to be a good one," he said with a shrug. "You, sir, were a very good customer. You paid me in advance!"

"I like treating the people who work for me with respect. They are doing something I cannot. They deserve my respect."

Pierre smiled warmly at me and said, "What can I do for you today?"

"I do indeed need more tables and chairs. In fact, I'm placing the exact same order as before."

"Pourquoi?"

"Why? Well, our restaurant got attacked and was demolished. We've started rebuilding now." I didn't feel like going into an explanation about a bomb, so I left that out.

"Quel dommage, monsieur. I'm sorry to hear this. You are a good man. It's terrible what happens today. What is your timeline?"

"The building won't be ready on the inside for eight-ten months. So I think you have lots of time, no?"

"Yes, that is plenty," he answered. "Oh, by the way, just in case you may have needed additional, I made a couple of each to keep in inventory. Come look please."

I followed him back deep into the workshop. You could smell cut wood, and hear the buzz of various machines at work. I stopped a second to watch someone work a machine that put notches in wooden legs so they could be joined without screws. It was brilliant! When the two pieces of wood were put together, it looked like one piece of wood.

The tables I had ordered before were set up as a display, stacked with the smallest on top. It was nice to see them there, assembled and looking lovely.

"Justin, do you want the same finishes and colors?"

"Yes, Pierre, exactly the same. No changes," I said, handing him my AmEx card. "Please charge me the whole order now, so you have the funds to go shopping."

"*Merci*," he said. "If we cannot match the fabric, do we contact you?"

"No, Pierre, I have complete confidence that you can select the appropriate fabrics. You know my taste, and what era we are going for."

"Merci, monsieur."

My next stop was to repurchase cutlery, linens, glassware, and anything else we would need. All this would be kept in storage until we could deploy it. I wanted to get things as close to the period as possible. Again, we had to have the cutlery made for us, but I returned to the same supplier. The glassware was simple enough because it was off the shelf.

The linens were easy. White and Aubergine, in sets of opposite colors to be able to dress the tables either way. I found the same candelabras for centerpieces in flea markets and stores in the area. I also found wall sconces and chandeliers that mimicked the candelabras. The wall that had been covered in bookshelves was gone, but luckily I salvaged most of the collection of books. I went hunting at estate sales to get more. I found bookends and knickknacks, too, which all went together really well.

With most of the decor ordered, I needed to touch base with my executive chef, Marcel Divigne, about ordering the kitchen.

"Marcel, I need a new list of what you want in the kitchen," I asked him when I got him on the phone.

"The same thing, please."

"Marcel, I don't remember everything you asked for. Please send me a list. And, if you discovered anything that didn't work as it was supposed to, or was missing, include that on your list please."

"Alright, give me a day or two please," he said. "By the way, I appreciate that you have continued to pay me during this investigation. When do you think we can get back up and running?"

"I think it's going to be a year, Marcel. If you want to work somewhere else in the meantime, I don't mind. Don't get stale."

"What about doing a food truck? We could use it for catering later," he suggested.

"Hmm, let me think about that. It may be an interesting idea. Have you got more data on that?"

"As a matter of fact, yes. I've been thinking of it for about a month now. I hate being idle, and I thought it could be something I do while I wait."

"How far have your plans gone?"

"I have the license and I've been shopping for a truck," he said. "I haven't got a menu or a name yet."

"Cool, let's brainstorm on that in a day or two. Get me a list for the kitchen first please so I can get it all ordered."

"You bet."

A food truck! *Why didn't I think of that?* "That's a great idea!" I said out loud.

43— Food Truck Launch

Justin

I got off the phone with Marcel and couldn't clear my mind of his idea of a food truck. It would be at least a year before the new building was finished and we had a restaurant again. I didn't want to wait that long, and clearly I couldn't pay Marcel to do nothing that long either. A food truck was a spectacular solution. Montreal had quite a few trucks operating, and most of them were frites and hotdogs.

I could envision a different kind of food truck, specializing in good food, like four-star dining, without the table. I had to do some research.

Calling Marcel back, I asked, "Why don't we do a simple menu that is derivative of the food we will have in the restaurant?"

"Such as what?"

"Such as a fish dish and a meat dish. Perhaps we could do wraps, or on baguettes. Fish and rice or meat and rice. The meat and fish can be prepared for grilling, into strips that would easily fit in a wrap or baguette. Then fill with veggies and a sauce."

"I like that idea. The meat and fish could be "of the day" so we aren't tied to one in particular," suggested Marcel.

"Yes, and we can bake the bread on the truck. We could also have a soup of the day."

"Soup requires containers and utensils," said Marcel. "Instead, what if we have a menu that is entirely 'green' to eat—no waste to dispose of."

"Oh, that's good, Marcel. That's amazing, and very now too. So, if we wanted to make soup, we could put it in a bread bowl."

"Great idea! Now I'm getting excited. What shall we call it?"

"How about 'A Taste of l'Escalade'?" I asked.

"Un Goût de l'Escalade," he said. "I like it. It will keep the restaurant's name forefront, and can work back and forth on business."

"Okay, then let's do this. Go and find a food truck for us and get it registered and I'll start working on recipes and menus."

"Where do we want to set up?"

"Close to our location?" I asked.

"That may be possible. I will go and check the area to see if there is room. Then I will make sure the truck has what we need for cooking. I think a grill, an oven, fridge of course, a press?"

"Yes, make that two ovens if possible."

"Will do. This is exciting. Thank you, Justin."

"My pleasure. This is fun!"

Within five weeks, we found a used truck that fit our needs, had it painted, settled on the location, and set up a menu. For our first day on location, *tomorrow*, I was busy prepping some of the food at home and Marcel was packing the truck. He had two dozen small baguettes ready for baking already. We had all our sauces ready, the meat prepped, and the salad ready to go. I was just making vinaigrette to take with us.

Sitting on location, we were across the intersection from the building where the restaurant would go. There was no other restaurant on this corner, so it should be lucrative. We got the grills running, the bread baking, and I had several pieces of fish and steak already cooking slowly. It was almost noon. We were holding our breath.

Our food truck's awning was open but I didn't have the window open yet. I was leaning over to do that when I saw several people walking toward the truck.

"*Bonjour!* Would you like something to eat?" I asked.

"Bien sûr!" said our first customer. She selected the fish of the day in a baguette and a 7Up to drink.

The second customer chose the same, and it kept going until we had no more food! We were sold out in twenty-five minutes! I ran to the market, purchased supplies, and ran back to the truck, where the two of us were happily chopping, cooking, and making more lunches for the people around us. Marcel and I were in our version of heaven—cooking for others. We shared that love and a vision for what could be done.

We sold out a second time by 1:30 that afternoon. We happily closed the awning and took the score of what we sold. All of our wraps sold, and the baguettes went first. Based on sales, we'd need a minimum of fifty baguettes for tomorrow. I went through three pounds of fish and six pounds of beef. Even portioning it out to one-ounce sizes, that didn't nearly go far enough.

The next day, we were prepared for an onslaught of fifty to seventy-five people this time. We were not disappointed. With a different fish and meat this time, we paired different sauces. The variety made the same people come back and order something different. The portions seemed to be good, because we didn't have people ordering two. If one wasn't enough, then it was too small.

It became clear, very quickly, I needed to get Marcel some extra hands. I figured we could fit perhaps another two people inside the truck. One working at the grill/fry area, and another chopping.

We were getting requests for desserts too. So Marcel went down the street and visited a bakery. He ordered two dozen of their pastries for the next day. He also brought some of their business cards. These pastries were a hit, and we established a running order with the pastry shop for two dozen per day. The owner of the shop came and set up a refrigerated display case.

So far, the truck was a huge success! We left a tip jar and a suggestion jar on the counter, and got lots of ideas from our customers on what they thought would be good to try. Marcel and I had fun in the mornings coming up with recipes to make some of them. Soon, we had enough recipes that we could have something different every day of the business week.

Two new cooks started with me at home, and I taught them our food prep procedures. They worked for me for a day, then I had them meet us at the truck for duty the next day.

"Marcel, I've hired you some hands, because I may not be able to be on site every day with you. I've trained them with the basics at home. May I present Michelle and Carson. They both have culinary training, and have gone through hospitality training as well."

"Welcome, kids. Which stations would you like to work first? I could use one on the grill/fryer, and another on chopping/prep?" asked Marcel.

They weren't kids, but to Marcel and I they seemed like it. In their early twenties, they had the energy of rabbits! Their help was welcome, and orders were getting prepared quicker and with the same care we would have. All of a sudden, the truck was pumping out meals like crazy.

Our next improvement, suggested by our customers, was a coffee maker. Our new employees were delighted with that too, because both of them had had short terms at places like

Starbucks, so they were trained in coffee art. They both shared that job.

We streamlined the beverages by having bottled water, three different sodas, and the coffee bar. We'd see how that went. Beverages took up a lot of room in the fridge. Positive feedback included the fact that there was no garbage waste if they finished their lunch. Even the soup in a bread bowl was a hit, but we needed spoons for that. Marcel located some wooden spoons for eating. We were asked numerous times for straws, and we had to say we didn't have them until Marcel suggested we have a stock of non-disposable straws for sale. That became a hit too.

We ended up doing about five hours of prep work every morning, which sold out in two hours for lunch. We opened for lunch at 11:30 a.m. and extended lunch to 2:00 in the afternoon. We usually had to send either Michelle or Carson to the market for more ingredients. But so far, everything we made was sold. No waste. If we could keep that up, we'd be making profit soon.

I got a call from Falon. She said they were having a big BBQ party and asked if the food truck would cater. Marcel was happy to get that booking. I suggested that he get together with Carlos; the two of them would have an amazing business. If the truck could get catering jobs for holidays and weekends, and then be busy for lunch during business hours, we'd have a profitable business.

44— Labor Day

Falon

Mark kept his promise to buy us a new home, and with the baby on the way he went big. A house down the street from Rick and Lora's came up for sale. It was nearly as large as theirs, with a pool and it was on a two-acre lot. The important thing was it had a large kitchen and dining area so we could have large parties.

We moved in early April and settled quickly. Mark hired painters to freshen up the house, so that was one thing we didn't have to do.

When the snow melted, we got our first look at the garden. It was a mess! Things were overgrown, and the deck was cracked. So, Mark hired a landscaping company to come and redo the backyard. It was a big job and took two months, but when it was finished the pool had a new liner, there was a cabana out back, and an outdoor kitchen similar to Lora's. There was even a pretty koi pond integrated into the landscape. It was a favorite spot for me to sit by in the morning on a swing having a coffee. It helped center me for the day.

We wanted to celebrate our move and new backyard, so we decided to host a Labor Day party. We invited the whole gang. Justin's immortals-only party inspired me. Our group needed more time to mingle and form a community together. So an end-of-summer party seemed ideal.

During that Labor Day afternoon, the youngest kids were playing in the splash pool while the older ones watched. That gave us adults some downtime. Mark wanted to play chef, but I told him that I had hired Justin's new food truck to cater for us. So Mark played bartender.

Lora told me that the witches had been working on a special surprise for the party. That was planned for the evening. Until then, we had music playing and people were dancing. We set up a karaoke machine and everyone was having fun taking turns on the stage.

I was standing off to one side watching the crowd; there were some new couples forming. Duffy was sticking close to Mary, the witch living with Margaret. They seemed to be getting along really well. Mary wasn't a woman easily denied, so Duffy was definitely taken. Anita, Lora's housekeeper, and Seamus, a male witch who was staying at Andrews' old condo, were also a couple. They were over in a corner Anita sitting on his lap, staring into each other's eyes. I suspected more was happening than was visible.

The third couple I noticed was Justin and Lucas. While more reserved among the crowd, they didn't seem to stray too far from each other, touching one another frequently, like a hand here or a shoulder there, or brushing past each other making skin contact. It was nice to see. I originally thought Greggory was going to hold Justin's attention. But perhaps becoming immortal changed his mind.

There were still a few singles among our crowd. I guess we'd see who ended up with who. I walked over to check on Marcel, who was running the food truck tonight, to see if he was okay or needed hands.

"Nope, everything is under control," said Marcel. "Carlos has been a big help. I think we're almost done. All the food has been consumed, the dishes have been cleaned up and stacked in your kitchen, and we're just about ready to leave. How would you like to pay?"

"What would you prefer?" I asked.

"Visa, Mastercard, American Express, cash, whatever."

I checked the bill, and told him to wait while I went to see if we had cash on hand. I returned with our platinum card. "Sorry, not enough cash on hand. Here's our card."

He took it and swiped it on the machine, asking me to authorize it. I added a twenty percent tip and he gave me a receipt.

"Thank you for your business, Falon."

"Thank you for doing such a great job!" Walking back to the party, Rick caught up to me.

"Falon, I made a tray of pastries for dessert for you. Where would you like me to put them?"

"Oh, Rick, thank you! How about leaving them on the table where the plates are?"

"Done."

I continued to the party and looked for my husband.

"There you are!" he said as I sidled up to him. He wrapped his arm around my waist and his other hand gently rubbed my belly. "How's the little one doing tonight?"

"He's dancing up a storm," I said, as I felt the baby move inside.

"Oh! Look at that, a foot. He's going to be a break dancer."

"I wouldn't be surprised," I said. "I'm going to sit down. I've paid Marcel and Carlos."

"Thank you. I'll come and join you, so get a lounge chair."

I found an empty lounge chair close to the waterfall by the pond and claimed it. A few minutes later, Mark came and sat behind me and pulled me between his legs so that I could lean back against him. Both his hands were around me and on my belly. He nuzzled my neck, and kissed and nipped me, sending tiny doses of venom coursing through me.

“Can you believe our life?” I asked him.

“Not what you had expected?” he teased.

“No, not at all. I had dreamed of having friends like this, a husband, a family,” I answered, rubbing my baby belly. “But it was a dream, and I never expected it to happen. Everything is so perfect, I am afraid to blink. Remember what a mess I was when we met?”

“I don’t remember a mess,” he said gently. “Haunted, hurt, lonely, yes, but not a mess.”

“You’re being kind.”

“No, I’m not. You were beautiful that night. In my eye, you glowed as if a spotlight was shining on you. I couldn’t not notice you.”

“I remember seeing your eyes the first time. I almost fell into them and onto the floor. I fell in love in a split second. If you had not noticed me, I fear I would have become a stalker,” I said in jest.

“I love you so much, Mrs. Chisholm,” he murmured into my ear. “I’m so happy you’re having our baby. I’ve dreamed of this for so long, ever since that first night.”

“I love you too, Mr. Chisholm,” I answered him. “But I hate to tell you this, you’re not the father of this child.”

“No? Who is?”

“A Greek god is the father.”

“Oh that scoundrel,” he said with mock rage. “Figures it’s him. It’s always him! I may just have to find him and give him a thrashing. How dare he put his seed into my wife!”

“His seed is superior.”

“You wound me, wife!”

I laughed. We played these little conversations sometimes—usually in private, but they were a game of ours. Since knowing his ability to change faces, our favorite game was making love with a new face, or the first face, Zisis.

I closed my eyes and leaned back on his chest listening to our friends. I heard Lora chatting and calling for everyone’s attention. I opened my eyes and saw her walking toward the middle of the pool deck.

“Everyone! Please can I have your attention?” called Lora. “At ten o’clock, the witches and I have a special presentation to show you for Labor Day. So if you will all find a seat out at the back of the yard facing the house we can get started. All witches, come with me into the house please.”

I checked my watch and it said it was 9:45 p.m. “Hun, would you get me a blanket and a drink before the demonstration?” I asked Mark.

“Of course.” He got up and disappeared.

Everyone was grabbing chairs and arranging them in a semicircle at the back of our yard. Once we were all seated, Lora came out of the house with all the witches. They were all wearing flowing, long, gossamer, rainbow-printed robes with hoods with wide sleeves. Walking in a star formation, they walked as far as the pool deck before stopping. Some of the witches turned around on the spot so they were all facing outward.

“Ladies and gentlemen,” Lora shouted like a circus barker. “In honor of Labor Day, we present ... magical fireworks!

Lora stepped away from the formation to the side and used a remote control to start music. Then she conducted the group of witches like instruments. The witches threw their heads back in unison and hummed in the same key, then tossed their hands up high in the air. Balls of light left their hands and soared up into the sky and burst like fireworks.

Everyone in the audience *ahhhhhed* and *oooooed.*

All eyes were skyward to watch them create different shapes in the sky that changed colors. Some were animals, like horses that were running with flowing manes and tails. Some were throwing more single balls of light, while others sent up huge complex fireworks. A couple of witches were making circles, and passing them back and forth as they danced in the sky. The show was pretty spectacular.

They continued for about fifteen minutes, before it looked like the witches were tiring. But instead of stopping, they all started building balls of white light again. We watched as the balls merged into the one in the center one at a time, until the ball in the center was as huge as a hot-air balloon. They raised it up slowly and started spinning it. It went faster and faster until it burst open in a finale of light, creating a dome over the whole yard. It looked like a soap bubble with multiple colors dancing across its skin, and thin ribbons like aurora borealis coiling across its surface. It was really beautiful; green, red, and amber crisscrossed the sky.

Everyone applauded and cheered at the spectacular sight.

At that moment, I heard a strange noise. I shouted at Andrews to get his attention and he walked over to our chair.

"Andrews, do you hear that?" I asked him.

He listened for a moment, then started searching the sky. "Yes, it's a drone."

We both started scanning, but it was difficult to see anything with all the light being thrown around. I got up and we started walking away from the pool.

"There!" he shouted at me. "On the south side of the house, I see something."

I looked where he was pointing and I saw five large, black, spider-looking objects flying low. They sounded like overgrown bees. "Andrews, are those drones?" I asked.

"Yes, they are military-grade, heavy-duty quad-copters, and they're carrying payloads."

He pulled out his phone and dialed someone. He had an urgent conversation with that person for ten seconds before hanging up. "Falon, the attack that I told everyone about when I got back from New Orleans is happening now. I'm going to go get some gear from my car. I'll be right back. Go warn Lora and prepare people to get to cover."

I ran up to Lora and whispered in her ear that there were five armed drones inbound.

"Can you do anything?" I asked her.

"Okay, witches, this is what we've been practicing for," shouted Lora. "I know you're tired, but dig deep. We have a problem. We need to hold this dome over the party. Cover everyone and everything. On the east side, make sure the dome stretches over the house, please!"

"How long do we hold it?" asked one of the witches.

"As long as we can!" cried Lora. "There are five drones coming toward us and they're carrying weapons of some kind. We have to protect everyone and the babies inside. We have to!"

I ran back to my seat beside Mark.

"What's up?" he asked, seeing that I was anxious.

"Andrews and I have spotted five drones flying toward us carrying weapons of some kind. The attack has started. Lora and the witches are going to hold this dome as a defense for as long as they can. Help me get everyone under it now!"

"People, please stand up and walk toward the witches under the dome. There is an attack underway, and they are holding that dome as a defensive measure."

All our guests got up without fuss and formed a circle around the witches. If nothing else, we would defend them, with what speed, strength, and ability we could.

Meanwhile, Andrews had returned with several large crates. One was a ground-to-air launcher complete with a small missile. Another was a complex-looking radio device. I walked over and asked if I could help.

"This is a jamming device. Put these on, and monitor the band for any signals. When you hear something, press this button," he said, handing me a pair of headphones.

"I can do that." *I think.*

Andrews picked up the rocket launcher, then walked over to Lora and spoke to her for a few moments. He pointed to the sky where the drones were coming in. She followed his signal and her face grew grim.

"Witches, I want everyone to turn toward the direction Andrews is pointing," shouted Lora. "Keep your energy in the dome, but now we're going to focus it in that direction and track those buggers."

Andrews came back toward me where I was listening for signals and grimly set up the rocket launcher.

"Andrews, I thought the New Orleans police were going to arrest this guy."

"I thought the New Orleans police were going to keep an eye on him at the very least! I gave them the information I had about his next plot. I told them he was planning this. They assured me they would take action."

"So they didn't?"

"It would appear not. That's why I called my contact in New Orleans first. I'm hoping she can have the police raid the location where they should be controlling these from."

"They can be controlled from that far away?"

"Oh yes. It was these types of drones the US used in the Middle East. They can be controlled from a different continent."

"What will they do? The drones?"

"They are carrying Hellfire missiles. They are anti-tank devices that explode on contact and spread extreme fire across a large area. They're designed to utterly destroy anything and turn everything into ash. It looks like whoever's flying the drone intends to drop the Hellfires on us like bombs, rather than launch from a distance. Doing so allows them to tweak the targeting down to the last second."

"Oh my God. Will Lora's dome protect us?"

"I don't know. It's why I'm working on two other ideas at the same time. If we can jam their signal, perhaps we can prevent them from crashing or dropping their payloads. If we cannot jam the signal, I'm prepared to take them out while they're still aloft."

"With that?"

"Yes. This is designed to take out aircraft."

I looked over my shoulder at the drones. They were close now; the angry buzzing of their motors was loud and distinguishable. I then looked at Lora and saw the strain on her face. She was contributing to the dome, throwing her magic into it. They all looked exhausted.

"This is good, guys, keep this going," Lora urged the group of magic wielders. "There is a spot on the northside that looks thin. Someone help cover that! We can do this! Everyone, breathe and focus, you're doing great!"

The huge dome now covered a third of the entire property. It still looked like a soap bubble, albeit very stretched, the colors thin and swirling around. *And then it just pops suddenly?* I was afraid that would happen.

The buzzing was much louder now. We could all hear them. Everyone was watching the sky nervously, except the witches and Lora. They were focused on the dome. Many of them had their eyes closed in concentration.

The drones were nearly on top of the house. I hadn't found any specific frequency that seemed to match the drones. Andrews pulled out his laptop and was furiously typing code into it. He had somehow found a channel to communicate with the drones and was trying to reprogram them. Suddenly there was silence… All the drone motors cut out.

A cheer rose from our guests, that turned into a drawn-out *oh!* An eerie silence fell on our party. The drones were no longer flying, they were falling. So not yeah, the drones were out of control and coming down right on top of the back yard. Then their motors sputtered back to life. But now they were much closer to the ground.

"What just happened?" I screamed. "Why did they come back on?"

"I'm not sure!" yelled Andrews. "Perhaps the pilot was able to override my jamming. Get everyone inside now!"

"Everyone, inside NOW!" I yelled, turning away from Andrews to get everyone to safety. The partygoers scrambled to get around the witches and ran into the house as the first drone struck the bubble and its Hellfire exploded. A terrifying wall of flame engulfed the sky for a few seconds. But the bubble held. The witches had succeeded!

Andrews launched his rocket from the edge of the property and took out one of the drones mid-flight. The fireball that erupted was hot enough to catch a close-by tree on fire. The top of its canopy sparked and sizzled. He prepared another rocket, but not before another hit the iridescent bubble. The fire spread across it like a burning oil slick. But the dome held, the fire did not come through.

On the far side of the group, one of the witches screamed in pain and collapsed. She was shrieking and waving her hands about as they burned. They looked like red-hot coals. I grabbed a towel and ran to her, throwing it in the pool to soak it with water and wrap her hands.

The witches next to her shuffled into her place, closing the hole that happened when she fell, bolstering up their section of the dome. But they were all getting very close to the end of their energy.

Lora screamed, "Keep it up, people! If we don't, everyone will die!"

We all felt Lora's fear and urgency. I wished there was something I could do to help her. For the one I helped, she thanked me for the towel treatment. When I suggested she go to safety, she refused.

"I will stay here, in case I feel my energy come back, then I can fight again!" she explained.

There were two drones left. They were not close together, so Andrews could only take one of them out. He fired off the last rocket and it hit the target, but it was close to the house. It nearly set the ground on fire as the Hellfire shattered across the asphalt and grass. Luckily, without fuel to feed it, the fire blew itself out.

The last drone kept coming without anything to stop it. When it hit the dome, it was like a punch in the gut. The fire exploded bigger than ever, and eventually snuffed itself out. But not before it damaged the bubble. I watched helplessly as the bubble burned through. The missing sections looked like smoldering holes in a burning sheet of paper with the edges of the rips glowing with fire.

The witches started dropping like flies. As the fire consumed itself, it ran out of oxygen and fuel. The bubble disintegrated. All the rest of the witches collapsed as one.

Lora was the last. As she wobbled, I saw her glance toward the house to see that her family and friends were safe.

Rick screamed her name and rushed out to her side. We watched as he tried to pick up his wife, but she was limp.

I ran to check on the others. They were unconscious but alive. They must have been exhausted. I ran over to Lora to find her cold and not breathing. Rick was holding her against his chest and rocking back and forth. A wail like I have never heard before rent itself from his throat as the animal inside him screamed in agony.

Lora's heart was not beating, her body lifeless.

Epilogue

PI Adams

My phone rang while I was preparing some of the food for our Fourth of July party in a few days.

"Hello?"

"It's Andrews. The attack is happening now. Five drones in the air."

"I'll mobilize the police now." I hung up feeling my gut in my throat. *Good luck, Andrews. You're going to need it!*

The only thing I could do was call the police and make sure we raided that warehouse to see if they were controlling the drones from there.

"9-1-1, What's your emergency?"

"I need to report a bombing."

"What do you mean, miss?"

"There is a person in a warehouse at the address 26 Wharf Road that is operating a drone strike in Canada."

"A drone strike? Do you mean a military operation, miss?"

"No! He's a civilian and it's unauthorized. Just raid the location! You'll find lots of illegal weapons on site."

"I'll dispatch the police, miss."

"Thank you."

I hung up and called my father the captain.

"Dad, the drone attack we warned you about? Yeah, it's in progress right now. We've got to stop it. He's using satellite-linked drones to attack civilians in Canada!"

"Okay, hun. We'll go investigate."

I threw my phone down in disgust and grabbed my own weapon and ran to my car. The hairy trip down to the Lower Ninth was heightened by my fear that I would be too late.

Arriving, there were no other cars, no sirens, no police, no fire, no nothing! Argh! I crept up to the building and looked through the window where I had seen the crates of drones. Sure enough, a dim light was on, and Douglass was sitting at a desk with a computer in front of him. He was using a joystick to control the drones from here. He must have programmed them before liftoff. According to what Andrews had taught me, those birds would fly autonomously until they were close to their target.

Very quietly, I crept inside. Checking all corners, I didn't hear anyone else in the room. He was alone. It was pitch black inside, and I had to close my eyes for a few moments to equalize my vision, else I would not be able to navigate the room without making noise.

Tiptoeing up behind him, I was lucky he was so intent on watching the screen in front of him. It was clear from where I was that the machines were nearly at their target. The screen had five images that must have been from the five drones. Suddenly one had a flare of light on it and the screen went blank.

"Fuck!" he said. "Fuck that shit. Goddamned vamps, they have rockets! Well, catch this, you fucking vamp!"

He tweaked the control and one of the drones zoomed in faster. On the monitor I could see some kind of shimmering canopy over one of the houses. When the drone was close he swore again.

"Fuck, fuck, fuck! Now what happened?" He furiously pounded the keyboard but could not get control back. "Fuck!"

I watched as the drones fell silent. Andrews had managed to cut their motors. I felt my spirits buoy. Douglass swore and started pounding on the keyboard again. Suddenly the drones came back to life and I watched as the first drone fell into the canopy and exploded.

"Teehehe," laughed Douglass. "That'll teach you fuckin' vamps."

I was almost right behind him at this point, so I planted my feet securely, and placed the muzzle of my gun up against the back of his head.

"Game is over, Staung. Put your hands up where I can see them."

"Who the fu—?" He wheeled on me, but I was faster. I had him by the hand and my cuffs were already on one wrist. I had his arm twisted to the point of dislocation before he stopped moving and started whimpering. Grabbing the other wrist, I forced him to turn around and I cuffed his wrists together.

"Now, on your knees until the authorities get here. And don't bother moving, because I have a gun on you."

"Fuckin' bitch!" he swore.

"Yeah, that's right, call me names. Stupid incel."

I watched the rest of the drones attack in horror because I had no way of knowing what to do. I could only hope they were alright and had a way of protecting themselves. Just as the last of the drones hit the canopy, a squadron of police burst into the warehouse with guns ready and big floodlights.

Once they found out who I was, they grabbed Staung and carried him out to the squad car waiting for him. My father and I stared at the monitor in horror; the last image was frozen on the screen. It showed the fireball that happened when the last drone struck its target.

“Oh my God!” said my father. “God in heaven, help those people!”

“It’s bad, Dad. I will reach out to Andrews and see if there is any news.”

“I’m sorry, Marcy, that we couldn’t do anything sooner.”

“I know, Dad. It’s the law. You can’t take action until a crime has been committed. At least now we have ample evidence to hang this guy, and perhaps implicate the rest of them.”

Information on Drug Tests

In our story we used the example of a real product that was invented by three teenaged girls in Miami, Florida. Read their story here:

https://www.intelligentliving.co/three-young-girls-invent-straw-to-detect-date-rape-drugs/

———

For more information about the real Smart Straws (TM) look up the girls' social media sites:

https://www.instagram.com/smartstraws/?hl=en

https://www.facebook.com/smartstraws/

https://twitter.com/smartstraws

If you, or someone you love has been the victim of such a crime, please report it and seek help. Here are some places to start.

Helplines in Canada for sexual abuse.

Reporting to Law Enforcement - RAINN

Excerpt from Book 8

IMMORTAL CRIME

Karen Armstrong

Spring 1958, Dr. Karen Armstrong, working on a small dig in a little known area on the far side of the plateau west of the Valley of the Kings, uncovered an unmarked tomb of a nobleman and his family. Inside she found all the normal things like sarcophagi and Canopic jars. There were stores of food, grains, and amphoras of wine that were all included in the materials the family would need in the afterlife. But one thing was really out of place: it was a male body. Nearly mummified, lying on the ground in a position of repose, but not wrapped or prepared. And yet the body was in nearly perfect condition. She also noted the surprising lack of rats or mice in the tomb, which usually contained hordes of them due to the food left.

I told my small crew of three workers to focus on the funerary objects in the tomb while I tackled the body. I wanted to bring it back to the university lab so I could examine it closely. A crate arrived and two of my men brought it into the tomb and helped me lift the body and place it in the crate. I then had it transported immediately to the hermetically sealed chamber. It had acrylic walls and was completely transparent from all angles. There were CCTV cameras positioned outside each corner and one overhead to monitor the contents of the chamber. The video was automatically recorded to a new device called a VCR. The system was part of the university's new security, but it wasn't monitored.

Following the body back to the lab, my thoughts went wild with speculation. Who was this man? Family members? Slave? Worker left behind? His clothes appeared well-made, so it was not likely to be a slave. But I would only know once I had taken samples and looked at them under the microscope. Considering this tomb had not been raided or opened since burial, and we thought we knew who the family was, we should be able to put a date on the tomb's closing. It was tradition that when the head of the family died, his wife and servants were buried with him.

Could the man be a spurned lover of the wife?

I had the crate carefully opened and the body lifted and placed on the stainless steel table. The first thing I would do was weigh him. The table served as a weigh scale as Well, as an examination table, so I didn't have to move the mummy by myself. It was just shy of 75 kilos. That's almost as much as a healthy male's weight. Huh! I measured his height at 198 cm, a very tall man in his time. I would need a complete set of measurements so I could create a model of him on the computer.

The next task was to undress him, taking lots of photos of the fibers and samples for analysis. As I unwrapped the layers of clothes, I felt my heart start pounding with anticipation. His body was not shriveled anywhere near as much as a mummy would be. In fact, it simply looked dried out — that simply washing with water would bring it back. But that was ridiculous. He'd been in the tomb for at least 2500 years!

What remained of the outside garment was delicately removed with the help of one of the interns who worked in the lab. It took two people to lift the body carefully. I examined the fibers under the microscope. They looked like fine linens and there was some evidence perhaps of dyes in between the fibers. The fibers were consistent with clothing made during the time in question, so this definitely was not a modern person.

That's enough for today, I thought. Bending over a body with a magnifying glass and tweezers leaves you with a crick in your neck and a headache. I left the lab locked up and went home for some dinner and my favorite romance novel.

The next day, I planned to clean off the body thoroughly. The body had not been mummified or prepared. My first observation was that since his body was exposed to the air and light, it had lost the gray hue it had in the tomb as if it was still alive.

Grabbing my brushes, I gently started brushing away the dirt and debris from his face. What I uncovered was a very handsome face. I was captivated by its perfection in spite of the age of the skin. Using tiny brushes I was able to remove dust from the creases in the skin and then using a squeeze bottle and a solution of water and salt, I irrigated the skin so I could clean it better. Before my very eyes, the skin absorbed the water.

"Huh! Just like a sponge." I continued working on the head until I had removed as much as I could, then I started to go through the hair, because the body still had a head of hair. I expected it to come off in my hands as I picked it up, but it did not. The long tresses were very dry, but still firmly attached to the scalp. Again I used water to rinse away dust and clean the skin gently and remove the dirt from the scalp. The water drained through but seemingly got absorbed too.

Once I was finished with the head, I went and made my notes. I wanted to document everything I found, taking photos with the big camera, as Well, as making drawings of small details I observed. By eight o'clock, I was again tired and hungry, so I locked up the chamber and went to leave. At the door I felt the urge to turn back.

"Good night handsome," I said to the body, before closing the door behind me.

Over the next weeks, I established a working pattern of cleaning a section, photographing it, making my notes, then repeating. After eight hours on my feet, I was exhausted and hungry, so I'd leave to go home.

Occasionally, I'd find what I thought was a bite mark on his body. But they were healed, which would suggest that he went into the tomb alive, not dead. How horrible! What would cause a person to entomb themselves alive? And then to be bitten by rats and survive there long enough to heal?

In the quiet of the lab, a transformation was happening. Any water that pooled or beaded on the surface of the skin got absorbed and the skin plumped up a tiny bit. Water that drained off the body and accumulated on the steel table underneath also got absorbed into the skin. In fact, the body absorbed nearly every drop of water the doctor had washed it with. That led to a remarkable result: The body started to revive.

Several mornings later, those minute changes had accumulated enough that they became obvious to the casual observer. That day, when I stood over him ready to start my work again, I saw spots where the skin looked like skin and not like the leather it looked like the day I brought him to the lab. It was weathered and old skin, but skin nonetheless.

"Hmm, I have a hunch."

I remeasured the circumference of his wrist again and found that it had enlarged by 0.25 cm. I rechecked my data from a week ago, and yes, the measurement I took then, was different.

"I know my measurements are accurate, because I measured them five times before recording it. So the wrist has become larger. I wonder if that has happened all over?"

I activated the scale function of the table and retook his weight. The body was nearly a kilo heavier!

"Ah ha! It is changing. Now, why?" I continued my work.

At midday, I was called to the director's office. So I took a break, turned off the lights to keep the body in the dark, and closed up the lab. I didn't want to have any damage due to artificial light. I grabbed my lunch bag and walked over to the building figuring I would eat after the meeting with the director.

Meanwhile, back in the lab, in the dark, the body continued its revival. Being exposed to water again, had revitalized the skin. With the addition of the water, the skin was able to absorb oxygen and that was carried inward to the body's vital organs. Because the body had not been mummified, all the organs and blood had remained and simply dried. So now, the body was a huge sponge, and with every drop it absorbed, the healing continued.

I didn't get back to my lab until the following day. When I turned on the lights and opened the chamber, I discovered a light layer of dust covering the body. I felt compelled to rinse this off. This time, I didn't use a small bottle, but I used the overhead shower tap. Washing the body from head to toe, I gently used my hand to rub off the whitish film that had appeared. I was surprised to discover it was like an outer layer of dermis. It came off as small flakes, just exfoliating a living person.

After showering the entire body and removing the layer of dead skin, I was amazed to see the skin underneath looked like skin, and not old skin, but healthy middle-aged skin. Was it de-aging? If so, how was it de-aging? Glancing at the clock I saw it was late again. Geez, time flies by when I'm so engrossed in what I do. I really need a time machine! I closed the lights and locked up quickly, leaving for the night.

In the darkness, the body started breathing. Quietly at first with barely any rise or fall to its chest. The shower of water had done much to restore its internal organs. While the doctor had been focused on cleaning off the skin, the body had been absorbing all the water she poured onto it. While no consciousness was awake, the animal of the body was, and had revived enough to live again. Soon, it will have healed enough to awaken the brain and to wake up fully.

By the third week, I had finished taking my initial examination of the body. Now, it was ready for me to get blood and tissue samples. I was excited for the work today, because it may discover what he was, or at least how old he was. I was walking to the lab with a spring in my step. When I flipped the lights on I stopped dead.

The body in the chamber was sitting up.

Recovering my wits, I walked around the chamber, as it was a free-standing structure, and looked at the body carefully from every direction. Other than sitting upright, nothing appeared out of the ordinary. It was not being supported by anything, nor was it tied. How was it sitting up?

"I'll bet the night staff is playing another practical joke on me. That must be it." I said aloud. My observation of the body told me the skin looked smoother today.

Dropping my purse on my desk, I walked up to the keypad to enter my code to enter the chamber. It didn't work. Huh! Why is that? It worked yesterday. I called the technician to come and take a look. He arrived in ten minutes and looked at the keypad.

"There doesn't seem to be anything wrong with it," he said. "Are you sure you entered the correct code?" Condescending S.O.B. I thought.

"Yes I am sure. 5 7 9 2 is the code," I said.

The technician entered the code and got a red light. Then he hooked up another device and told me to come up with another code and he'll reprogram it. I gave him 7 2 9 7.

With the keypad working again, I entered the chamber and approached the body.

"By the way," said the technician. "How is the body sitting up?"

"I don't know. I suspect someone is playing a practical joke on me."

The technician left me alone in the chamber with the body. I walked up to him and touched his shoulder. I jerked my hand back because his flesh was warm. I gingerly touched him again, and confirmed the skin was warm, but not only that if it felt normal, not like mummy skin at all. It was soft too.

I placed my hands on his shoulders and pressed them back toward the table, expecting the legs to rise up. They didn't. The joints were supple enough that the body laid flat again. I walked to his head and was standing behind him looking down at his face. I suddenly saw his face. It was that of a young man in his thirties.

I couldn't help myself, I lifted one of his eyelids expecting it to be the milky white of death, and instead saw perfectly clear emerald green eyes. Startled, I jumped back and swallowed. Calm yourself Armstrong. There has to be a scientific explanation for this.

Approaching the table again, I lifted both eyes, and sure enough, they were the same. They were not looking back at me, but they appeared perfectly fine and not dead. Letting the lids close, I decided to continue my 'restoration' work. The director wanted me to present this mummy at a symposium next month. That was what he called me into his office for. The university wanted to make a splash about this find, and that meant getting more funding. For me, it's about science, but the university was always short of funding for projects. He told me this would ensure I could continue to work on the dig.

Did I have a choice? No. So, in spite of the questions running through my head, my focus now had to be what the mummy represented for the university and the symposium next month.

Torion wakes up.

His consciousness is not quite ready to think, but the brain is coming back on line. His head twists left, then right, taking in what little he could see in the pitch blackness. Not much. Without being able to see details, his eyes close again, and he falls back into oblivion.

It's the day to travel to the symposium. I have finished the preparation of the body, crafted similar clothes to what he would have worn and packed them with the body. The mummy was repacked into the wooden crate and straw was packed tightly around him. With the crate closed, it would be secure until the shipping company would take it off her hands and transport it to the symposium.

The symposium was in Paris, and the most prestigious archeologists would be there from around the globe to present new ideas on man's historical life. The university had paid for her travel and hotel. Her mummy was going to turn the archeology world upside down. He represented a completely different portrayal of how Egyptians buried their dead and this was why the university insisted on presenting. This body hadn't been mummified, and yet it was perfectly preserved. He was also not put in a coffin, but laid on the bare floor like a slave, also very unusual. So they had to tell the community.

Torion wakes up again. He is lying in a wooden crate packed around with straw, as if he was some treasure. When his eyes opened, it was still dark. He discovers that he cannot move and his breathing is difficult. He has no memory of who he is and the only thing he recognized was the materials surrounding him.

There is a loud humming vibration all around him, and there is a little light filtering through the slats of the crate. The humming was grating his teeth and causing his body to feel like ants were crawling all over him. The only thing he could do was go back to sleep and wait.

The plane landed in Paris, and was unloaded and transported directly to the museum. I followed the crate to make sure it was left in a secured place and that it was hermetically sealed. Satisfied with the arrangements, I went to check in at the hotel and get something to eat. My stomach was grumbling after spending over five hours on the plane.

Inside the crate, Torion feels the movement of the crate as it is removed from the plane, carried by men and put inside a vehicle. The jostling makes him bump and sway inside. He squints as bright light assaults his eyes through the crates slats. He still cannot move, but this time, he thinks it's because his limbs are restrained.

When he stops moving, all sound stops too. His crate was plunked down on something and whoever had carried him left. The light suddenly disappears leaving him staring straight up at the underside of the crate. He cannot see much because it is dark, but his eyes can pick out the grain of the wood. Through the gaps in the wood, he can see machinery beyond. There is a specific smell that he doesn't recognize that is a strong acrid odor. It almost burns his nostrils and makes his eyes water. He lies there trying to figure out where he is.

His preoccupied thoughts are interrupted when light suddenly returns and the top of the crate is pried off. A woman is looking down at him. Impulse or instinct drove him to glance at her. As soon as his eyes moved, she screamed and ran away. He closed his eyes quickly and waited. He heard her hesitant footsteps as she came back. When he sensed she was leaning over the side of the crate again peering at him, he opened his eyes again, and she screamed again, but this time she didn't go away.

I stared into the crate and wondered how his eyes were so beautiful. I had screamed when I first saw them move, but I couldn't help myself, I had to look again. When I witnessed him open those eyes and look at me again, I fell into a bottomless pool of cool green water. Captured by his gaze, I forgot to wonder why he was alive.

What's Next

The next installment of the Immortal Stories is *Book 8 - Immortal Crime.*

- Andrews hunts down an immortal criminal
- PI Adams helps out on investigation
- Lora is critically injured
- Falon has a baby
- Mark gets serious about finding a secure place for "his group" of immortals to live
- The Amazon woman makes another appearance
- They find the immortal who has been impregnating women

About The Author

Linda Ashton Trott

Ms Trott, a native of Montreal, Canada, currently lives in the nation's capital with her husband of twenty-four years, their four cats, and eight Japanese Koi.

When not writing, Ms Trott can be found in their backyard relaxing by the pond or editing her husband's stories.

Ms Trott has always had an interest in all things supernatural, the occult, UFOs, aliens, and the paranormal. It seemed natural to combine one or more of these elements into a unique universe in which to tell interesting stories.

These are not children's stories. "It's funny, I never sat down with the intention of writing Adult books," Linda once said. "But here they are. I wanted to express physical love honestly without cutesy acronyms and vague names."

These stories contain explicit language and hot, steamy sex scenes that will leave you panting.

Books In This Series

The Immortal Stories Series

The Immortals are a race of beings that came to Earth many tens of thousands of years ago. Their stories stretch across time and have become woven into the history of humans. Their society is hidden from humans even though they live among them. Forbidden from developing romantic liaisons with humans, some break the rules and form close bonds and get married. But this always comes with consequences.

1 - **Immortal Desire**

One immortal and one human.

As Zisis' world collides with Falon's, she is left to cope and deal with the blowback. Their love affair is erotic, passionate, and stirs the soul, but it is ill-fated. This is a story of romance, heartbreak, hardship, and survival. The sex is hot and steamy, the highs euphoric, and the lows devastating.

---

2 - **Immortal Fulfillment**

What a twist! What has Mark done?

After a nasty life twist has her rethinking a relationship with her Texan, Falon needs to decide which direction to go. Is she back to square one? Certainly not! Between hurricanes, hot tub invites, and road trips with hot, sexy guys, there is plenty of action and adventure.

---

3 - **Immortal Peril**

The Family is NOT happy!

Lora meets Rick, a talented dessert chef in an up-and-coming restaurant in Atlanta, Georgia, while visiting her best friend, Falon, who is on contract work there. Lora and Rick hit it off in ways she can't believe—one hot weekend in Miami and she can't get him out of her mind. So, when invited to Atlanta again, this time by Rick, she doesn't hesitate!

When Mark disappears without a trace, Falon is left to find out what happened.

---

4 - **Immortal Victory**

Out of the fire and into the frying pan!

Falon gets out of one problem only to find herself in danger again. An ancient enemy is targeting the immortals and will stop at nothing to eliminate them. Dodging assassins and traps, Falon decides to end homelessness, one person at a time.

Her BFF Lora discovers that true love sex generates magical energy while she looks for her ancestors.

Gwen finds a partner in Andrews.

---

5 - Immortal Hunt

Having just survived a coordinated attack from an ancient enemy, the immortals rejoice and celebrate their success. Attention turns toward locating their ancestors when a news item catches Lora's attention and gives her a very important clue to finding them. The immortals are off on a great adventure to distant places. Pirates, witches, time travel, spooky castles, and volcanic caves are some of the encounters happening this time. Don't miss out on the adventure!

---

6 - Immortal Nexus

New is old, and old is new

Surely, saving a coven of witches from a pocket dimension would be a highlight in life. But it's not. The immortals return home to everyday life; family, moving, school, raising teens, and of course, spicy lovemaking.

We meet a new character with a deep past. And when a new couple moves in across the street, Falon notices some familiar characteristics. She makes it her mission to meet the new neighbors.

Family matters are front and center in this story. The close-knit group of immortals is becoming a family, and some stories need sharing like Andrews' tale of being hired by aliens.

Justin and Rick finally open the new restaurant. It was a New Year's Eve celebration with a bang!

---

7 - Immortal Generation

Short Stories

First Contact: An Immortal Origin Story

The Immortal's Origin Story started 33,000 years ago, when they arrived on Earth. *First Contact* follows the story of how the immortals meet the first humans and what happens when they interact and live together.

Praise for the Series

What are readers saying about this new series?

"Yet again I've got an ARC for this author and I've got to say that these books just get better and better. I loved this one [Book 6] and it is my favourite so far out of the series. There is now so many new people with there own stories that I don't think it will get boring any time soon. My favourite couple were Falon and Mark but I have quickly fallen in love with Margaret and Abeo and I didn't see the twist and turns right at the end. Brilliant book by a brilliant author."

*... Sam ***** Amazon*

"Linda Ashton Trott has a real gift for crafting intricate sex scenes that are highly charged and also entirely believable. She really brings you into the bedroom in a joyful way. The will-they-or-won't-they story keeps you wondering, right up to the plot twist at the end, which sets readers up for Book 2."

*... Amy **** Amazon*

"Ohhhhh! This book was good! Hot hot scenes with enough of a story in between to keep you hooked. We all need to become

Leopard Ladies! Nice quick read. Can't wait to read book 2 of the series!"

*... Josée **** Goodreads*

"Brilliant book loved the storyline and I couldn't put it down once I started. I loved the characters and got really absorbed in to their lives and feelings.

all I can say is Wow I loved every part of it (#3). I'm really sad that the book ended the way it did as I wanted to carry on reading and finding out what was going to happen. I love this series and all the characters. Hopefully there should be another one."

*... Sam ***** Amazon*

"Picking up where the first book ended, this installment of the series was the heroine's journey of self-discovery in order to make the right decisions for her, something I really enjoyed!

This book was sexy, fun and the character development was great! Ioved how the heroine slowly took back control of her life and found empowerment in her spontaneity."

*...Nikita **** Goodreads*

"wow! amazing, fast paced and enthralling new world! Wonderful characters that charmed me from the beginning. Honestly this was a wonderfully perfect read to help me escape from the world for a bit.

Amazing (#3). I love this world and it's characters. Great storyline and Well, written. This series has been amazing to read. Definitely need to pick them up."

*... Naomi ***** Amazon*

"Yet again I'm absolutely totally blown away by this book (#4). I love the characters and the story line. Linda has written a fantastic book with steamy scenes that I didn't think were possible but brilliant. I loved the fact that we're now starting to see smaller named characters have a bigger role. It's very Well, written and can't wait to read more of the series."

*...Sam ***** Amazon*

Being an Indie Author

I've chosen to publish independently. This means I don't have the big machine of a traditional publishing company behind me. Reviews are very important on Amazon because they determine how visible you are in the marketplace. That makes your review, and every other review I receive, the most important tool in my marketing toolbox. If you've enjoyed reading this book, please consider spending a few minutes leaving me a review on Amazon. It doesn't have to be long.

Thank you!

See my website at www.lindaashtontrott.com to join the mailing list. You will not be inundated with mail, I promise! It will let you know when the latest book is released and if there are freebies.

Visit my Amazon author's page at https://www.amazon.com/~/e/B09TG29J19